BOR
DREAMS

Cynthia Arsuaga

Erotic Romance

Secret Cravings Publishing
www.secretcravingspublishing.com

A Secret Cravings Publishing Book
Erotic Romance

Born Again in Dreams
Copyright © 2012 Cynthia Arsuaga
Print ISBN: 978-1-61885-487-2

First E-book Publication: September 2012
First Print Publication: December 2012

Cover design by Dawné Dominique
Edited by Ariana Gaynor
Proofread by Rene Flowers
All cover art and logo copyright © 2012 by Secret Cravings
Publishing

PUBLISHER
Secret Cravings Publishing
www.secretcravingspublishing.com

Dedication

To my parents, who have been long passed away, even though you aren't physically with me, you are forever in my thoughts and dreams. I hope I've made you proud by pursuing my dreams by working hard and not compromising my standards which you helped in molding. Thank you, I love you. To my rock, my everything, and my husband, Mike. You stood by me when I had doubts about making those dreams come true. Thank you, I love you.

Acknowledgement

As always, I couldn't get this story off the ground and into the hands of my readers if not for the magnificent Secret Cravings Publishing staff. Thank you Ariana, Rene, Dawné, Michelle, and Beth for making this all happen.

"A dream is your creative vision for your life in the future. You must break out of your current comfort zone and become comfortable with the unfamiliar and the unknown." ~
Denis Waitley

BORN AGAIN IN DREAMS

Cynthia Arsuaga
Copyright © 2012

Chapter One

Four Years of Darkness and the Awakening

What is happening to me?

The pitch blackness enveloped her. The sound of distant voices reverberated in her head. The only distinguishable ones were of her parents, but the deeper monotone of the man's voice sounded unfamiliar, strange…*no, who is he talking about? Me?*

"I'm sorry, Mr. and Mrs. Travers. There's nothing more we can do. Now, it's up to your daughter and her will to live. We had high expectations when we took her off the ventilator and she breathed on her own, but she hasn't awakened, and that isn't a good sign. My best recommendation to you as her legal guardians is move her to a facility which can provide the proper care for all her basic needs. The body is healing nicely, but her brain, well…"
The grave sound of the man's voice scared the young woman lying in the bed.

What did he mean my brain…my brain what?

"With every passing day your daughter doesn't regain consciousness, the likelihood of her ever coming out of the coma becomes less likely. If she ever does recover, there is a strong possibility she would be in a diminished cognitive neurological state. She could awake and appear normal, but if the perceptive part of her brain ceased to function, she would be unable to respond to her surroundings."

"Doctor Davidson, do you mean she won't be the same? She's a freakin' vegetable and might as well be dead!" The shrill voice of another man in the room was loud enough to wake the dead, but not the patient.

Robbie, are you there? Ohmigod, Robbie. Get me out of here!

The distraught sound of her mother's words drew Merliah's attention. Her mother scolded her boyfriend, "Robert Jessup, she can hear you. Don't talk like that. Merliah is going to get better."

Merliah listened to the muffled sound of sobbing. *Mom? Please don't cry. I'm here. I'm okay. Why can't you hear me?*

"While there's always a chance, I thought I should prepare you for the worst as well," the officious voice of the man she recognized now as Dr. Davidson said.

The doctor continued speaking. "I've seen this condition many times in my practice. Family members hold out for hope their loved one would wake up from a coma. I don't wish to sound heartless, but the prognosis from my experience is grave and your daughter will no doubt succumb to the complications from her injuries either through death or the remainder of her life spent in an institution."

I'm awake doctor. I'm not in a coma. I hear you.

"No, doctor. I can't believe my Liah, my little girl isn't coming back to us. Her brain will heal. She's young and strong," Merliah's mother said.

"I understand you believe that, but the left side of her brain has been severely damaged from the car accident. There is nothing more we can do, Mrs. Travers."

Merliah understood what Robbie said may have been crude and hurtful to her parents, but he was correct. The doctor was trying to be kind, but she really might as well be dead.

Dead? No! I'm not dead. I'm here! The car accident hurt me, but I'm better. Ohmigod, help me someone!

With all the strength she gathered together, she attempted to open her mouth and speak. Anything that even possibly made an audible noise, she tried with little results for her efforts. First, she struggled to move a limb, then the twitch of a finger, or a blink of an eye, anything to show anyone in the room that she was aware of them. She failed.

"No she isn't. You know what the doctor told us. Her brain is pretty much dead. The vamp blood didn't even work," Robbie said.

Robbie I'm not dead. I'm alive. I'm over here. Help me, please. I can't move. Robbie, what's going on? Help me! Mom? Dad? Why can't you realize I'm conscious and understand you?

"What vamp blood?" Dr. Davidson asked. "Tell me you didn't give her tainted blood from one of those dead beings?"

"I did, but a lot of good it did. I paid a lot of money for a small vial. I think the guy I bought it from ripped me off. He said the stuff was fresh and should cure her."

"Robert, you didn't. You ran the risk of killing her, son," her father said.

"When did you give this blood to her, Robbie?" Dr. Davidson asked.

"About a month ago, after her last surgery. I hoped it would help her recovery. A couple of my buddies told me they tried the vamp blood and it worked on them for curing their little problems and ills after they went to the local vamp club. I...I thought it was worth a try. I didn't want to lose her."

Oh my god Robbie, you didn't. I'm in a vampire coma. That's what this is. I've heard about what vampire blood does to some humans. Bad things. I'm dead. You killed me. No. No. I can't be. I must fight this, find a way to let someone know I'm alive. I feel like I am. Oh no, I can't be dead. I can't stay like this. I will fight with everything inside me.

"I'm afraid any effects the vamp blood had on her were only to heal the incisions we made during the surgery. Her brain is too severely damaged to recover. You shouldn't have given the blood to her young man, but I understand why. I may have done the same thing myself if in your shoes." Merliah heard a soft sound, like a pat on the back and assumed the doctor touched Robbie in some way.

"The vamp blood didn't harm Liah, did it Doctor?" her mother asked.

"No, probably not. Any effects, we would have seen by now. Most medical doctors don't put much credence in the healing properties of vampire blood, but just in case I'll order more tests before we discharge your daughter. Let me know what facility you plan to move your daughter and we'll help with the arrangements. If there aren't any further questions, I'll send the nurse in with instructions and a social worker will also come in with a list of facilities you may want to consider. Again, I'm sorry there's nothing else we could do to bring her out of the coma, but she's comfortable and we intend to maintain this level."

But there is something you can do Dr. Davidson. I'm here. I hear you. Why can't you fix this? Mom, Dad, stop him. Oh God. Why can't anyone hear me? Why can't I move? Robbie, if you did this to me, you better help me. I love you despite what you've done. You have to find a way to get me out of here. I'm scared.

The nurse came in, checked the monitors, and Merliah heard the scribbling she made on a board. "I think we can take this IV out and disconnect these monitors. Her vitals are all stable. The doctor tells me you are transferring her to a permanent facility. There is a very nice place about an hour's drive from here. My sister works there as an art therapist on the weekends. She really loves working with the patients. She says everyone at the facility is an inspiration."

"It sounds like a perfect place for Liah. Do you have the contact information?"

"Sure. It's the Berger Institute. The social worker can get the information for you. Ask her when she comes to see you." Merliah felt the needle and tubing being removed from her arm, then a clinking noise. By the sudden silence in the room she could tell the other monitors had been shut off. Merliah assumed the nurse was the one tucking in the sheets and then adjusting the pillow. "Oh my, how interesting," the nurse said.

"What is?" the mother asked.

"Um, nothing, I thought I saw something. No, it was nothing." Merliah felt a gentle touch across her cheek. Someone brushed away a tear escaping the corner of her eye. *The nurse? She saw my tear. Now, she can tell everyone I'm awake.*

Help never came that day. Or the next. As the days blended into weeks, weeks into months, then into years, Merliah's mind sank into a deep, dark place. She thought voices came from a distance, but witnessed nothing but blackness and vague sounds. Lost, frightened, and unable to find her way back home, she succumbed to the solitude of darkness.

After four years wandering in the darkness of her mind, ready to succumb to the grim pain, Merliah experienced such desperation, depression and fatigue, she wanted to scream and find a way to end the misery. The strong survival instinct brought her out of the coma initially years ago, but her strength to fight remained hanging by a thread. This wasn't living, awake and aware but unable to communicate in any form was like death. When the pitch-blackness first happened, she tried repeatedly to call out, but her voice couldn't be heard. Relentless, she tried over and over, to move a toe, a finger, and she even cried to draw attention. The nurse, who witnessed the one tear, all those years ago, dismissed the physical plea.

Merliah's parents had her moved from the hospital to another facility. She understood the distant voices calling the new place, Berger Institute. The first reaction was of shock. *Ohmigod, I've been put in an institution with crazy people. Am I insane?* She refused to believe Robbie abandoned her, but after leaving the hospital, she never heard his sweet voice again. The man she loved gave up and left her without saying good-bye and her imprisonment became more painful and lonely. Her parents' voices faded as well. Time ceased for her and she slipped deeper and deeper into the gloomy abyss, existing on a different plane of consciousness. She could hear and feel on the outside, but remained in the darkness of her mind unable to communicate to her loved ones. Time seemed to cease to exist. She'd occasionally heard the staff celebrating a holiday, but after a few coming and going, Merliah stopped counting. The instinctive will to survive faded.

One more cry out into the emptiness before she resigned to death's call was made as a last resort, and to her surprise and elation, a voice answered. First, faintly, then it grew louder. A deep, melodic, and velvety voice broke through the darkness reaching toward her. It was a man, with a beautiful deep tone. His voice consoled her, wrapped around her and pulled her toward the light. She cried tears of joy and then a slight fear overtook her thoughts. *Am I dead? Is he the Angel of Death from the stories I've read?*

Up to that point, everything that made sense in her black world evaporated. Minutes, hours, days, months slipped by slowly and now someone reached out to her. How long she wandered aimlessly in her mind, often time curled up in a ball in the depths of the bottomless pit, she didn't know. Time meant nothing without any reference point. The sweet-sounding, shadow man had found her, and brought her into the light. Who was he and how did he find her when no one else could? She didn't know and didn't care about the details. He had found her, the only thing that mattered.

From the murky shadows, arms outstretched to clasp on to reality. She jolted when his cold hand touched hers, swiftly pulling her toward the light with his commanding voice guiding the way. Feeling the strong power moving her forward, she feared he was the Dark Angel of Death and not salvation to the world she had known before the blackness became her present life. She pulled back from the stranger, frightened more than relieved. As she battled with the fear, she glanced up but was unable to view his face, only sense the touch which set her skin afire.

Several seconds ticked by, and a little more of the self-control eroded away. His dominant presence began to put her at ease, and with one foot in front of the other, he guided her through the prison of hopelessness.

"Come with me, you'll be okay. I won't hurt you." The voice spoke softly, a low, lyrical, and heavily accented one. *Where is he from?*

The power he exuded surrounded her again and his efforts to save her worked as she fell under his spell and into the tight embrace. Fear, anger and desperation had driven her to this precarious position. She either had to trust him to lead her home or believe he was Death, or allow him to eliminate the misery of her present existence. Either way, the hellish nightmare would end. Could she leave the nightmare and be born again in the make-believe world of her dreams? Apprehension still held her back because he could be nothing more than wishful thinking on her part.

"You scare me. I called out for a long time and you're the first person to answer my cries. Am I dead?" The words were tentative, barely above a whisper.

"I don't sense you are. Blood runs strong through your veins. Your skin is warm and your eyes are bright. You are definitely alive," the shadow man's velvety voice soothed her.

Ohmigod, this man's voice could melt icebergs. He certainly did a good job of bringing life back into her desolate reality.

Merliah's senses screamed as if she were freefalling over a cliff, becoming light-headed and the wind knocked out of her lungs. Between his seductive words and the sensuous touch, the hunger of desire clawed her insides to be released. The arousal continued with thin fingers tickling up and down her spine. The light touches lit nerve endings on fire and caused her pussy to contract. Her clit ached for attention, a simple caress to ease the need she had not felt in God only knows how long.

The world she once remembered swirled in heat and desire. She swallowed hard and tried to stifle the passion building in her core. The power of his presence shoved right back. Merliah stumbled backward and gasped as the energy surged upward when gazing into the glowing red eyes piercing through the darkness. The stare was one of a predator, a carnal stare which stole her breath and sent her head spinning. She tried to breathe through the fire consuming her.

A firm hand settled on Merliah's shoulder. With a flutter of heavy eyelids over crystal blue eyes, she looked up again and gazed into calm, steady, obsidian eyes with golden flecks. Tender fingertips trailed over her cheek. Turning into the touch, her lips connected with the stranger's palm. Without hesitation she kissed the soft skin. Desire simmered in her veins, and for the first time since the black imprisonment, she knew freedom drew close.

Merliah closed her eyes and kissed his hand a second time, inhaling the scent permeating from the man, a mixture of musk edged with something wild and exotic. The effects of his cologne rushed through her. He pulled his hand away, then cupped her chin, and leaned forward. The arousal for this imaginary man surprised her. Was this the way she now coped with her torment? Sexually explicit encounters with a make-believe shadow man? She decided yes and gave into the fantasy. A dream. *This is so real and vivid. I can see him clearly, smell his cologne, and feel every taut muscle through his clothing.* The echoes of her life before him usurped their power over her. Never had any dream past or present had such strong senses of touch and smell, which confused her. When he lowered his lips to within inches of hers, she lost all thoughts of confusion.

The first touch of his mouth was tentative, hesitant. When she didn't push him away, the kiss became more. She heard his heartbeat in her head. Merliah hungered for him to sink deep inside of her until they were one. She felt strong arms wrap around her. He pulled her close. When their hips touched, she felt his erection pressing against her stomach. Her pussy contracted. Desire filled her heart. She wanted to feel every inch of him inside of her. The carnal thoughts played out in their most base element, more than she ever experienced before she fell into the darkness. *What is happening to me? Is this real or my over-active imagination?*

Hesitantly, she broke the kiss. Her breath came out in soft pants. Desire threatened to crest over her like a tidal wave. She looked up at him. The golden flecked onyx eyes drew in her gaze. She studied his features, from the highbrow, to his sculpted cheekbones, aquiline nose and sensual lips. What shocked her most were the scars prominently slashed through his cheek which dragged the right side of his mouth down.

She reached up and lightly traced the fine white line of the mark.

He grabbed her wrist. Fear of having done something wrong caused her to look away.

"It's okay, little angel. The wounds are old and don't hurt, only the memories. Besides, I'd rather have your nails tearing up my back making new ones." He smiled and she almost melted into a puddle at his feet.

An electric thrill sparked through her from his sensuous voice. *Am I crazy to feel this way so intensely from something I've conjured up in my mind?* Heat flushed her cheeks, then she couldn't help but imagine their entwined legs as their bodies moved together, racing toward climax. *Ohmigod! Where did that come from? My imagination is running wild this time, or I'm really dead and this is heaven. He did call me angel, didn't he?*

"I'm Sorin, come with me. Do not be afraid."

With an overwhelming sense of trust, she extended her arm and placed her hand in his, and with his gesture he brought her into the light.

I'm awake! Her excitement faded when her limbs remained stubbornly immobile.

For the first six months after awakening, she'd struggled with the memory of him helping her find the way back to reality. Unable to make sense of what happened, she pushed it out of her mind. She enjoyed the way he made her feel, but at the same time saw him as a powerful unknown danger. Once in the light, his image faded and she never saw him again, and his voice didn't answer her calls. Although grateful for his guidance, she traded one nightmare for another. Alone again, trapped in a body unable to move or speak, in daylight instead of darkness. Then, after desperation and a final attempt, her cries for him were answered.

Almost every night he came to her in dreams over the past eight or so weeks. Their erotic rendezvous kept her alive and hopeful that a life after the accident could be possible. Only wishful thinking on her part, the dreams faded in the light of day when the reality of her physical condition painfully reminded her that the stranger who saved her wasn't real.

* * * *

"Merliah, this is beautiful. Your eye for interpretation of the human form is incredible. Here follow through with this down through the torso and you should have it," Abigail Mann instructed. Her clear, precise, and caring manner, as well as for the other patients at the Berger Institute, never faltered. Merliah, as one of the newest students in Abigail's class, learned the sculpting skills quickly as well as enjoying the new art form.

The appearance of this talent confused Merliah too. "I've never taken classes before and the only talent I thought I had involved finding the best priced shoes or clothes. At least that's what I remember." The words took a while for her to express. Speech was difficult. The thoughts were perfect in her head, but her mouth couldn't seem to get them out fast or coherently.

At twenty-nine years old, Merliah learned upon wakening, she in fact resided at the Berger Institute, a facility for those with mental and physical disabilities. Her physical impairment, recovering from severe head injuries sustained from a car accident—almost five years prior. In a coma for almost four and a half of those years and according to her parents, they never gave up hope she'd gain consciousness and return to them. The boyfriend abandoned her three months after the accident. The story the nurses told gave her shivers, telling how the doctors declared her dead twice before stabilizing to the point of operating to repair the damaged parts of the brain and body. The frail scarred form healed, but the brain remained shut down.

She awakened to a changed world, her mind and body altered by the ravages of the collision. The doctors had no plausible medical explanation for the recovery. Her parents called it a miracle. Merliah knew better, but couldn't express the difference yet. Fragmented memories surfaced, a life of a young woman who looked like her, but the face staring back looked different. Confusion. Anxiety. Pain. Deformed. Disfigured.

"Merliah, are you sure you never had art instruction before? I mean before your accident. Sometimes those skills are latent and suddenly return."

"N–N–No, Ab–bi–gail," Merliah stuttered. With therapy speech slowly returned. Six months ago she was in a wheelchair and several weeks before bedridden, only sitting up with assistance. Although she walked with the use of a walker, mobility had returned. Progress came fast, but not fast enough for Merliah.

"Well, you could fool me. You are a natural. I've never seen anything like this."

Merliah blinked at Abigail. *It is natural to me, Abby. I want to learn more.*

"I wonder if you can do other things. I'm going to speak with your doctor and see if I can work with you more than once a week. You have so much potential."

Merliah raised her shaking arm, straining to speak. "M–m–more."

Abigail chuckled and placed a hand on Merliah's. "Let's see what we can do."

The next day, Merliah, with Abigail's assistance, sat in the reception area of her doctor's office waiting for what seemed like forever. The cognitive sense of time still appeared out of whack for her. At last, the nice lady sitting at the desk put down the telephone receiver and said they could go in to see the doctor.

Abigail helped Merliah to her feet. Merliah moved slowly into the office pushing the metal framed walker a few inches at a time, while Abigail led the way to the doctor's office.

"Doctor Wright, thank you for seeing us," Abigail said.

"Hello, Merliah. How are you today, young lady?"

Merliah tried to speak, thought hard about how to form her words. She'd struggled for months to speak clearly and not mumble. "H…Hell…o, Doc…tor. I–I'm good."

He smiled and she felt proud she got the words out without stumbling too much.

"So, what can I do for you Miss Mann?" the doctor asked.

"I've been working with Merliah for months and she's exhibiting exceptional talent in sculpting for someone who has awakened from a coma several months ago. Can you tell me her history?"

"Miss Mann, you know for privacy reasons, I can't discuss any information about any of the patients with you."

"I'm not asking details about her medical history, sir. I want to start working with her more than once a week. Do you think she can take extra classes without interfering with her structured treatments? I know she has a lot of physical and speech therapy scheduled every day, but I really would like the opportunity to work with her on an on-going basis."

"Doing what exactly? You see her now once a week for what, an hour maybe two? What kind of extra time are we talking about?"

"A couple more days a week, for a few hours each day. I want to expand her development."

"The woman is barely walking, and can't vocalize clearly, and you want to develop her what…painting stick trees, molding odd ashtrays, or weird strange shaped human bodies as an expression of their artistic mind? With all due respect, Miss Mann, Miss Travers won't be capable of having more than the mental capacity of a six year old at best."

I'm sitting right here, Dr. Wright. I'm smart. I'm not six years old.

Abigail glanced over at her, and Merliah smiled. *Tell him Abby.*

The art teacher returned her attention to the doctor. "Merliah understands us. Please don't dismiss her. I may not have a doctor's degree, but I know talent and she has it. I've never seen this from any of the other patients I've instructed. She has a natural ability and tells me she didn't pick up a paint brush or lump of clay before my classes. Maybe she can't remember because of her injury. Just talk to her, please. She can tell you for herself. I assure you, she wants to do this. Don't you, Merliah?"

"Why do I get the feeling I'm being double teamed?" He smirked.

"Hmm, maybe because you are." Abigail grinned, turning in the chair to face Merliah. "Go ahead Merliah. Tell Dr. Wright what you want to do."

"Wait just a minute. I need to get my assistant to pull your paperwork." He pushed the telephone intercom button. "Sherry, could you transfer Merliah Travers' records onto my computer desktop, please."

"Yes, Doctor," the woman on the other end of the intercom said.

He returned his attention to Abigail. "I will have her recent tests shortly, but until then, would you like to tell me what else makes you think she's talented. I've seen nothing during examination. What has she shown you and not me that intrigues you?"

"You'd have to see for yourself, and then you'd understand."

He tilted his head slightly, with eyes squinted, he didn't answer immediately. "Maybe I should."

Sherry Jennings, the secretary, knocked on the door, opening it slowly. "Excuse me. Merliah's file is up on your screen."

Dr. Wright opened the document and perused the contents.

Abigail patted Merliah's hand and smiled.

After a few moments, the doctor looked up from the computer monitor. "I see some slight changes in the last CAT scan but nothing significant is leaping out at me from her file, Miss Mann. The most recent test shows significant brain activity in the damaged area since she awakened, which is interesting but not noteworthy. The physical rehabilitation is progressing, as well as the speech therapy." He peered over his glasses, giving Abigail a quizzical stare. "There's nothing here to indicate she warrants additional art classes as therapy. I'd like to see other therapies increase before painting stick figures or sculpting clay ashtrays."

Merliah sucked in a deep breath. *I don't paint stick figures, Dr. Wright.*

"In all due respect, doctor. I teach my students beyond elemental or useless art. She has surpassed the basics. Nothing she learns will hurt either," Abigail bluntly stated.

Dr. Wright leaned back in his chair, crossing his arms across his chest. "No, I guess not." He glanced at the young woman. "Do you want to take more art classes, my dear?"

Merliah raised her head slowly, stared blankly at the gray-hair man for a few moments, not speaking a word.

"Do you understand what I just said? Do you want to take more art classes with Abigail?" He asked again, enunciating the words slower.

Abigail placed a hand over the young protégé's and squeezed gently. "It's okay, take your time. Tell Doctor Wright what you told me earlier."

Merliah stared intently, getting the reassurance she needed from her friend and teacher. Then she turned to the doctor and concentrated on speaking clearly. "I w–w–ant m–m–ore, A–Abby to show me m–more."

"You want to make pretty things with Abby?"

Merliah nodded, her insides doing flip-flops. She wanted him to say yes so bad, she could taste it.

Dr. Wright glanced at Abigail, back to the computer screen and then to Merliah. After several minutes, he spoke. "Okay, I see no reason why she can't spend a few extra hours a week with you, Miss Mann. The therapy schedule is posted at the ward nurse's station. Work around her sessions because I don't want her regular commitments disrupted."

"Thank you, Doctor Wright. Your approval is all I needed to hear." Abigail stood and assisted Merliah with the walker, escorting her from the doctor's office.

Before going back to Merliah's room, Abigail checked the schedule at the coordinator's desk for Merliah and made arrangements for the next art instruction.

"Okay, we can start your additional lessons Wednesday. I hope you're up to this because I'm going to push you, Merliah."

"I–I'm read–y." As they walked back to her room, Merliah had been waiting for the opportunity to ask Abigail to use her nickname. Her parents and a few friends called her Liah. Abigail Mann had become more than an art instructor over the past couple of months and Merliah wanted to tell her how she came to trust the young teacher. "Ab...by? Can...could you call me Liah? I like to be called Liah."

Abby chuckled. "Sure. You've never said anything before."

"You're my best friend."

Chapter Two

Master and Commander of His Domain Awakens

As he stepped onto the balcony to take in the evening's offerings, the stars, the snow and the fire intertwined their magic into his senses. This was the middle of winter in the Carpathian Mountains, and Sorin Bochinsky's homeland was dark, cold, bleak and depressing. His mood wasn't much better. Bright stars dotted the clear sky. Since the night before, fresh snow had fallen, blanketing the ground several inches deep. Sorin watched the remnants of the thick-flaked flurries fall. They formed icy, splintered patterns layered on the skeleton trees, a striking contrast with white against the black limbs, as if wearing clothing. A movement in the underbrush caught his eye, a slight shift in the shadows. His exceptional night vision spied a small animal scurrying for shelter from the larger predator making chase.

Blue-gray smoke swirled out of chimneys from distant cottages and from his stone manor house as well. The odor of burning wood wafted through the air and his nostrils flared. The scent was a mix of different woods—oak, pine, ash, and something else. Not wood, flesh! The putrid smell of wild game cooking, not human. Pangs of hunger surged through his gut. Squinting eyes, lungs filled to capacity, and fists clenched, Sorin sucked in a tight breath, then shuddered. With a heavy exhale, the warm breath left a trail in the night as he turned and leapt off the balcony. A sharp, cold crack of air rushed out from under Sorin's six foot five inch muscular body as he hit the frozen white landscape below. He growled, scrambled back, and stood prone. Long fingernails and fangs flashed, as he bent over and clawed at the snow, raised a hand arcing overhead, creating a long spray of loose white powder, solidifying in a lacy arch over him. With sure foot, he stole into the cold darkness in hunt of his own prey.

At one time he had loved the winter nights, the brightness of the icy snow sparkling bright, bringing light to his soul, but those were times he shared with his blood mate, his wife. His ex-wife,

Anya. With complete surrender came trade-offs and her jealousy, her dominance, her insatiable desire to control him had reached a point where they could no longer be together. Sorin became Master and Commander of the Eastern Europe Blood Family and with the position came responsibilities which Anya couldn't accept. He had lived in an emotionally unsatisfied relationship for two centuries and had to let her go or lose his sanity.

Over all the years of his existence, he had learned that existing, rather than living was a better choice. No pain and no hurt for a lost love. He'd exist for the blood and sex and no emotional ties to anyone. With his long self-induced solitary lifestyle he may not have any enjoyment or fulfillment in the arms of another, but neither would he suffer the loss that came from loving a woman who could betray him again. *It's easier this way.*

Hunt and fuck indiscriminately. Command his family with an iron fist. Those were his only priorities and needs at present. Before now his existence had been lost in deep memories of another life. Something threatened that life and the unsettling urges building within left him grasping for answers as to why. He shirked the thoughts aside and went in search of prey to satisfy the current desires—sex and blood.

Upon returning from the prey mission a couple hours later, Sorin walked into a solemn house, surrounded by his knight and sergeant vampires. The blood clan of warriors owed him loyalty or he would destroy them. He didn't tolerate distrust in his territory and his word maintained the absolute law of obedience by all.

The heavy mahogany wood door to the study creaked as Sorin pushed the eight foot tall panel open, and then flipped on the lights as he stepped in. He stripped off his black leather overcoat and flung it over the side chair next to the window. Without breaking stride, he continued to the credenza and poured a goblet of blood wine. Taking a seat at his massive desk, he peered out the picture window watching the continuing snow fall of slow-dancing lace crystals. He took a long sip from the gold-rimmed crystal glass, the dark liquid held the aroma of copper, and the finest mix of fermented grapes with the hint of black currant. He let the silky smooth substance linger in his mouth before swallowing. "Ahh, exactly what I needed to wash away the taste of the filthy human whore."

The sound of the study door opening drew him from his thoughts and he spun the chair around. "Good evening, Master," Maksim Chernovski said. "I completed the accounting for the month. I also received a call from Liam Langston in New York requesting an opening for a new trainee. He wants to send her over for the next training session if space is available. I told him I would clear the transfer with you, but we would most likely be able to accommodate his request."

"Yes, that is fine. He is an excellent client. Confirm it with him," Sorin said as he leaned back in the leather upholstered chair.

"Very good," Maks said. "And if there's nothing else to review tonight, would you like to take one last look at the trainees before we return them to their respective masters tomorrow?"

"Yes, let's get it over with, Maks, I'm tired." Rising from behind his wood-carved desk, Sorin walked toward the office doors. The night was young and Sorin's body felt drained even though he just returned from hunting. Perhaps, feeding from prostitutes who harbored diseases wasn't his best choice in blood donors, but the nearby village didn't provide much to choose from. Deep down, he knew the women available weren't the real problem.

Lately, he questioned his sanity, slowly feeling his mental acuity slipping away, especially if he continued down the current path. He had to confide in someone and in such a way as not to undermine his absolute power and authority.

"Master, may I speak freely?" Maks asked. The two men weren't only Master and Sergeant Palatine, but old friends. Good friends. The subordinate vampire had served him well for over a hundred and fifty years.

Sorin stopped abruptly and turned. "I do not wish to speak about it, Maks."

"There's something wrong. I haven't seen you like this before. You're lethargic, can't concentrate, and you're not interested in training. This strange behavior is definitely not you. I'm saying this as your friend, and I'm worried." Maks paused, and added, "Tell me you didn't contract the Vamp Virus from America."

One dark brow arched, and Sorin shook his head. "No, of course not. I do not wish to discuss this right now. Can we go?"

"Whatever you say, lord."

As the two men proceeded to the training dungeon, Sorin's mind wandered to his troubled thoughts. If he were honest with himself he'd tell his friend. In his heart, he agreed Maks was right. Sorin recognized something was wrong, terribly wrong, and he couldn't stop the pain tearing at his insides. The dreams, actually more like nightmares, started six months ago, haunting him, disrupting any chance of rest. Was he going insane? Pushing the thoughts aside, they arrived at the dungeon. Hissing out a breath, he turned to Maks and blurted out, "I'm having dreams."

Maks stared at Sorin, wrinkling his brow. "We don't dream. What are you talking about?"

"You wanted to learn what is wrong with me, I'm telling you." *Christ, now my second suspects I'm crazy. I probably should have waited.* Sorin didn't let Maks answer. Instead, he pushed open the dungeon door and herded him inside, closing the door behind them.

The sounds of a whip cracking, a hand slapping flesh, screams and stern commands from a male vamp master could be heard as the two vamps entered the dimly lit room. Sorin and Maks witnessed a sub trainee being flogged on the St. Andrew's cross. She thrashed her head from side to side in the throes of a climax. Maks leaned close to Sorin, chuckling. "Derrick hasn't lost his touch with making the slaves beg for release, of course, he's not as good as you, lord."

Sorin nodded with his arms crossed. Sub and slave training was an art in his opinion. Running one of the most successful enterprises for the past hundred years meant great importance. He and Maks watched the scenes play out before them—five interns finishing a three-month intensive training program. After tonight, they would be sent back to their new masters ready to take their place as certified Erotic Re-Imprint or ERI graduates. ERI was Sorin's company, owned solely by him. The instructors took the trainees through the final lessons, led by the senior master instructor, Derrik Lungu, six foot three inches of steely brawn, a true dominant vampire. He had been in Sorin's blood clan for over two hundred years and personally trained by Sorin.

The submissive under Derrik's tutelage turned her attention away from him, catching Sorin's eye. "Lord Commander we're honored you are here to see our trainees on their last night. Do you wish to inspect them personally before we ship them to their owners?" Derrick asked, stepping away from the woman.

"Thank you. As always, I trust your skills. From what I can see so far these little subs look fine indeed." Sorin moved up the line of five naked women in various positions on different apparatuses. They were each either ball gagged, blindfolded, or handcuffed. On a few, all three restraints or devices were used.

Sorin took pride in running one of the most prestigious and well-known submissive/slave training schools in Eastern Europe, perhaps the world. Known more through the vampire community, he recently saw an increase with interest from the human population for his services. He wasn't sure why, but he didn't particularly care, the increase made him a rich vampire in the process, rivaling most of the American Grand Masters and Commanders. One day he could be Grand Master of all Europe, an honor he'd gladly accept from his peers if the position were ever created. Grand Master and Commander of his eastern section of Europe a worthy position and comfortable, but he had ambitions of uniting the territories under one rule. He was sure the other MCs had similar aspirations and a long drawn-out bloody fight would ensue. The possibility of an extensive war kept them from ripping each other's hearts out. Modern times put a significant damper on such ideas. Dragos tried in the States and he met with his own demise, a path Sorin didn't wish to travel anytime soon.

"Would you like to try any of the women, my lord?" Derrick asked.

"Hmm, tempting. But they belong to another. I don't wish to lose control and mark them by mistake. I know you have done an exceptional job as usual. Carry on Derrick."

Sorin couldn't concentrate on the trainees. He normally tested their education, but not this night. After confiding a few minutes earlier to Maks about dreaming, he sensed the uneasiness and had to discuss the matter further to alleviate the tension.

After departing the dungeon, he and Maks walked halfway down the torch lit corridor without a word exchanged between them. Then, Maks spoke, breaking the silence. "Not to question your authority, lord, but what the hell was the ambivalent response back there? You never pass on fucking at least one of the trainees. What's going on?"

"Nothing, and you *are* questioning my authority, friend. Be careful." Sorin released a low growl.

"Forgive me, Lord Commander." Maks bowed his head.

Upon the approach to the grand room of the manor, Sorin inwardly questioned his anger toward Maks. The poor vamp wasn't to blame for his foul mood. The cause was the infernal lack of rest. The dreams, the haunting nightmares plaguing his thoughts over the past six months were the reason for his disagreeable disposition.

The large wood double doors opened wide into the room. Six other knights lounged on various pieces of furniture. Several talked amongst themselves, another silently read a book from Sorin's vast collection of antique volumes, and Serghei tended the burning embers in the fireplace. All turned their attention to Sorin upon his entrance into the formal parlor.

"Leave me," Sorin motioned with a flick of his hand, walking toward the elevated ornately wood carved credenza. He took the crystal stopper from the top of the bottle and poured the blood wine into a glass.

All the other vamp knights left the chamber, except for Maks. "I'm assuming you didn't mean for me to leave, my lord."

Without looking up from pouring the wine, Sorin asked, "Would you like a glass, Maks?"

"As you wish, my lord. I can't have you drinking and enjoying the night alone."

Sorin harrumphed. "No, I don't think I should drink on my own. A bad habit to be sure." He grasped both drinks, walked toward the divan in front of the fireplace, and handed one of the glasses of blood wine to Maks, and then reclined upon the velvet-covered sofa.

"Thank you. I think I'll need this."

Sorin took a sip of his drink. *Yes, you may very well need this and more.* "From the expression on your face, you want me to tell you everything, don't you?" Sorin asked, his eyes narrowed and could have indicated the same thing without uttering a word.

"Of course, I have thought of nothing else since you confided in me. Your actions the past several months make sense now."

"Hmm, are you saying I'm failing in my duties as Master and Commander and question my authority, Maks? If you believe that is true, I will show you how much in control I am."

"Oh, no Sorin, never. I'm not questioning your abilities, only curious about what you said. I've never known any vamp to dream before. Is it a phenomenon only occurring for the elders?"

"No, I don't think so. I've never heard of it happening either. Trust me. It's a curse, not a blessing. I haven't told anyone until now." He ran a thumb along the rim of the glass, and then took a sip of the blood wine.

"Maybe if you talk about the dream, get it out in the open, we can figure out how to solve the problem."

"A problem? Yes, the dreams are becoming an annoyance." Sorin's brow wrinkled as he caught Maks staring at him. He began to doubt the decision of trusting his Sergeant Palatine with the personal information, but he took the leap of faith. "My dreams are filled with blood and lust...and pain. These dreams have come almost every day over the past six months, especially more intense over the last several weeks."

"Every day when you are sleeping?"

"Ah, the true crux of the problem, Maks. I'm not resting. This woman, a beautiful woman, called to me to rescue her. I went to her and pulled her from a dark place, so black and forbidden I barely found her, but I did find her. I thought at first the cries for help were of a human crossing over, lost and unable to find their way." He paused and took another sip of blood wine.

"Was she?" Maks asked.

"Was she what? Crossing over?" Another sip of wine touched his lips as the anxiety built.

"Yes."

"No, but I didn't know the state of being until I found her. At first, she was frightened of the blood and me. I didn't sense death. She was very much alive, but trapped in the darkness. I led her out and into the light."

"You did what?"

Sorin shook his head slightly. "Yes, I know. Strange isn't it. I walked in the light, briefly. She faded away from view, or at least I did, back to where I was when it all began."

"Which was where exactly?"

"Miami while I rested. About seven or eight months ago the first meeting happened when I went to help Stefan with the Dragos situation. The day after the siege, I was awakened by the faint call from the woman. I thought the voice was a psychic connection from another vamp, but…"

"But, it wasn't. The woman is human as you stated. What else happened because you are shaken like I've never seen you before? Was it really a dream or did you save her?"

"Oh, it happened and continues to happen, every day. About six weeks ago they became more intense and increased in frequency. I hear faint calls from her and I can't rest soundly. I gaze into those crystal, sapphire eyes and I'm transfixed by her beauty. I can't escape her siren's song and imploring eyes."

"Did you feed from her? Maybe you made a blood connection which needs to be severed, if so."

"I didn't take any blood. I've had only mind touches. I don't know where she is or even if she is real. She's like a ghost haunting me."

"Sorin, there's no such thing as ghosts."

"Yes, I know, just like we don't dream. But I am, and if there were such a thing as ghosts, she'd be one. She has pale skin, golden hair, the bluest eyes, and a light shining around her." His breath hitched. "She takes my breath away."

"She sounds more like an angel, not a ghost."

"Hmm, you're right. She is an angel. My angel. I must find her, Maks. I sense she needs me. She continues to call for me, but I don't have any idea where to begin to look."

"Start from the beginning. You said this connection was strongest in Miami? Why not start there. I'm sure you can make an excuse to do business with Master Stefan."

Sorin thought for a few moments, running his thumb along the rim of the wine glass. He finished sipping the wine and put the glass down on the coffee table. "Yes, Maks, thank you for your counsel. I will go to Miami after I take care of a few loose ends with some family affairs. A couple more weeks shouldn't make a big difference. The lead time will give Stefan a chance to prepare as well."

"Anything I can do for you? Arrangements for the trip, perhaps?"

"Take care of my travel plans and any correspondence before I depart. Everything has to be in order. I'll leave you in charge while I'm absent. I shouldn't be gone for more than a week. Two at the most."

"Consider it done, my lord."

Maks left the room, leaving Sorin to his own thoughts. The woman, this angel and he were bound together, mind and soul. How, he didn't know for sure, but he was determined to find out, why and how. If the nightmares were to end, he decided binding them by body and not only through their minds had to happen. Though Sorin didn't know what could come of such an arrangement or how it would happen, he was certain of one thing. He'd stand against the forces of the universe if necessary, to protect her and make her his despite the torment he'd endured the past several months. His beautiful mystery angel would be his. That is, once he found her.

The shadows of the flickering flame danced on the wood-paneled walls, writing in their secret, ever-changing message. If only the encrypted code could decipher his dreams, his nightmarish existence would cease and the beauty would be his. He cursed under his breath.

Rest...a restful sleep is much needed. I never seem to be able to get enough with this apparition haunting me.

Chapter Three

The Rouged Princess

The dark lover's large hands ran across the pale nakedness with familiarity and wanton desire. The tender touch of fingertips swirled circles along the abdomen, then across the delicate underside of small, round breasts and rested at the hollow of the neck. Drops of blood trickled from the wound of the exposed nape. He leaned over to lap up the last of the beauty's elixir of life. As he tilted his head to the right side, he ran a moist tongue over pencil-thin, blue-flesh lips in delight. A wicked grin emerged viewing the body with satisfaction. An adrenaline rush filled his veins staring into the motionless, glassy-eyed blonde he picked up at the nightspot, Club Euphoria.

"Such a fragile human female, unsuspecting, and wanting a blood fix and sex." Obliged, he gave her both, and more.

Now, she'll be a pretty little bitch forever. Get on with it. Time is slipping away.

"Shut up. Let me do this my way."

Every nerve awakened as he continued to pose her, every vein coursed with burning life force in anticipation of the final piece of his artwork. He took his time making the adjustment to each limb, ties of silk scarves around the wrists and ankles secured at the bedposts. The foul odor of her stale perfume and their sex saturated the bed linens necessitated washing her body. The chore would slow him down, but an unavoidable one, else his identity be discovered before he intended. Fetching a bowl of water, soap and a washcloth from the kitchen, he returned to the muse's bed within minutes.

Positioned on her back, he methodically wiped her flesh with warm water and lemon scented detergent. Soon, the breathless body lay on the mattress perfectly arranged, and cleansed and scented with lemon-fresh detergent. The sleeping princess of his dreams was ready for his artistic touch. The lethal lover dressed her in white lace bra and panties.

After the monster within him was satisfied with the specifications for the muse, he reached into the duffel bag he'd brought, and pulled out a compact. Red rouge. A deep crimson.

With a long middle finger, he dipped into the smudge pot. A dab of the cream was applied to his human canvas, first on one cheek then the other. From the apples of the high cheekbones of the demure beauty, he swirled over the cool skin several times and lightly blended fading away into the hairline. Pleased with the deepness of blush, he smeared the rouge upon the fixed smile of the angelic face glaring back with a glassy stare.

"Beautiful. You are art for an eternity, little princess." Finished, he retrieved his camera from the satchel and prepared to click off a picture, but paused. "Almost forgot." Next, he pulled out the black velvet box from his bag and removed the rhinestone tiara. Carefully placing the mini-crown on his female model, he set the fastening comb just right, cocking his head back and forth deciding if the position was perfectly placed on her brow.

With the digital camera ready, he towered above her beside the bed and zoomed in, capturing her fine features. With a finger poised on the shutter button, he frowned at the close-up image in the LCD screen. He stopped and lowered the camera, and then adjusted a stray hair. His art composition had to be perfectly done. The presentation for the authorities and his audience would come under scrutiny if one detail was imperfect. Once corrected, he stepped back and reset the lens first from one angle, then another.

After snapping a few pictures with her face, he zoomed out and took in the entire body, taking more shots for the unfinished canvas at his studio. Excitement rose within him at the thought of the impact his work would have on both the person who found the deceased female and those viewing the finished portrait. Inside his trousers, his cock grew hard. His breath hitched. The beast driving him to seek out and kill for his art growled in triumph.

"Exquisite." The artistic murderer leaned over and captured her mouth one more time, smudging the blood-red lips. He tucked the camera in its case and put it back into the duffel. Next, he pulled out a pair of latex gloves, sheathed his hands and exited the room. He planned not to remove them until he departed the building. Cleaning and trying to erase any evidence of his presence was unnecessary, but he had to make sure. When he returned to the new princess's apartment, they went straight to the bedroom and he'd been careful not to touch too many articles, doorknobs or furniture. He washed and dried the bowl and with the wet dishcloth, wiped down any counters and other hard surfaces.

Satisfied with the clean-up in the front room, he revisited the bedroom and made a clean sweep as he did in the living area. When completed, he picked up the cordless phone seated on the nightstand and with gloved hand punched in 9-1-1.

After two rings, a woman's voice said, "Nine-One-One. What is your emergency?"

Covering the mouthpiece slightly, the killer spoke. "Yes, my mother is having a heart attack. Please send the paramedics. Please, please, she's unconscious. Help me." He disguised his voice with a southern accent, which added to the pathos of the cry for assistance.

"Yes, sir. Calm down and tell me your name."

"Who cares what my name is? Just send an ambulance."

"Sir, I need you to calm down and tell me exactly where you are."

"Yeah sure. Apartment Three C, One…Nine…Six…Three Addison Street. Please hurry." His breath sounded labored.

"Paramedics are en route. Stay by your mother. Is she breathing?"

"No, um, I can't tell."

"Do you know CPR, sir?"

"No!"

"Sir, please calm down. Is anyone else there with you?"

"No!" *I've had enough of this idiotic banter. Hang up on the bitch. We have other things to do before the humans arrive.*

The killer dropped the phone next to his beauty, leaving the connection open. Why did he care who heard now? No fingerprints, no voice trace, no way to link him to the young woman. No one even at the nightclub could recognize him. He made sure he sat in the darkest corner and kept his head down. A quick change of clothes and all camera recording would show a man dressed in black with sandy blond hair.

The sound of the emergency dispatcher continually called to him over the phone. The killer moved from the bedroom after surveying the area and continued to listen to the escalating tone of voice coming through the cordless.

One last minute check of the living room for any misplaced tell-tale evidence and he quietly slipped out of the apartment, leaving his latest canvas for discovery.

"Ah! My masterpiece for the entire world to see. Those so-called art critics think I've no talent." He stomped over the wooden floor toward the front door. As he turned the knob, the anger built to the boiling point within him. With a fisted hand, he punched the side of the wall, leaving a small dent in the wallboard and him with bloody knuckles. "Juvenile, common, not worthy to be called an artist, is what they bellowed in their reviews."

Yes, they'll all pay, won't they my dear boy. Every last one of them will receive what they deserve. I'll help you.

The fanged-killer lover slipped undetected from the walk-up flat as he caught the muffled sound of sirens of the emergency vehicles break the evening silence. When he reached the second level landing, he took notice of the voices of men running up the stairs from the first floor. He slipped behind the corner of the side hall to wait.

"Carlos, you got everything man? The call came from the third floor. Shit! I hate these old buildings without an elevator."

"Hey, stop the complaining. You could use the exercise. Stacy said you were getting a little paunch on you," Carlos said, chuckling.

"Well, all I can say is you've got room to talk, dude. More than beer has been filling out your waist."

"I work out. This here's a tight core."

"Yeah, right."

The two men started up the third flight of stairs. The killer came from around the corner and decided to stay and listen. A wicked grin crossed his chiseled face. The temptation to wait and witness the exquisite scene unfurl gripped him. The adrenaline flowing through his veins gave him such a high, half the thrill came from watching the pathetic humans scurry about trying to solve the canvases he created. After a brief hesitation, he decided departing the area a better choice.

With sensitive hearing, he smirked when he overheard the first rescue worker find the beauty, his latest masterpiece, perfectly painted lips and cheeks accentuated with red rouge.

"Jesus, this isn't a heart attack call. I think this is the work of the Tiara Princess Killer I read about. Call the cops, Troy. Don't touch anything. This is a crime scene now."

"Wow, dude. She looks like a freakin' Barbie doll, all dressed in sexy underwear and a painted face. And with a tiny crown. Whoever did this is into some kinky-ass shit."

"Yeah, pretty little thing too. Fuck! Who the hell would do something this disgusting?"

"A sick bastard, that's who. Eww, this is giving me the creeps. I think I'm going to toss my cookies, man. Ach."

The killer grinned again. As he rounded the bend to slink away under the guise of night, the desire to remain and watch the law enforcement types figure out what happened compelled him to sneak back into the building. "I have a name now. Interesting. I wonder what else they have on me." He chuckled and decided to go with his first choice and leave, not hang around and be discovered. He turned the corner of the next brick building.

"Another time I'll stay and play."

It's too soon to show your hand. There's more art to create before dawn.

Chapter Four

A Couple of Paint Brushes and a New Canvas

"My goodness Liah, I can't believe you've only been painting for a couple of weeks. This is incredible. First, sculpting, now painting." Merliah observed Abby's enthusiasm for the landscape canvas, which she couldn't contain. "Are you creating this scene from a memory? Comparing what you started painting the first day until now shows immense improvement."

Merliah stared at Abby for a few moments unsure of why she asked the question. She had problems processing questions and answers to the queries—her brain couldn't get the message to her mouth with any consistent accuracy. Frustration mounted daily along with the incessant headaches and the tingling throughout her body for the last several weeks. *Why can't I be normal again?* The doctor and speech therapist told her after more than four years the brain function to sync back with the rest of her body would take some time to regain full functionality. *But after six months, I still don't feel in sync.*

For Merliah, tomorrow wouldn't be soon enough. After almost five years locked away from everything she used to have, the time lost felt like an eternity. Getting on with the rest of her life the way she lived before the accident became her number one priority. The painting techniques Abby taught her were fun and relaxing, taking her mind off the pain of the other therapies and bad memories.

The words formed finally. "I played here once." She lied, not knowing the truth. The wildflower field came from the dreams. The fantasy world she conjured with the dark stranger who saved her.

"Really? It looks like a nice place, but the field doesn't look like anywhere in Florida I've seen before. Was this meadow somewhere else when you were a little girl?"

Merliah shook her head, not sure why she was so quick to answer. *I have been here, I think. But, when and where is this place?*

Abby placed a hand on Merliah's shoulder. "It doesn't matter because the painting is beautiful, so full of life and imagery. I could step right into the field and touch the flowers. They appear real." She stood staring at the painting. "Strange, I swear I'm being drawn into the meadow. It's powerful and moving." Abby extended her hand to touch the canvas.

Merliah gently restrained Abby's hand, "I–I'm not finished. You c–can touch when I–I'm done."

Abby chuckled. "Liah, I'm not serious. You can't transport into a painting except in your imagination, but that's what makes a great artist. I think you're on your way to becoming one, sweetie. I can't get over the effective use of layering and colors."

Smiling, Merliah picked up a brush and continued painting. The landscape remained unfinished, but a few more strokes and she'd apply the final touch.

"Amazing," Abby said, shaking her head. "Look at you. I'd have never thought of using various brush strokes and shading to create these effects until I'd been painting for years. Liah, this is like a mini-masterpiece. I have to do something special for you."

Abby left the studio, but asked Merliah to stay until she returned. A half hour later, she finished the painting project, and slipped into deep thought, almost in a trance. Reflecting on the most recent dream, she sensed her mysterious companion had an urgency to find her. She wanted him too. He'd become more than her salvation to recovery. The dreams had progressed to the point she wanted them to become lovers. She sensed he wished for the same. Was this her brain's way of healing, finding her way back to sanity, to real life? Whatever or whoever he was, he did save her from the darkness, but where was he? If he really existed beyond her imagination, she wanted to see him in flesh and blood.

The dark man called out in her dreams some nights, other times she called to him. The stranger, who brought her into the light and out of the nightmare, now haunted her. He aroused a sexual desire within her she now craved, almost like an addiction. He couldn't be real, no matter how desperately she wanted him to be, and the frustration began to overwhelm her day-to-day activities. Six months ago, the doctors couldn't explain the spontaneous awakening either, but something changed within her, a burning inside. Indescribable. Yearning. Desire. Knowledge. Except, the headaches and body-tingling she tried to express and they only treated her with medications she hated taking. No, somehow she felt the dreams were related and the man in those dreams could save her as either her lover or savior. *He has to be real.* She was certain the latest encounter affirmed her hypothesis. He was the key to the changes within her, but she didn't know how to prove the point.

> *The hard angles of his outline were visible even though he stood back in the concealing shadows of her night-filled bedroom. Slowly he lifted his hand, beckoning her.*
>
> *"Come closer." His quiet tone was darkly sensual, sending shivers through her entire body.*
>
> *"Who are you?" She cringed at the sound of her breathless voice. He was the one causing her to feel breathless and shivery. All these feelings and she hadn't even seen his face.*
>
> *"Maybe I'm the one you're searching for." His hypnotic voice beckoned her closer and she couldn't resist. Before even realizing it, she moved toward him, forcing herself to stop a foot away from his shadowy form.*
>
> *Too close, yet not close enough. Her mind warred with her body, leaving her confused in front of the sensual power he so easily wielded, and fighting a desire threatening to envelop her completely.*
>
> *Forcing air into her lungs, she breathed out. "Why are you the one I'm searching for?"*
>
> *Only a few words, but they had the compelling power to send her senses into overdrive.*
>
> *"Because you need me."*

The need to be with him drove Merliah to make identifying him her number one priority, longing to know the answer to the question of who he was. She was falling in love with a dream, a figment of her imagination. Yet, in her heart, she felt he could be real and all she had to do was find him. Painting the landscape was the way, the conduit for their meeting again. Not knowing how or why, she felt compelled to paint to find the answer. Something inside yanked at her core, energy, a compulsion, she couldn't explain. And create she did.

Another hour slowly ticked off the wall clock as Merliah finished the newest canvas. With some dexterity difficulties, Merliah managed to clean the area where she worked, putting the brushes in cleaner as well as wash her hands, then tossed the apron over the back of chair. Although she made great progress in regaining motor skills, she had more months of rehabilitation ahead. Patience began to wear thin. She wanted her life back, the one she remembered, with her parents, great job, and friends. All had been lost because of the accident and the only person in her life who offered continuity was Abby.

And the shadow man.

The room where Merliah resided at the facility was comprised of four white walls enclosing a space of approximately a hundred square feet, a small bathroom, twin bed, small dresser and an upholstered chair. When her parents visited, they went to the common areas instead of staying in her dreary little space. Upon returning from the art room, Merliah's energy waned and navigating the distance to the patients' domicile wing took all her strength. All she wanted to do was crawl into bed and rest.

Within a few minutes of easing down upon the bed, a knock rapped on her door, startling her to an upright position.

"Hello. Come in."

The slow movement of the doorway had Merliah thinking the visitor was one of the nurses' aides checking on her. They rarely bothered her, but when they did, they did so to make sure she attended therapy or meals. When she first came out of the coma, and before she gained control of her legs, attendants always wheeled her to the dining room. Now, she could get around on her own with a walking cane.

The familiar face of her teacher peeked around the edge. "Liah? It's Abby. May I come in?"

"Yes. Hi, Abby."

"I'm sorry if I'm interrupting, but I checked out the art studio first and you weren't there. What I had to do took a little longer than I expected. I'm sorry if you waited for me, but I do have exciting news."

"W–What is it?"

"I called a friend of mine in Miami. He owns an art gallery and has graciously said he'd like to take a look at your work. I told him all about you and the progress you've made in a short time. He's interested and I'd like to take him a few of your pieces to show him. If he likes them, he has a special exhibition for new artists in a couple of months. Isn't this exciting?"

"M–my paintings? No, I can't."

"Why not? They are amazing considering the amount of time you've been painting. At the rate you're improving, in a couple of months they'll be remarkable, and quite marketable in my humble opinion."

"No, I can't do it. They're special."

"Exactly my point. You have to share this talent with the world, Liah. You can inspire others by showing how you've overcome many obstacles and created such beauty. Please, let me take a few of your pieces to show Antoine and let him make a determination."

"No, they can't be touched. They are special, Abby."

"Okay then, how about I bring Antoine here. Let him take a look with you present. Would having him stop by be acceptable?"

Merliah stared at her friend, and teacher and confidant. Could she confide how special her painting really was? Something could happen when someone touched the finished canvases, something unexplainable to normal science and she didn't want anyone to know. She recently discovered the new world she created, but would others? Even Abby? The idea of showing others how she overcame all the obstacles, some of which she still worked on, then exhibiting her art could be a good thing. The slow healing powers every time she returned from visiting the world in her painting at first were unremarkable. Until she understood how and why they occurred, she had to keep the secret. "If I can be in the room, okay. I'll let him see my pictures."

Abby leaned over and hugged Merliah. "Oh, this is great."

"When? When does An–Ant–wan come here?"

"How's tomorrow? I can call him and set everything up."

"Okay, if I'm not busy."

Abby laughed. "Oh, yes. You are such a woman of many activities. I'll make the arrangements for the meeting after your lunch. How's that sound?"

"Good."

As promised, Abby had all Merliah's canvases set up in the studio on easels ready for her friend to inspect after lunch the next day. As she sat on a stool, tapping her feet in anticipation, a collage of emotions bounced around in her head and filled her with anxiety. She couldn't let the stranger touch her paintings after she imprinted them. *Look, but don't touch.* A saying her mother always told her as a little girl. She snickered to herself. The large-faced clock on the wall ticked off the minutes until at exactly one o'clock the door to the studio opened. Abby and a distinguished looking man walked in.

Merliah eyed Antoine Rousseau, the man Abby introduced as the owner of the art gallery. He seemed nice and interested in her paintings, and she liked him. Then he spoke in whispers to Abby. He stared at her more than her work making her uneasy and she got the feeling it wasn't about the paintings.

"Why does she wear a veil, Abby? Something wrong with her?" he asked, speaking softly.

"Merliah is self-conscious about her looks since her accident. Please don't make a big deal out of it. You're here for her art not her appearance, Antoine."

"Hmm, yes, yes, I am." He turned his attention to Merliah. "You young lady are *merveilleux.* Incredible is all I can say, my dear. But, I'm a bit confused. I thought your name is Merliah. Who is Phoenix?"

"I am."

His eyebrows crinkled.

"If I may, Merliah doesn't want anyone to know who she is. I call her Liah, but for her art, she wants to be called Phoenix, like the mythological creature which rises from the ashes. Not unlike her life after awakening from the coma she was in for four and a half years," Abby explained.

"What a fascinating story which adds to your charm. I'm very interested in showing your works with the other two new artists

I've signed on. Could you produce, say another five or six pieces in the next sixty days?" Antoine posed with his left hand under his right elbow and his right hand resting on his lips. Then, the corners of his mouth turned up and his long eyelashes fluttered.

Merliah stared at him like he was unreasonable with the outlandish deadline. How could she produce what he wanted in such a short period of time?

"Liah, you can do it. I have faith in you. You are so focused lately. This is a great opportunity for you," Abby said, as her expression was nothing short of a look of excited expectations, one of a little child finding out they were about to ride a merry-go-round for the first time.

"Do I have to meet people at your gallery Mister Ant–wan? I–I don't want people to see me...like this."

"You should, helps the public relate to you, but I think if you dressed with some mystery, the appearance will add to the hypnotic effect your art has. Oh, *mais oui*, you will create a real buzz with interest as not only how intriguing your work is, but you shall be captivating as well. Yes, yes, yes, this could be the best showing for the gallery yet." The eccentric gallery owner paced the floor in front of the three easels displaying Merliah's paintings. "Three distinct artists—one a really dark and morose *avant-garde* multi-media painter, a photographer and a mystery woman named Phoenix painting in the style of Monet and Van Gogh will grace Rousseau Gallery. I love it. Just love it, love it."

"Oh, I like Antoine's idea, Merliah. The mystery woman, dressed in red, or black with lace. What do you think?"

"I–I guess. Maybe, my mom can make me a nice dress with a matching veil in lace. I like blue, not red."

Abby and Antoine laughed. "Anything you want, little Merliah. You will be the hit at the show. You will see. Abby, you can help with the preparation once she finishes each piece, if you don't mind. Will she be able to come by the gallery at least a week before so we can go over all the paperwork? Is she...you know, legally competent to sign?"

"Good question. I'll find out and let you know. In the meantime, I think we need to leave Liah so she can get to work."

"Very good." He paused. "Do you wish me to call you Liah, Phoenix or your given name? I need to put which name you choose in the promotional materials."

The two women looked at one another. Merliah shrugged her shoulders and didn't say a word.

"I think Phoenix will work best. Liah is shy about people knowing who she really is," Abby answered.

"I understand. Phoenix it is."

What have I committed to?

Over the next several weeks, Merliah spent every free moment painting. At night she drew inspiration from her mystery man. He had become her muse, encouraging her to create the beauty surrounding her. Deep down, she knew he wasn't real and the ideas came from within, but he always seemed real when they were together in the dreams. Before she realized what she'd done, eight finished pieces were completed instead of five pieces promised Antoine, as well as smaller ones for some of the patients at the institute. Only those for the fellow occupants and one special landscape did she add her personal touch. For the wheelchair bound boy down the hall, she created a personal scene and showed him how he could escape his paralysis, if only briefly. The look on his face made painting all worthwhile. Her secret of the special places she created would be kept by those she shared her skills with. Besides, some couldn't speak and others knew if they said anything, they'd be committed to a life worse than where they were.

After a particularly vivid dream occurring during the daytime, her shadow man inspired a painting filled with vibrant colors set in a meadow and a wooded area in the background. The place depicted the surroundings in her dream, a peaceful mix of wildflowers with a forest in the background, blue skies and bright sun. It was her favorite and all her energy went into perfecting the paint strokes.

Chapter Five

A dreamer finds his way out of a nightmare

Before his departure for Miami the next night, he thought long and hard about how he'd find the angel of his dreams. Hours were spent pacing and gazing out the open window of his bedroom into the unforgiving Romanian winter sky. A partially covered full moon lit up the night, but cast shadows on the frozen, snow-covered ground.

His heart pounded behind his ribs in anticipation of leaving within a few short hours. If he breathed deep enough, Sorin could find the scent of her skin, of her heat surrounding him. On him. He gripped the window mercilessly, wanting to throw his head back and howl with rage.

He breathed deeply of the late winter air flowing over him, the cooling breezes of the night's darkness soothing his stressed sex. Gradually, his reaction to the dream faded. His tensed muscles relaxed until he could stand at his full height without animalistic need clawing through him, without the desire to be sated spearing him with a viciousness never experienced in his lifetime. The breeze entering his home through the window danced over cooling skin, teasing shoulder length black hair, raising a ghost of the sparking touch he had yet to experience, yet knew too damn well regardless.

Sorin's head sank forward a fraction, his gaze focusing as adrenaline continued to resonate through his blood with the hunger of his unsatisfied sexual dreams. He wasn't disappointed with any of the women he'd shared an occasional interlude with, none had met his long-term expectations or his deepest desires. What did bother him was this unknown vision tempting him, drawing him into a world of seduction and sex, every night.

Since her initial invasion of his dreams, no other woman had raised more than a whisper of attraction or appeal. Even the thought of slackening the lust with another woman was impossible.

Any woman other than his dream-induced siren left him cold and disinterested.

His seductress was mystery, desire, hunger, and maybe something more he couldn't put a finger on. Something called to him almost as strongly as her voice and scent, a hidden element he knew he recognized but couldn't place. And with just a dream, she could make him experience things he'd never felt wide awake and in bed with a flesh and blood woman.

Needing to escape the torment of his dreams prior to the departure for Miami, Sorin stepped away from the wide window and inwardly called to the heat of change within. He craved the rush of blood, the changed tempo of his heart pounded in his ears. He needed the beast clawing at his insides to be let loose like a dying man needed forgiveness. The fanged creature of the night begged for release and he allowed it.

Leaping through the window with a fluid movement, he sprinted into the moonlit night. His long, harried gait carried him miles into the woods where he slid to a stop in the complete stillness, breathing heavily, trying to leave his misery behind, and knowing he failed. He let out a long, piercing song hearing the reverberation of his voice combined with the echo of nature. Gradually, peace calmed his erratic pulse, though it was only temporary, until he slept again tomorrow. Tonight he'd quiet the beast and worry about the trip later.

The long flight across an ocean began upon awakening at sunset the next night. Evidently, coming to Florida in the States would be the answer to his torment. Her call for rescue had grown stronger since landing on the faraway ground.

The two vampires, dressed all in black, eyed one another. Stone-faced expressions on both as the distance between them narrowed. "Sorin, my brother, nice to see you again. A good flight, man?" Stefan, the Master and Commander of the Southeast Region, asked.

"Stefan, yes, I slept the whole way." He laughed deep in his chest. "Good to see you again. Thank you for allowing me to come and stay with you." Sorin descended the stairs from the private jet on the tarmac.

They shook hands and patted each other on the back.

"A bit warm here compared to the mountains I left. Snow a foot deep covers the ground near my manor." Sorin added and cocked his head showing curiosity. "What's this?"

"What?"

"Color? You never wear anything but black. Like me."

The host vampire lowered his eyes, and then slightly shook his head. "Alex. She says I need more vibrancy in my wardrobe. She especially prefers lavenders and blues. You don't like my new, modern look?"

"I never thought I'd see the day when a woman would dictate to you what you wore. Hmm, interesting. Anything else she controls, my friend?"

Stefan scowled. "Love tends to do unusual things to a person. Last I checked you're the one who's traveled thousands of miles to find a woman who may not even exist. How long has it been? Has there been anyone since Anya or are you the modern vampire and play the field?"

Sorin ignored his friend's amicable jibe.

"Let's go, she's waiting for us." The vamps took a few steps, then Stefan broke stride. "I can't believe you don't like my new modern man look. I think the colors reflect onto my skin and give the illusion I'm human."

"I believe the word is frou-frou and you're not human, brother."

Stefan motioned for his driver to attend to Sorin's bags. "Don't let Alex hear you say such a thing. She's determined to have me blend in as she tells me every night. I know she means well, but sometimes I want some breathing room."

"Clingy is she? I knew she was trouble the first time I met her. Why do you keep her around if you can't have her submit?" The men walked toward the waiting company vehicle.

"Our relationship isn't like that, Sorin. She's a modern woman with a career she enjoys." The driver opened the back door to the black SUV and the two vampires slid into the backseat of the Escalade.

"I understand. I left Anya during Victorian times. She was liberated and ahead of the times then. With her strong will, we didn't work as before."

"Sorry, brother, but I never thought Anya was the woman for you. I told you once and I should have known better. Now there's a woman haunting you, driving you to near insanity. Isn't that what you said several weeks ago? Well, I'm not saying anything more. Let's change the subject."

"Wise choice."

"Fine. Maybe you'll return the favor of my hospitality and allow me a vacation to your manor in the Carpathians. I could bring Alex."

"After living in this balmy South Florida climate perhaps a winter in our homeland would be a welcome reprieve in more ways than one." One side of Sorin's mouth turned up.

"Ah, winters in the mountains. No, I'd prefer spring thank you very much. I've become spoiled, I'm afraid. Alex doesn't do the cold weather either. She's definitely a sun baby."

"Yes, she seems that way, but I do have to agree winters are a bitch. Late spring is the best time of year and my favorite as well. You remember those times we spent battling with rival families, don't you?"

"I try to forget, my friend. I try to forget."

"Well, hopefully, if I find what I'm looking for, I'll be back to enjoy the season."

Pleased to see Stefan again, Sorin and he had been friends for centuries, more like brothers. Dragos Munteanu happened to be his sire as well and shared in Sorin's distrust and hatred of the ancient vampire. Fortunately, the detested one had been vanquished months earlier in Virginia by their mutual friend and fellow Master and Commander, Gregori Van Zant. Sorin had risen through the ranks and led the family in Eastern Europe, an old and strong blood clan. Dragos never challenged him after he took the position and moved to South Florida, creating the Blood Family. Stefan inherited the clan when Dragos was imprisoned for crimes against humanity and the vampire realm.

"Ah, speaking of what you're looking for, you want to fill me in on why you're here, Sorin? Surely, not for pointers on my fashion sense."

Sorin furrowed his brow. Since when had Stefan developed a sense of humor? He grumbled. *Must be the human woman.*

"Seriously. You were a bit vague on the phone weeks ago. I owe you a favor, but I'd still like to know what I'm getting into."

Sorin sucked in a deep breath, eyeing his friend looking for any signs of doubt as he explained. "Ever since I was here in Miami last year...I've been having dreams." He waited for Stefan's reaction before continuing.

"Dreams? We don't dream, Sorin." Stefan's voice was low and disturbingly matter-of-fact.

"I know." Sorin stared out the tinted windows into the darkness of the night. Street lights flashed by at almost a blur of amber. "But, I am. A woman, a human is haunting me there in my mind and I cannot rest. I think I'm going insane." He raked fingers through his shoulder-length ebony hair.

"Jesus, Sorin. Are you sure this woman isn't in transition and you've tapped into her thoughts somehow?"

"No, she's not turned. Besides, no transition to our kind takes six months. She has called to me in dreams more in the past several weeks than in the beginning, but what difference does it make. I'm dreaming, and you know that's impossible."

"So what is she doing with you, or should I ask?" Stefan grinned.

"Don't ask." He paused, and then looked directly at Stefan. "She's beautiful. Like an angel with long blonde hair, her eyes are as blue as a spring sky, cool and crisp. She's like no woman I've seen before. Her voice is soft and melodic. I swear, she's a real, no-kidding angel."

"You are dreaming. Well, let me know how I can help."

"Can we go to the club first? After I visited here last, the dreams began. Maybe she was a customer and saw me there."

"Let me call Alex and let her know we're taking a detour before returning to the penthouse."

The conversation ceased for the remainder of the drive to Stefan's club. After Sorin assisted Stefan in taking down the previous Master and Commander Dragos Munteanu, Stefan inherited the property. The Club Euphoria had been the scene of several murders and ground zero for the drug *Blue* Dragos used to launch his attack against humans and vampires. Sorin returned to his headquarters in Europe shortly after the showdown, but not before he went to the Club Euphoria with the other MC's for a celebration. In the silence of the car traveling back to where it all began, his thoughts slipped to the first time he met the haunting woman, who changed everything.

For seven hundred thirty-two years, Sorin had lived a satisfied vampire's existence, sharing with his blood family, having never really sought out another for his own happiness. He'd never been compelled to be proactive for the one woman who would be his. All his energy centered on surviving the travails of humanity and the politics of the vampire world. Then, he befriended Stefan and they worked together to be stronger as a team. He sought his help now with the woman who invaded his mind through dreams.

As he recalled, the first episode came the night after taking down Dragos. The merciless assault on his regenerating sleep continued almost every night since. On the first encounter with the beauty, he saved her from the darkness. The subsequent nights were less detailed and vivid, except for the awareness of her presence. He craved the time with her, though he silently decried it when awakened during the shroud of night. The nameless angel had become Sorin's captivating plague. To make matters worse, for the past six weeks the frequency and intensity increased with her calling to him almost every night.

A woman of uncommon beauty, every time he imagined the vision, his breath halted. Her ethereal quality left him speechless and not even his ex-wife Anya surpassed the exquisiteness of his angel. Her hair was like liquid platinum cascading over her shoulders. Her eyes were like cut sapphires, hypnotic and exotic like the crystal blue waters flowing from the mountains during winter snow thaws in spring. Helpless in his sleep, he tossed restlessly as the image of the woman enthralled him, made his blood sing, creating sparks of flaring desire, which never really faded when awake. During the nights, he could hear her occasionally in the back of his mind, just out of reach, a distant cry.

After a few encounters the cries of help turned to cries of want and desire. The passion between them escalated. At first, he welcomed her, but the lack of rest began to wear on his sanity.

Within the hidden secrets of his dream, his gaze would sweep over her with a hunger he'd never experienced. He longed to feel the silken sweep of her lustrous hair which fell straight and brushed her mid-back. The long platinum blonde tresses defied its own glow, a shimmering white and soft gold fire in the full moonlight slicing into his room, as though there were flames hidden within the heavy fall of midnight. With his keen senses, he realized a wild, untamable burning flowed through her, moved with her. Even in a dream, the surging heat lingered under his skin, everywhere she caressed and teased him. He tasted her essence in the air. When she moved, her hair swayed with a scalloped motion, a natural wave which called out to him to touch, to worship and he followed hungrily, feasting on all of her like a starving man who hadn't fed in a week of Sundays.

This woman had become an enticement, a temptress of unfulfilled desire as he rested every day. She beckoned to him, calling to him by name—Sorin. The one word was all she ever said, a seductive whisper enticing him to love her, the sultry sound made him ache for more than their make-believe life.

In every sequence, his angel would appear slowly, only her eyes at first, the thick eyelashes batting and teasing him. His vision panned out, opening wider to enjoy her completely, one part at a time. Her features focused until he could see her entire face, smooth fair skin crowned with the full, rich glow and lightness of her hair. Delicate features, high cheekbones forming to a lush perfectly sculpted mouth painted ruby red, parted with the promises of passion once he could press his lips to hers. She glided over him with a graceful presence as he hungered for the next moments of the dream. After so many encounters, he knew what to expect, and she never failed to deliver. She'd become an addiction, unable to completely sate his body, craving more each time they met, which became part of the growing insanity.

Her body was long and lean with supple hot skin, arching and writhing beneath his ministrations. She brought the same burning hunger he bore when she invaded his dreams. Long, pink tipped manicured nails, sharp but purposely teasing, brought him to a fever pitch, stroking, holding, tempting his cool flesh. The sensations were electric, and tightened his skin until breathing became almost painful. He never questioned her weight as she rose over him almost as if she were floating, taking him deep inside of her heat, like a velvet caress. In the back of his mind, he knew this was a fantasy but refused to accept the reality because the aberration felt so good and so real. She would cry out and he would moan in pleasure as they met, the ends of her long tresses of hair brushing the heated skin of his thighs with her rocking movements. He quivered when she raked his stomach with her nails, the blue depths of her eyes blazing with possessive ecstasy, daring him, challenging him and begging he fulfill every wish.

Sorin participated with complete abandon in his dream, falling in-between the world of real and make-believe willingly. He'd been with hundreds of women over the past several hundred years. None had brought him as much pleasure as this imaginary woman. Any regrets about not finding her in the real world would be a conversation for another time. The lack of sleep from the dream sessions left him craving more. When he lacked sleep from the pretend sessions, the cold stab of deception mocked him. His existence there, with her, seemed more human than the creature he was in reality.

The vague remembrance of a time hundreds of years ago surfaced, the time when he was complete with one woman in his existence. With the one in his dreams, he imagined every word, every caress, every desire he knew he wanted. Desires this woman wanted, they both wished to share, drove him forward to find the mystery woman. Her cries filled his ears, her spine bowed tight, moonlight streaking over luscious breasts like a beautiful offering to the gods. Rocking over him, he reveled in the fire burning between them. Smooth skin flowed like heaven beneath his fingers, heat roared up his arms to settle in his chest with every caress.

Until he couldn't take any more. Until he thrust his hips, dying to feel her heat. Until he buried himself inside her silken sheath. Until he was wrapped intimately by her. Until the ecstasy overwhelmed.

Sorin always awakened groggy and weak at sunset and exactly at the point he climaxed. How many times he snapped straight up in bed with the lingering images of their love-making in his mind just as his body finished what had started in the dream. He groaned thickly as a fierce orgasm would rip over him, his hips clenching in release unable to stop the result of her daily visits. Clutching cool bed linens in shaking fists, snarling his frustration with a loud echo in the dark room, his head reared back at the cruel misleading vision of passion. He was alone with nothing but a fading dream, again.

The sapphire-eyed vixen tortured him for over six months and she wasn't physically there with him, never had been, and she appeared only in his imagination. Had his years on earth neared the end? Was this how insanity began?

Day after day, he'd been trapped in the vicious cycle of repeating her torturous seduction as he strained to rest. She'd reached a point where she began to invade his nights. That's when he told Maks and then prepared to return to the States and seek Stefan's help. He thought his sanity teetered on the edge of falling into the darkness, the same place he found her. Maybe she wanted to snare and bring him into her world. For the first time in his long existence, he felt helpless. *What is she doing to me?*

None of this made sense to him. Vampires didn't dream, but yet he did, day and night. Last night had been no different. She came to him again, awake. Sorin hoped traveling back to Miami would help him find her in the flesh. She couldn't be a dream, she had to be real and she had to be located where it all began. The angel of seduction didn't have a name and he would be guided only by his keen senses of tracking. He'd sworn a vow not to leave until he found her. When she came to him last night, he set the plan in motion. The woman who tormented him with an unbelievable body and a voice spoke of promise and pleasure would lead him to her. With one word, she'd invite him. With only one word, she'd seduce him, and then he'd have her.

The journey for redemption and satisfaction began.

"I'm coming sweet angel," he murmured as he stared out the side window of the SUV.

Chapter Six

A Mystical Force Comes on the Night Mist

"Did you say something?" Stefan asked as he flipped the cell phone shut, shoving it into his leather jacket pocket.

"What? Oh sorry, I was thinking out loud."

"The woman? You know, I can't ever recall you acting like this. This dream woman has you really shaken. We'll get to the bottom of this, I assure you."

"I don't think I'm the only one with woman problems. How are you and Alex getting along? She's still human, right?"

"More than ever." Stefan huffed out a tight breath.

"Real trouble in paradise, huh? I could have told you living with her wouldn't be easy. I witnessed her feistiness at the operational meeting when I first met her. I knew then you were in for a long road if you stayed with her."

"You did? Look, don't get me wrong. I love Alex, it's just…you know, she can be a handful sometimes. All the qualities I fell in love with occasionally rub me the wrong way. Her damned independent streak is frustrating. She takes unnecessary risks with her job. Actually, our problems began with her dangerous choices in her career and have manifested into the stupidest little things in our personal life. She's upset with me for not coming straight back to the penthouse with you. What kind of stupid shit is that?"

Jokingly, Sorin gave his opinion. "Bro, you need to send her to me for a few weeks. I'll get her to realize who the Master is in your relationship."

"Uh, our sex life is not the problem and you know I am not a passive dominant in a relationship. I give my women what they need."

"Ah maybe that's the problem. Do you continue to have other women?"

"No, I didn't mean women, *now*. I mean my women of the past."

"Okay, so she's not jealous. Do you push her limits and she doesn't respond?"

"She has hard limits both in and out of bed, but unfortunately we've hit a wall to the amount of control I have over her career. She's quite agreeable in the bedroom, relinquishing power, but everywhere else there's a point of contention. She thinks I have an anger problem. We had an argument earlier tonight before I came to pick you up. She set a meeting about this art exhibition. I lost my temper with her. She thinks I'm avoiding her and the appointment by staying out with you."

"Well do you?"

"Do I what?"

"Try and avoid her when you get angry? You know you can just drop me off and go to this engagement with her. I'm a big boy and you won't hurt my feelings. I think I can handle being alone at the club for a few hours. I can meet with you later."

"No, I won't hear of it. Alex can go to the meeting without me. She's running the entire affair anyway. I'm just the artist. I'll show up for the opening night and make small talk. If I make a sale, big deal. My self-esteem doesn't revolve around my art. Alex on the other hand…"

"An *artiste*? Since when did you start this new vocation?" Sorin snickered, putting a hand over his mouth to muffle.

"Nothing is funny about it. Alex liked my art from the first moment she discovered my photography in Virginia Beach. She found a gallery which will showcase new talent and I'm one of three artists exhibiting. There's some kind of event in a couple nights. All the last minute preps I'm letting her handle. I don't have time for all the shit involved with a show. The family comes first."

Sorin's snickering increased louder to an all-out hard laughter. "Oh no, you really have her mastered, brother."

Stefan narrowed his eyes at Sorin and a low growl escaped the back of his throat. "I'm letting her do this. Planning my *newest career* as she calls it, makes her happy. So I indulge her. Crucify me."

"I thought she worked for the FBI. Did she quit?"

"No."

"And you're still okay with her tracking and hunting vamps?"

"No. But, either she works for them or she told me she'd renew her Vampire Hunter International Membership." The sarcastic tone in Stefan's voice didn't go unnoticed by Sorin. "She meant it and I did too. I lost my composure and control of the entire argument. Ever since then she's suggested I seek anger management classes. Is that fucked up bullshit or what?"

"Damn, man. I knew you've always had a temper, but take classes. I find her assessment of your personality funny. I still say you need to send her to ERI if you have to go to anger therapy. A fair trade in my book."

The SUV came to a stop in front of Club Euphoria. The driver exited and opened the passenger door.

"I need a drink with something extra. Let's go." Stefan motioned to Sorin.

"Sounds good to me."

The two male vampires stepped quickly past the bouncer and into the club lobby.

"Master Stefan, we didn't know you'd be here tonight, sir," the hostess said as she leaned on the countertop, resting on her elbows and cupping her hands under her chin.

"Last minute decision. How's it going tonight, Chantelle?" Stefan asked the spiky-haired tall woman.

She raised her eyes and glanced over at Sorin. He grinned and acknowledged her with a slight nod.

"I'm fine, Master Stefan. Oh, I mean it's rather slow tonight. Probably around ten o'clock we'll pick up, usually do."

Stefan turned attention to Sorin. "You want to wait until then?"

"I'm okay, are you?"

"You mean is Alex okay?"

"Yeah."

"She'll be at the gallery for a couple of hours, so visiting with you is more pleasurable than sitting alone at the apartment. I'm good with staying."

Three hours later the two vamp friends sat viewing the crowd increase from a few couples scattered in the dungeon to full capacity. The scenes playing out on the raised stage area and surrounding spaces were all occupied. Sorin became numbed by the sounds of flogging, caning, spanking, and the cacophony of the moans and groans interspersed with normal conversation in the tables and booths spread throughout the large room. The only sound he wanted to hear was her voice, the whisper of the woman of his dreams.

Sorin neither sensed nor heard anything. He hadn't heard the sweet sound since he'd arrived. *Was this a mistake?*

"Stefan, baby. Are you enjoying the evening with Sorin?"

The female voice sounded all too familiar and when she stepped from behind the high back of the banquette, he realized why. Alex, Alexandra Carlton, Stefan's human girlfriend came into view.

Sorin couldn't believe how his friend fell all over himself jumping from the booth to greet the red-haired woman. Sorin knew the evening would be ending soon, at least the time at the club. Staying would only interfere with the plans Alex no doubt had for the rest of the night.

"*Prinţesa*, I didn't expect you." Stefan kissed her on the cheek, and then wrapped his arm around her waist.

"Sorin," she extended her hand. "So nice to see you again. You look well."

His brow crinkled. The woman was quite pleasant and he sensed no anger. "Alex, a pleasure to see you too. Thank you for your hospitality opening your home for me to stay with you and Stefan."

"Absolutely. I can't ever thank you enough for assisting Stefan and I at SGM last year."

"Not a problem. Dragos was a bad vamp who needed to be taken down." Sorin took a sip of the cognac and blood cocktail. "I hear you're with the FBI and not freelancing. Stefan says you're working on a new case. A serial killer, I believe?"

The expression on the girlfriend's face was one of surprise. *Oh fuck! I think I screwed, Stefan.* The words left his mouth before he could retract them. Alex narrowed her eyes and glanced from him to Stefan, then back. Deducing Stefan divulged a confidence he probably shouldn't have and Sorin's betrayal of the confidence weighed heavy on his shoulders. *The poor man is in trouble tonight. Shit!*

"I am and enjoy the work. Although working for the government is different from working with my family." She looked over her shoulder at Stefan and smiled. "And, the case I'm working on now has got me stumped. I've hesitated asking Stefan, but I think I need help on this one." She turned her gaze back to Sorin. "Maybe, since you're in town, I could pick your brain about the case, since it obviously captured so much public notice that I'm working on it now."

"I...uh...would like to help, but I'm here on business. I have my own agenda, but if you need to run anything by me while I'm in town, I'd be glad to listen."

"She thinks the perpetrator is a rogue vamp, a sophisticated one. A loner, right *prinţesa*?"

"Ha! He's more than sophisticated, babe. He gets off terrorizing these young women, and then continues to humiliate them after he's murdered the poor innocent souls. Sick, a real nut case."

"Why do you think a vampire is the culprit? Anyone can be a serial killer, Alex," Sorin posed the argument.

"Simple, the women are drained of blood and marks are on the bodies...well shall we say, penetration occurred."

"Okay, you have me there."

Stefan snickered. "She's good, Sorin. You can't challenge anything about her job and think you'll win. Believe me, I've tried several times and failed miserably."

"Do you have any other evidence? Fingerprints, surveillance video, or a link between the victims possibly?"

"If we did, Sorin, I wouldn't be asking for help now would I?" Her sarcastic tone reminded him of the first time he'd met this woman. He shook his head knowing what his friend dealt with. "Have either of you heard about a rogue going off the deep end lately?"

"I arrived here a few hours ago, so unless the killer recently came over from Europe, I know nothing."

"Now there's a thought. Anything like this happen where you were and stop without warning, say about a year ago?"

"You didn't tell me you've been working this case for a year? Why didn't you ask me sooner, *prinţesa*?"

"Because I only had it charged to me six months ago, not a year. The locals determined a vamp was involved and called us in. Such rookies. They thought they could solve it on their own, like duh, they couldn't. I didn't tell you sooner because my boss asked me not to. After the Dragos debacle, Washington didn't want to get you involved."

"The government doesn't trust us to take care of our own now? Great, what's next, the High Tribunal rolls over for them and rounds us up and imprisons us, or worse?" Stefan asked with his voice and body tensing, the anger spewing from his mouth.

"Stefan, calm down man. Alex is only doing her job."

"See, this is why I don't tell you anything anymore. You yell and fuss and blame me. You have a problem, Stefan. I try and help you with your art and you don't show any interest." She stood to leave. "I love you, but I'm about to give up on you. Get some help or I'm leaving and I don't just mean the club, I mean your life." Alex turned and began to walk away.

"Stefan, you need to go after her. You know she's right even though she's being a brat. We've always known the High Tribunal vamps were a bunch of puppet politicos only interested in kissing up to the Feds. The North American Grand Master is a self-centered prick, but we've always handled our own. The European GM is the same. If this rogue vamp is in your territory, take care of it. Alex doesn't need you going snake-shit on her since she works for the FBI. Go after her."

"Yeah, yeah, I know. I'm frustrated with her. We went into this relationship working as a team and somewhere along the line, we stopped. She's taken over almost everything we do. Even my photography isn't really my stress reliever anymore. I'm wound tight and feel like I'm about to snap."

"Shit, that bad? Good thing I came when I did. How can I help?"

"You can't. You have your own problems. The dream woman, remember?" Stefan rubbed his hand over the one-day stubble on his chin. "No, Alex and I'll be fine, but you my brother need to find out who this woman is or you'll go insane without sleep. I can sense the unrest and confusion within you."

Sorin harrumphed. "Maybe we'll both go mad together. I think we're getting too old for this living forever shit. What do you think?"

Stefan let out a short exhale. "You're probably right. I thought about ending my dark existence right before I met Alex. She saved me. I should remember how grateful I felt the next time I yell at her."

"I need a drink and not the alcohol type. Where's the best place? I don't want to break any of your family rules."

"Let's get out of here. I need fresh air and blood too."

The two vamps rose from the booth and stalked across the room in a blur, departing the club in search of blood.

"You wouldn't personally handle Alex's training if she agreed to go to ERI, would you?"

Sorin grinned, not offering up a verbal answer, and then he got a scent of an ideal prey to sate his thirst.

Enticing the prey to bend to his glamour flowed from his essence as easily as the blood flowed, thick and sweet like honey, down Sorin's throat. When he had first been changed seven hundred odd years ago, he had abhorred the idea of drinking blood from someone. Most times, he killed the victims due to his own incompetence. Now feeding was second nature, a necessity, one that he enjoyed and took pride in not losing control of the beast within. Pulling his fangs from the stranger's neck, he licked the wounds, closing them. The female was a pretty morsel, brunette and dark brown eyes. Meticulously made up and wearing a scant piece of cloth women of this century considered acceptable attire for evening club hopping. He couldn't remember the last time a woman wore more feminine clothes, the kind a man with lust in his pants wondered about what lay beneath the silken dresses. He supposed those days were long gone and would never return.

As Sorin sent the woman on her way, he placed a thought in her mind not to remember what happened. In the morning, all she would recollect was how tired and achy she felt and nothing more. Shoving his hands deep into his pockets, he strolled down the streets in search of Stefan. He sniffed the air. Stefan was close by. The United States had strange people, unlike his. In the Old World, humans had a healthy respect for vampires, but not here. There were fanatics who would just as soon kill him for sport as accept him into society. Their kind of fear of vampires wasn't idolized as in the Carpathian region of his homeland. *How can Stefan stand to remain in this hot and humid climate? Or among the concrete buildings and congestion of motor vehicles polluting the fresh air? Give me the mountains, clean air and quiet.*

Cloaked in black leather from head to toe he could remain hidden in the blackness of the night until he found his friend. His ebony hair contrasted sharply against his pale features. His dark eyes scanned the darkness. In an unfamiliar region always made Sorin uncomfortable, especially in the New World. Having fed could have drawn unwanted attention to the act, although he surveyed the area to ensure no one else was hiding in the shadows. Becoming a victim to a hunter was not on his list of things to do on his visit to the States. While the humans typically let vampires remain in the world and only because of the pact made back in 1905, there were a select few who kept the advantage on the human side...the bounty hunters, like Alexandra Carlton. Alex was a feisty one and Sorin understood how his friend and brother vampire could fall for her. But, humans and their kind did not mix well. Sex most definitely worked, but any long-term relationship was doomed to failure. At least in his opinion.

"Sorin? You ready?" The deep voice came from the behind the oleander bushes.

"Stefan. Yes, I think it's time to call it a night."

Within a half hour, the two arrived at Stefan's penthouse and settled in. Sorin wandered out onto the balcony to take in the last few hours of the night before retiring to the sleeping quarters. The night was clear and warm. He sat in the chaise lounge and glanced up at the stars and then closed his eyes.

Sorin? Where are you? Come to me, please.

Chapter Seven

Pieces of a Shattered Dream

After a long session of painting, Merliah retired to her room. Closing her eyes, she rubbed at her stiff neck. She ached all over. Painting was hard work, probably more difficult than the physical therapy she endured several hours a day. She was exhausted but it was a good tired. "A nice hot and steamy shower, a restful night's sleep, and I'll be ready for tomorrow's work." The words bounced off the walls with no one to share or respond. The fact she was alone hit hard. *Is this all my life will ever be? Alone and isolated in a building full of people?*

"No!"

Tomorrow, the day she'd dreamed about for months, would start to offer her the independence she craved. She leaned on the cane to assist her walk toward the bathroom. She'd been using the aide more than usual lately, which disappointed her. Over the most recent months she'd struggled in therapy to improve, not digress. Determination to regain full mobility without the assistance became a primary goal. She realized working relentlessly on the canvases for the show wasn't helping, but she didn't want to disappoint those counting on her to complete the paintings. Most importantly, she didn't wish to fail in the goals she set for herself.

Running her fingers through the short, wispy patches of hair which remained on her head, Merliah surveyed the little room, satisfaction warmed her heart. The day may have been long, but she finished the final landscape. The energy she expended was draining, but the pleasure derived from completing it delighted her. Wrapping her head around the fact the exhibition of her art was in a few days, she hoped and prayed this would be the turning point in her life. She'd be able to make money, get healthier and leave the institute to find a place of her own. Moving in with her parents could be an option. At almost thirty, she'd lost her freedom being in the coma and didn't want to be confined to her parents waiting on her, not allowing for that independence. She'd feel smothered. *I have to break away on my own.* Tomorrow Abby would take her on a trip to the gallery and finalize the preparations. The excitement mounted and she didn't know if she could sleep even as depleted as her mind and body were. She'd imagined this event almost every day since Abby introduced her to Antoine Rousseau. The vision was almost realized.

Over the past months she'd never believed the metamorphosis of her life would happen so quickly. She'd worked hard at restoring her life to some semblance of what it had been before the accident. Coming back from the pitch black depths of her mind, to awakening to a new world creating beauty seemed almost miraculous. Content and at peace, but not completely happy, she hoped with the success of her art, success in the love department would come also. Someone other than the dream man.

Deep down she knew the possibility of finding a new man in her life wouldn't happen. Who would have her? "Me, myself and I," she whispered. "I'm the only one who can make the happiness in my life. If I'm ugly and can't walk without help, so be it. I can still be happy. I'll always have my dreams and paintings as an escape to a temporary life of perfection."

The mask of sleep wouldn't prevail tonight. She tossed and turned for what gave the impression of hours. The attempt to go to bed and get a good night's sleep before tackling the last touches on the works in progress she thought was a good idea at first. But, she failed miserably at the effort.

A prickly tension rippled across her skin most of the late afternoon and early evening. Something inside her head changed. Not a bad feeling, but definitely a different sensation than she usually experienced. The power radiating there arced up. The strokes she made while painting intensified as well. She pushed through the odd sensation, but as she attempted to rest, the unusual feelings resurfaced.

In recent weeks, the dark angel came to her in dreams, a welcome diversion from the intense work on the exhibition items. The erotic fantasies made her blush even in the dark. After calling for him, she began to believe he was nothing more than a figment of her imagination. Was it her brain's way of maintaining her sanity while she healed from the accident? Four long years were spent in darkness before her shadow man led her into the light. Doctors couldn't explain her recovery, and she couldn't tell them either. How would they ever believe her explanation? *Yes, doctors, I was found by a tall, dark angel who came to me inside my head and pulled me out of the pitch black and held my hand as he guided me into the light of day.* If she said anything remotely similar, she definitely would have spent the remainder of her days at the Berger Institute, locked up permanently on mind-altering drugs.

In those erotic dreams with her new lover Sorin, she was perfect. Her hair flowed in thick tresses down her back, long enough to cover her breasts as she lay naked before him. Her tanned skin glowed in the sunlight and blushed with the slightest touch of his fingers. Walking hand-in-hand in the wildflower field without the use of a cane excited her as well. No scars, no pain, no hurt. *Yes, my brain created Sorin to keep me from going insane. He doesn't exist so I need to get on with my life, even if it isn't much of one.*

Sleep came and with the repose the dream misted into view. First, nothing but darkness. Then, she called his name, yearning to find him. She missed him, longed for his delicate touch and to feel his lips on hers. The fire sizzled between them, and ignited thoughts within her mind to conjure up his image. *Sorin, where are you? Come to me, please.*

The hopelessness swamped her waiting to hear him answer the pleas. And then his familiar timbre reached her. A soft whisper, then gave way to a more distinct velvety plea. Suddenly, she paused. The tightening in her shoulders caused pain down her back. She willed herself to relax and swung her head around. His gaze slammed into hers with a fierce, primal lust that singed every nerve ending to her core. The bottomless obsidian eyes sucked her in, as she imagined his cock sinking deep into her pussy. Everything about this man screamed alpha and dominant. *God help me, I want him.*

He met her stare and refused to back away. "Angel, I've been searching for you. Where have you been?"

The illumination surrounded him and she let out a slow moan. She'd been so busy and pre-occupied, several weeks had passed without calling for her dream lover. How could she turn him away and deny both of them the pleasures they experienced in this shadow realm of illusion.

He lifted a hand, stroked fine platinum blonde strands of hair from her cheek, and trailed the backs of his fingers across her smooth unblemished skin. She trembled from his touch.

"Sorin…are you real? Are you alive…" She wrapped her arms around his neck, bringing her lips close to his. "…or only my imagination?"

She'd never know if he made the first move or if she yanked him to her. When it came right down to it, she didn't care. This was her dream, her conception and she had control of the outcome, and she wanted to feel his lips on hers. They were comforting, like home and tasted like the sweetest candy.

The dream lover growled his pleasure against her mouth just before he pressed hard, sending heat pulsing through her body. They kissed deeply and frantically, as their hands sought out every inch of their flesh. Tongues tangled, their teeth nibbled, and lips crushed as if an eternity passed since they last embraced. To her, only weeks clicked off the calendar. Her mind tried to rationalize how a dream lover could make her feel so complete, aroused, and desperately wanting more each time they met in her fantasy realm. The moment she touched him, her body screamed for need, for satisfaction.

How can a dream be so real? She disregarded the question and delved into the imaginary role-play.

As he wrapped his arms around her, he dragged her body hard against his. She moaned into his mouth as his strong and virile body took command. She wanted to devour him and he did the same to her. The heat building between her thighs made her dizzy with wanton desire. She clung to his shoulders to keep from collapsing into a puddle on the floor.

Her lips parted eagerly for his tongue and then he plunged deep. She sought out his tongue, the craving want to taste him, the flavor lingering in the soft and inviting recesses of his mouth drove her insane. She sensed he felt the same and threatened to send her over the edge before they even began.

He broke the embrace. "Did my kiss feel real or fake, angel?"

She thought he'd already answered her question with the passionate kiss. *I guess I was wrong.* The sweet black currant taste of him lingered on her tongue and she didn't want his essence enveloping her to ever end. Every time she dreamt of their time together, it was good, damn exceptional more like it. This time also promised to be just as phenomenal, if not better as he framed her face in his hands and dove back into her waiting warm mouth.

Merliah moaned, the only response she could make. The reaction to his commanding dominance almost frightened, but aroused her at the same time. He echoed her thoughts out loud by his actions. This was her dream, but he acted on his own. So many unusual things happened since the accident, and if he were real, then she knew she wasn't alone in this situation. If he felt about her as strongly as she felt for him, she wouldn't be alone anymore. *Except this isn't real, only a dream.*

What had started with a slow burn of need quickly erupted into a fury of desperate lust. She began to tear at his clothing, and at first the leather jacket fell to the floor with ease. Unfastening the buttons to his black shirt was impossible and she ripped the fabric. He tore at her clothes, even though she couldn't feel any against her body. She clawed at his jeans zipper until he pushed her hands away and what seemed like magic, they disappeared from his body.

Stroking her hands over the bare skin of his chest, she murmured approval. His body fascinated her, hard and cool to the touch. Amazing how in a dream she could feel such distinctions. She wanted to touch him for hours, days, forever.

She tore her attention away just long enough to ask, "If you are real, then where are you? You disappear from view come daylight, existing only in my dreams. I can't take much more of this fantasy, Sorin. I have to find you."

Gazing into his dark, smoldering eyes, she begged for help with her blue crystal eyes.

"Who are you, my angel?" he murmured, his voice thickly accented, something she suddenly realized and never noticed before. She knew she was asleep, and he was a figment of her imagination, but why did he start taking control of the dream? Something seemed strange.

A raw voice reached out to her. "Help me find you, sweet angel."

"You know where I am. You found me, remember? If you want me, come to me."

Sorin's expression seemed unusual. The vision of his body began to fade. Then she realized she began to fade as well. Her body felt sluggish, hard to move and breathe. She frowned knowing the dream was ending and couldn't stop it from happening. She watched helplessly as his image faded more. He cocked his head to the side as if looking at another, then returned his attention back to her. "Tell me now. Where are you?" The tone in his voice sounded frantic.

"I'm here. Please. Find me Sorin. I need you."

The male voice replied, plaintively filled with wave upon wave of pain and exhaustion. "What is your name, angel? Where are you? I can't..."

She froze, her mouth went dry and struggled to speak. Her heart raced. His image faded to a transparent glow. Tears welled on the verge of tumbling down her face.

"My name is Merliah. I'm at the institute. Find me Sorin. I can't do this anymore without you."

Then his image disappeared into the dark.

Merliah bolted upright from the deep sleep. She broke out in a cold sweat and her heart pounded hard against her ribs. The vision of Sorin was nothing more than her imagination again. Merliah closed her eyes as if doing so would have Sorin reappear. She intensified her thoughts, forcing herself to conjure the dream back. But, she failed.

Chapter Eight

Another Princess is Crowned

The dark lover escorted his newest prey to the young female's home. He promised a night she'd never forget when he poured on his most seductive voice at Club Euphoria. After spiking the cocktail, getting the woman to take him back to her place didn't take much convincing. Within a half-hour, the drug's effects worked its magic. She was conscious, but barely. They stood at the entrance of her apartment when she collapsed on the landing. He found the keys in her clutch and unlocked the door, scooped her into his arms and carried her limp body inside.

If there had been a choice, he'd have taken her to an innocuous and sleazy hotel paid for by the hour, where anonymity was the norm, but the little bitch had remained lucid enough to insist on her place. Next time, the monster within told him to add more of the drug so deviations in the plan wouldn't occur. The location of his masterpieces had to be disgusting and the palette had to harness the lowest denominator of humanity. This apartment presented an adequate substitute, but he'd have to be extra vigilant covering his tracks. His women were to be immortalized and create a sensation in the tabloids. Every detail he meticulously scrutinized so as not to ruin his creative process. His cock always reacted with instant response once he was in play to capture his next muse and this one was an exceptional subject tonight. Almost too perfect.

Easing the front door closed, the sinister stranger glanced around the room. A dimly lit table lamp next to the chestnut brown chenille sofa provided sufficient illumination to the room to view the layout. He determined where the bedroom could be situated. A door at the end of a long hallway to the right appeared to be the answer and he strode toward it, and then kicked the six-panel wood door open with a thud. He carried the new princess to the bed and laid her down on the mattress. Unlike many of his former muses, this one had no scars from vampire kisses.

A virgin. She'll be a sweet addition. We've never had one before. I think I'm going to delight in this one.

"Yes, she will." The killer spoke aloud. "But, this will be my way, not yours."

The thick and shiny dark auburn hair fell across the pillow in a halo effect. With the precision of a doctor examining his patient, he pushed her eyelid up, uncovering the dilated pupils of a hazel eye. With his thumb and forefinger he separated her lips, revealing her teeth. They were clean and white as pearls. Her breath smelled sweet, the effects of the liquor and drug he slipped in her drink at the club. The monster residing within the dark lover stirred and clawed inside. The malevolent artist's cock came more alive, pushing painfully against the hard fabric of his jeans. He stroked his hardening flesh, begging for release.

Sitting beside her, he leaned over and ran his knuckles across her cheeks, down her neck and between her breasts. He slowly unfastened the buttons of the silk blouse, spreading the thin fabric to reveal a baby pink lace bra. His large hands ran across the tanned flesh with wanton desire. He relished the thought of taking her body and blood. Over a week had passed since he last indulged in luring another princess into his web. He thought he'd finished with the gallery owner's request, but he needed one more for the new canvas he began the day before. He chuckled, a deep wicked noise from the back of his throat. "The show needs one more piece," he said and this little one will do nicely."

Yes, I told you she'd be nice. We'll show all those critics and the world, you aren't second rate. Stick with me Esteban. You'll earn the respect you deserve.

"Enough. I was good when I was human."

Ah, but when you received my gift, we became stronger and better than any human.

"You make me do things I don't like. How is that better?"

Has anyone found us yet? Don't answer, I know. I always know everything you do.

"Stop. I have to finish and need to concentrate. You're throwing me off. I have to do this precisely right."

With time limited, he decided to dispense with his normal routine of preparations and since the pretty princess was already unconscious, he went straight for the blood, neglecting the pleasure of her body. Leaning closer, he turned her head to the side to expose the long column of slender neck. He ran his tongue over the pulsing vein, dropped his fangs and sank them into the delicate flesh. As he sucked voraciously, she awakened but for a moment and moaned. Within several minutes, he heard the faint beat of her heart slow. The skin began to pale and lose the vibrancy and warmth. Another few minutes and she'd be ready for the next stage.

He pulled away, swiped the back of his hand across his mouth wiping the residual blood from his lips. "Mmm, delicious my sweet virgin princess. I love blood mixed with the little something extra." A low growl vibrated in the depths of his chest as he ran his hands over his abdomen then between his legs, coming to rest at the rock-hard erection.

Damn, you should have fucked her before you took all her blood.

"I don't have time."

You always have time. I'm very disappointed in you. You know you want to as much as I do. C'mon. No one will know. Do it. Fuck her.

"No! She's already gone."

Do it. You're almost there. I feel your arousal. Do it, or I will.

"Ah, fuck." The beast drove him forward as he slid the zipper down on his pants, and pulled out his erection. He fisted his shaft, stroking only a few times. The thought of taking the princess after she had expired and crowning her brought him to an explosive orgasm, spewing his cum down his hand. Once he regained his composure, he cursed again. The beast goaded him to this and anger stirred in the deep recesses of his mind demanding satisfaction being forced into the act. He was the one in control, not him. As a creature of meticulous routine, he now had to spend extra valuable time cleaning up the mess he made.

After returning from the bathroom, he set about completing his creation. He removed the black mini-skirt from around the female's hips, folded the tiny piece of fabric in half and laid it across the foot of the bed. Reaching an arm behind her back, and with the free hand he removed the charmeuse blouse. The tender touch of fingertips swirling circles along her abdomen, and then to the delicate underside of small, round breasts, he stopped at the hollow of her neck. A few remaining drops of blood trickled from the wound he inflicted. Greedily, he lapped at the trail of the last of her essence. The dark man kissed a path to the slightly parted lips then traced them with his tongue. A last rush of the *Blue* drug filled his veins causing a quiver through his entire body. Closing his eyes, he let out a deep rumble. Shifting his position, he stared into the motionless, glassy-eyed dark redhead, and then grinned with contentment.

"Such a delicate and pathetic human female, unsuspecting, and wanting a blood fix and sex. Well, you got nothing, but I'll give you beauty in your death." Tilting his head in one direction and then the next, he gazed upon her lifeless body contemplating which shade of lipstick and blush to use. He wanted to fuck with the police tonight. All the other princesses he'd used red, but he'd change this one up. "What do you think, my dear? Shall we play fuck-fuck with the stupid lawmen?" He paused, as if he waited for an answer. "Yes, I think you're right. A pinky coral will look better with your complexion and match nicely with your lingerie."

Standing beside the bed, he began to position her hands and legs. He plumped a pillow and placed it behind her head, smoothing the chin-length hair. Every hair had to be perfectly in place so he could place the small tiara on her head when he finished with the other preparations.

The cooling body lay on the bed perfectly positioned, arms outstretched over her head and spread, legs straight and ankles together with the stilettos and stockings still worn. Grabbing his duffel from the floor where he dropped it when they entered, he rummaged through the bag and retrieved pink rigging rope. From his leather jacket pocket he pulled out latex gloves and proceeded to knot and wrap her limbs. When finished he took out a make-up compact. Coral Pink rouge for something different and matched the rope perfectly.

With a long middle finger, he dipped into the smudge pot. A dab of the cream was applied to his muse, first on one cheek then the other. From the apples of the high cheekbones of the demure beauty, he swirled over the cool skin several times and lightly blended fading away into the hairline. Pleased with the deepness of blush, he smeared the rouge upon the fixed smile of the cherubic face glaring back at him with a glassy stare.

"Beautiful. You are art for an eternity, little princess." How many times had he performed the same ritual, not deviating from the practiced moves over the past twelve months?

None, you have to do this exactly the same each time or the canvas will be imperfect. You have to be perfect.

Both his hands covered his ears. "Shut up. I've done it exactly the way you said to do. Word for word. Move by move. Leave me alone." His voice rumbled deep in his throat as he paced the floor a few minutes. Then he paused to retrieve his cell phone. He prepared to click off a picture, but stopped.

"I almost forgot again like last time. See, you need to be quiet or I'll miss something. Then, it will be your fault, not mine."

You can't blame me for your incompetence. You were nothing before I was reborn. That female creature made me strong. Now finish or I'll be upset and you know what happens if I do.

"Shut up." He retrieved the black velvet box from the satchel he dropped in the living area, and then removed the rhinestone tiara. Returning to the bedroom, he carefully placed the mini-crown on the lifeless human female. He made several attempts to position the fastening comb just right, cocking his head back and forth until perfectly placed on her head. Repetition to complete each step precisely on each creation had to be perfect. The beast within demanded his following directions to the letter. *No modifications, Esteban. You know I don't like it when you deviate from my plan and don't do everything the same. They'll come for us. You don't want that, do you?*

"No! I know what I have to do. Just shut up and let me finish." Anger spewed forth in his words and tone of voice.

He then picked up the phone and clicked off a picture for the unfinished and newly started canvas at his studio.

"Exquisite and unique. You will definitely be the showstopper at the exhibition, my beauty. Not to mention throwing the police off us." One last time the artistic murderer captured her lips with his, smudging the purple flesh. Returning the cell phone to his pocket, he found the cordless phone seated on the side table. With the edge of his jacket, he placed the call to 9-1-1.

After three rings, a woman's voice came on the line and asked, "Nine-One-One. Is your emergency police, fire or ambulance?" He loved to hear a woman's voice instead of a man's. *I can rattle them more.*

"Yes, an ambulance. My mother is having a heart attack. Please send the paramedics. Please, please, she's unconscious. Help me." His pathetic cry for help had a New Yorker accent added, disguising his real voice. *The accent should throw them off from the southern one I used all the other times.*

"Yes, sir. Calm down. Please hold on while I transfer you."

Dial tone, then two rings.

"This is Juan, County Ambulance Services."

"This is the Nine-One-One dispatcher, and I have a gentleman on the line whose mother is having a possible heart attack. Go ahead, sir." Then a slight click as the first dispatcher disconnected.

"Yes, sir, how may I help you?" The male dispatcher asked.

"I need an ambulance as soon as possible, sir."

"Okay, sir. What's your address?"

The killer's voice grew shrill, yelling non-coherent words. *Very good, Esteban. They'll never guess who you are.*

"Sir, I need you to calm down and tell me exactly where you are."

"Yeah   sure.   Apartment   Four   Eleven, Two…Nine…Three…Poinciana Avenue. Please hurry." His breath sounded labored for effect. *I'm such a good actor.*

"Okay sir, what's the phone number you're calling from?"

"Why do you need to know? Just send an ambulance." The beast within began to become irritated. He hated dealing with human males.

"Paramedics are en route, sir. Stay by your mother. Is she breathing?"

"No, um, I can't tell." *Such predictable rhetoric. Hurry this along, Esteban.*

"Do you know CPR, sir?"

"If I did, would I be calling you!"

The killer dropped the phone next to his newly made-up princess without breaking the connection. He could hear the dispatcher speaking and ignored his frantic inquiries. Cleaning the apartment of any fingerprints or any other possible evidence of his presence would be the next step. Like before, the fancy, know-it-all criminal investigator wouldn't be able to link anyone to the young woman. At the nightclub, he sat in the shadows of the room and selected this beauty because she was different from the other princesses of his images. Slipping her the *Blue* took some finesse, but when she turned to speak to another human customer, he walked by and dropped the drug in her drink. Within minutes, he pushed the male out of her sight and stepped in quickly to escort her out of the club.

The muted voice of the emergency dispatcher continued to echo in the bedroom. After a final check of the living room for any misplaced tell-tale evidence, the killer prepared to make an exit. He wiped the knob on the entrance door, inside and out. Before he departed, he peered through the bedroom door one more time.

"So beautiful. She will be perfection above the others and the ideal masterpiece for the entire world to see. Let the critics try and put me down then. She will show them. Won't you, princess?" He heard the sound of sirens of the emergency vehicles intrude further into the evening silence. *They're close. We have to go. Hurry.*

The fanged killer turned and slipped undetected from the apartment. He took the elevator to the first floor and as the doors slid open, he caught a glimpse of the emergency personnel striding through the front entrance. He stole past the opening doors, dropping his head and walked into the shadows to watch the paramedics.

"Wagner, what number is the apartment?"

"Four eleven."

"Hit the four button, dude," the first emergency medical tech barked. "The call a couple days ago was a real bitch. Three flights of stairs give you a workout wheeling a gurney."

"At least this place has an elevator. Joe and Julio are lucky this time. Glad I don't have to haul a gurney up three flights of stairs."

"Me too," the second tech said.

The elevator controls dinged and the doors opened.

"Three calls today in buildings without elevators have all been a real bitch. Thank goodness this will probably be the last one for this shift."

Then the doors closed. The killer stepped from the shadows around the corner. He sneered and flexed his itching fingers then rubbed each thumb over each one at a time. The tightness of the skin exaggerated when he stretched and then curled them over his palms. His insides tugged with curiosity. He debated to follow or leave. For the last princess he walked away from before the police arrived and regretted doing so. Now, another chance presented itself. Each time he created a new princess, the risk of being discovered increased.

A wicked grin crossed his chiseled face and the temptation mounted. The adrenaline flowed fiercely through his veins. The beast within clawed to be released. He could take care of the two EMTs and add a twist to the scene. The thought tickled his brain for a brief moment.

Take the risk. You know you want to.

"No, I won't deviate from my plan. Stop tempting me. I can't chance being caught," he murmured, deciding to fight the urge and leave.

The Tiara Princess Killer, content with his decision, skipped out into the night ready to complete the final canvas for the gallery show.

Chapter Nine

He dreams with eyes wide open

"Sorin. Hey, man. You all right?" Stefan nudged him a couple times.

The older vamp felt the tug on his shoulder, the violent rip away from the woman named Merliah caused the beast within him to growl and fight the binding chains. Leaving his dream lover too soon, his eyes flew open, and the vision before them blurred crimson. The overwhelming desire to attack regardless of who lay in his path struck him. The beast was unleashed with a fury.

"Fuck, Sorin, what's wrong with you? And Alex thinks I have anger issues." Stefan morphed to match and fend off Sorin's attack. "Compared to you, I'm a domestic cat."

The two vampires struggled for several moments before Stefan maneuvered Sorin to the ground, braced solidly above him.

Sorin blinked and relaxed. "Let me go," he expelled in a loud, deep voice.

Stefan backed off. "Are you all right, brother? What just happened? Was it the woman? Were you in a dream?"

Sorin blinked a few times and the red haze faded, the onyx color returned. "Stefan, what did I just do?"

"You attacked me, you daft bastard." His answer had a hint of laughter, but not much. "Are you sure you're under control?"

Stefan released Sorin from his grip, then shifted position and stood.

Sorin pressed to a seated position, and then rose to an upright stance. "I didn't hurt you, did I?"

His friend ran his hands over his arms as if dusting them off. "No, but you sure acted like you wanted to. You didn't answer the original question. Were you in one of those dreams with the unknown woman?"

Sorin shook his head to ward off the brain haze. "Yeah, an intense encounter. I got her name this time. Merliah."

"Interesting name. Unusual to say the least. What's her last name? Maybe we can track her now."

"Don't know. I was ripped from the dream." He eyed his friend intently, rubbing his hand over the stubble shadow along his jawline. "You pulled me out of it. I guess that's why I came out fighting. Sorry, man. I didn't mean to attack you."

"Well, I had to do something to wake you. If you haven't noticed, the sun is due up shortly. Couldn't let you stay out here and fry." He snickered and patted Sorin on the shoulder. "C'mon, we can work on this tonight after we've rested."

"Let's hope she doesn't visit me again and I can."

The two vamps retired to the sleeping quarters. The adrenaline flowed through Sorin's veins at a high level. After a concentrated effort, he relinquished control of the night and succumbed to rest.

As the sun set on another day, he awakened relaxed and refreshed. She didn't visit him and he did sleep for the first time in many months. The mysterious woman of his dreams was near. He sensed her. Tasted the sweetness of her lips on his. The sound of her voice softened his heart. Yes, she was close and he'd find her, soon.

Sorin found his friend and the live-in girlfriend sitting at the kitchen table when he left the sleeping chamber. They appeared to be in a heated discussion and Sorin debated whether or not to intrude into their space. Then Alex glanced up and smiled.

"Good evening, sleepy head. Did you rest well? Stefan said you had an interesting episode before you settled in this morning. Sorry I missed it." She spoke as if she really did miss witnessing his attack on her vampire lover.

"Am I interrupting anything?" Sorin asked as he closed the distance between the couple and him.

Stefan peered over his shoulder. "No. We're good. Planning the evening and it seems I have a meeting for last minute preparations for the gallery exhibition tomorrow night." He returned his attention to Alex. Sorin saw his friend wink at his lover.

He definitely interrupted something between the two hosts. "What plans are they? Involve me in any way?"

"They can. Join us, Sorin. Then we can go to my office and see if I can help you find this woman Stefan told me about. The division I'm with at the Bureau has a great database on vampires."

"Really? Interesting, but Merliah isn't a vampire, Alex. I'm not sure what she is, although she did say she is at an institute. Maybe everything happening is some type of experimentation." Sorin stood with his arms crossed over his chest. "I don't know what any of this means, but I'm determined to find out."

"Well, we have something to start with. A partial name and a place. Anything else?"

"No, other than I call her angel because she has a glow about her. I'd even go as far as say she's a ghost, but I know they don't exist either."

"Hmm, you seem pretty sure of everything she's not. A ghost, an angel, what else do you think she is Sorin? I've seen some pretty interesting stuff since I began working at the Bureau. I'm not familiar with these other paranormal phenomena, but you need me to help you and check it out. You never know what resources the Bureau has at its disposal until you learn how to manipulate the system and dig for the answers."

"Breaking rules now, Alex? I thought you lived by certain standards, Miss Vampire Bounty Hunter. Wouldn't your offer break at least one of them?" Sorin asked.

Soft laughter filled the air from the two lovers. "She probably is, but she's broken a lot of them since we hooked up. Isn't that right, *prințesa*?" Sorin spied another wink and the smile from her as a response.

Yeah, I've definitely come into the middle of something between these two.

"Okay, okay I know I've slipped a few times, but your devilish charm isn't saving you from the meeting. We have to go, Antoine will be upset if we're late."

"Antoine? You're on a first name basis with the owner?"

"Yes, are you jealous, babe?"

Stefan snorted. "No, of course not. I know he doesn't have anything on me." He pushed back from the table and stood. "If you want to go, let's go." He turned to Sorin. "You ready?"

"Who's Antoine?"

"Antoine Rousseau. He's the gallery owner," Alex said, as she turned to Stefan. "You have to go tonight, babe. I promise we won't stay long."

"Oh. So what is it exactly you have in this exhibition?" Sorin asked, eyeing his friend.

"You don't know, Sorin? It's his photography. Beautiful pieces." She rubbed her hand along Stefan's arm. "He's modest, but I fell in love with his pictures when I first discovered them in Virginia. I've been telling him they were exceptional and I finally found a gallery who was willing to show them. Granted he's with two other artists, but it's a start." She rose up on tip-toes and placed a soft kiss on Stefan's cheek. "I'm so proud of him." She smiled.

Sorin watched the two people before him with amusement. He was the one feeling jealous, not for anything other than they seemed happy in a weird kind of way and he hadn't had any type of relationship in years. *No, make that hundreds of years.* After Anya, he never indulged in the pursuit of love again and he couldn't imagine doing so with a human. *Maybe an angel would work.*

The twinkling lights of the city held Sorin's attention as the three made their way to the Rousseau Gallery in the Wynwood Art District of Miami. He hadn't paid too much attention to collecting art over the years after he settled into his position as Master and Commander. His manor was decorated with some pieces— paintings, sculptures, ancient weaponry and artifacts—but he didn't go out of his way to acquire anything contemporary. He could easily afford to increase his holdings, but nothing ever interested him. More important matters garnered his consideration, like building a reputable business and maintaining his position as head of the blood family. Grumbling to himself, he now figured he'd have to at least purchase one of Stefan's photographic compositions or whatever he did. In a few minutes, he would get the chance to find out exactly what his friend created and why Alex was full of pride.

The SUV pulled into the parking garage and the group made their way on foot to the gallery a few blocks away.

"This is where you come alone, *prinţesa*?"

"Yes, why?"

"I don't like this neighborhood. Your life could be at risk. You're not coming here by yourself again."

"Stefan, stop being so…so caveman with me. Do you forget I'm a trained bounty hunter *and* special agent with the *F.B.I.? Please.*" Alex trudged off at a faster pace.

"She always like this?" Sorin asked, and snickered inwardly at how she enunciated the letters with such emphasis. Almost as if she did it to annoy his friend.

"Yes, always taking risks she shouldn't. I've talked to her until I'm blue in the face. She will do what she wants and I can't stop her." Stefan grinned. "Then again I don't want to ever hold her back. I love her too much."

"I'll never understand your attraction to a woman who makes such decisions against your demands, brother. I'd keep her tied to my bed and so well fucked, she wouldn't be able to move. Then you wouldn't have to worry about her being out on the streets alone in neighborhoods like this."

"Don't let her hear you say such things. If ever I consider your suggestion, and believe me I've been tempted, she'd leave me."

"Is your relationship so tenuous she would return to her world? Doesn't sound like love to me."

"No, we are, but she's just an independent woman with a mind of her own. She loves me and tells me more than once every night. I can push her but so far."

"By the way, where did she disappear to?"

"See what I mean?" Stefan stopped, closed his eyes then opened them. "She's not far, and okay. We better hurry and catch up or I'll never hear the end of it."

Five minutes later they were standing in the lobby of the gallery waiting for Antoine Rousseau to meet with them.

Sorin glanced around the stark white room. Overhead lights dangled from the exposed beamed ceiling, again painted white. From what he could tell from his perspective, the art pieces which hung on narrow flat columned walls catered to contemporary styles. His Old World classics would look totally out of place at the gallery. The colors were vibrant and eclectic. A few odd-shaped sculptures were large and set upon the floor for display. He shook his head, questioning what someone saw in the strange and almost nonsensical pieces. Give him a portrait of a countryside he can recognize as something real, not a free-flowing structure open to interpretation. He guessed he'd never make an art critic. Then again, he didn't care to be one. His art entailed sculpting women, sometimes men, into a submissive or slave for their masters. Bodies and psyches are works of art in themselves and he took pride in those particular forms of talent.

Whatever the gallery owner talked to his friends about, Sorin tuned out. The conversation meant nothing to him. He wanted to concentrate on finding the haunting woman of his dreams. *Merliah.*

Stefan had been right about her name—unusual, unique, and beautiful. His angel. What if it were possible to find an angel on earth? Had he found a way to tap into another realm? Surely, his faith in God had long since faded, but what if this were redemption of some kind? *Am I tasked with saving this angel in order to redeem my evil ways as a vampire?* The thought of the possibility seemed farfetched and Sorin pushed the thought aside.

"You look bored," Stefan said, slapping Sorin on the shoulder.

"Huh?" Sorin stared, half dazed before recovering. "No, just thinking. Do you mind if I look around while you and Alex take care of business?"

Stefan leaned in closer. "Go ahead. I got a feeling I'll be awhile."

Sorin snickered, and then wandered off to the left away from his friends and the animated and vocal gallery owner.

The large, open spaces were divided into different sections as Sorin quickly discovered. With the high ceilings and the industrial like buildings they passed in the area, he figured this once had been a warehouse in a previous life. Now, the modern styling found a new life as an art gallery. Almost like a maze, sections for the different artists were cleverly laid out when he snaked through one room to another. He stopped briefly at a display by the artist who sculpted, or at least Sorin thought they would be classified as sculptures, of contorted shapes of industrial materials. Metal rods, plaster slapped on the various parts, nuts and bolts, and other odd pieces compiled the display. Sorin shook his head and walked on to another section.

As he slipped around the first corner, he spied a placard with Stefan's name and then the room opened up with the presentation of his friend's work. Sorin took a step back, the shock of viewing Stefan's handiwork astonished him. The photographs of sunsets and sunrises amazed him. He inched closer to examine the details. Impressed, Sorin stepped back with folded arms over his chest, and then studied first one then another, working his way along the room admiring each one.

"Well, well Stefan, I think you owe Alex a vote of gratitude. She was right," he murmured. As long as Sorin had been friends with Stefan, he felt strange not realizing his friend had such talent. If this was an art form to be admired, he'd certainly consider collecting. Maybe it also had a lot to do with the fact neither one of them had seen such a spectacle of beauty in eons. The subject matter struck a chord with him. Sorin could relate and understood the feeling behind each composition. How the old vampire captured the light and shadows of each picture stunned even his jaded conception of art.

After a few minutes admiring Stefan's work, he slipped around the next corner in anticipation of viewing more of his friend's artwork. To his disappointment at first then amazement, Sorin came upon another section. Not of Stefan's art. To his untrained eye, the paintings appeared to be watercolors. The usual criticism he had for modern canvases had him reconsidering this artist. The use of vibrant colors and scenes depicting nature intrigued him. The subject matter appeared familiar which drew his attention immediately. Compelled by the mesmerizing landscapes, Sorin drew closer, and as if in slow motion, the space between the art and him seemed to collapse in on him. One in particular captured his attention.

The field was of wildflowers interspersed in tall grass in the foreground and a clump of tall trees leading to mountains in the background. "Damn." *This looks like summertime back home, on my estate.*

Searching for the title and the name of the artist, he moved closer. The word Phoenix was scripted on the bottom right corner. The name was interesting but unfamiliar. Perhaps he was an up-and-coming one like Stefan. Sorin shifted his attention to the small placard next to the landscape. As he did so, something caught his eye. A quick movement. From the painting. He reached out to touch the canvas along the treed area. Something moved? *What the fuck was that?*

"No, no, no, *monsieur*." The voice of Antoine Rousseau boomed and jerked Sorin from his exploration. "You cannot touch the paintings. The artist left specific instructions. No one is to come within three feet."

"Sorry, I thought I saw—"

"You can see from behind here," he said as he pointed to the floor. "This line is here for a purpose. No one is to step and view any of her work any closer than this. No exceptions. During the show a velvet stanchion will take the place. Until then, do not cross the line."

"What's going on?" the sound of Stefan's voice interjected from across the room. "I heard Antoine's squeal from the lobby."

"I guess I broke a rule, the artist..." Pausing, he peered at the painting and then added, "Phoenix has strict rules not to cross this line taped on the floor."

"Well don't cross it. You know women and rules, they're the only ones allowed to break them." Stefan smirked.

A woman? I thought...

With narrowed eyes, Sorin glared at his friend. "I hope you meant the remark in jest, but I swear I saw something in this painting move. I was getting closer to see what it was."

"Oh, probably one of those nasty Palmetto bugs. They're huge and quick so you probably did see something, but it moved too fast."

"Bugs! I don't have bugs in my gallery. I keep a clean place." Antoine's indignant tone had the two vamps snickering. They had managed to get to the demanding little owner. Sorin found the voice of the man, well, irritating at best and had no use for the human.

"I'm sorry, Antoine. I didn't mean to imply you kept a dirty gallery. I'm just saying those filthy creatures can get in any way no matter how diligent you are to prevent them. My apologies."

"Hey, what's going on in here?" Alex asked walking into the area.

"Long story, *prinţesa*." Stefan wrapped his arm over her shoulder and pulled her close. "Are we ready to go?"

As the group left the area designated for the artist Phoenix, Sorin glanced back over his shoulder one more time. *I swear I saw a person moving, not a damn bug.*

Chapter Ten

The Dreamer Sees the World before the Dawn

The man on the other side turned and stared at Merliah. *Did he see me?* A strange mixture of desire and knowledge of her watching him seemed to gleam in his dark, sable eyes. The glance over his shoulder was brief but enough to send shivers up and down her spine. A corner of his mouth lifted in a quirky smile, reinforcing her belief he saw her.

Ohmigod! The man in my dreams. Sorin?

The man was real and stood within inches, further if he were to step inside. Was it really him or someone who appeared like him?

Not real, he was a dream. She shook her head, and her mind raced wondering how this was possible. Imagining the man looked like Sorin had been an activity she'd done quite often recently. A visitor at the institute the other day turned out to be the father of one of the kids in the pediatric section. From a distance she'd swear on her grandmother's grave the man had been Sorin. Merliah chided herself for acting like a fool stumbling over two feet while walking across the room to see him. Fortunately, the man was nice and didn't make her feel bad. After the brutal chastising she gave herself, she swore off falling into the daydreaming slump of thinking about running into her dream lover again. Merliah knew the fantasy was an escape mechanism for dealing with the chaos she felt within her body. "Your brain has survival mechanisms to keep the pain at bay." Dr. Wright had told her those words several times in their sessions discussing the matter. *Maybe he was right.*

But she liked the dream and Sorin. Inspired by her new abilities with the energized painting, she wanted to explore the possibility of creating a fantasy world while awake. *Is that even possible?* If so, it would be the one place she'd feel her old self, the person from before the accident.

Lights flashed on, illuminating the gallery brighter than before. Then another voice. *Antoine?*

Her eyes fluttered as she glanced around the tree she stood behind to take in more of the room. She closed her eyes, and then opened them.

A male figure moved into her line of vision again. With his back to her, she couldn't make out his face, but even from the backside, he had the same broad shoulders as Sorin, the same cut of jawline, the same shoulder-length, raven hair.

Merliah definitely recognized him from her dream, but how could it be possible. Something about this man wasn't easily forgotten, just like Sorin in the haunting dream.

"How can I ever forget his captivating face? Even the scar across his cheek was the same." Merliah carefully peered from around the tree she crouched down behind.

The extraordinary resemblance astounded her as she watched intently at the men speaking. The man on the other side definitely was the sexy man of her dreams, only this wasn't a dream she kept telling herself. He really did exist, and he almost discovered her in the painting. No one said his name, only the other one. His name was Stefan, and she recognized the owner of the gallery. *Say his name, please. Let me know it's my Sorin.*

The devastatingly attractive man, scars on his face and all, made her pulse quicken just as the male in her dreams. The mere sight of him made her feel the same. She exhaled softly. Tall with broad shoulders accentuated by the black leather hugging his muscular frame, his massive arms and legs looked exceptionally powerful in the body-hugging leather pants hugging him like a second skin. All taut muscle, just like her Sorin, created no doubt in her mind.

A woman walked in and Merliah's train of thought broke. Her heart thumped loud. Is she with the Sorin look-alike? *No, she just kissed the man named Stefan.* Merliah felt relieved. The others continued to talk and then announced they had to leave. Mr. Rousseau had been agitated by comments made. Covering her mouth to stifle a giggle from the comment about how her image in the picture looked like a bug was priceless. At least this experience gave her a perspective of how people would perceive those in the painting. *Oh no, they can't ever know this is possible.*

As she watched the group depart the room, she nearly choked when Sorin's twin glanced back and it seemed his eyes focused directly on her. Merliah sucked in a quick breath. Her heart beat loud in her ears, and it fluttered when his stare returned to and didn't leave the painting. *Did he see me?* Merliah licked her dry lips, her body leaned on the backside of the tree not daring to move one inch or else he'd return to check out the *bug* again.

A disaster would have happened if he touched the painting. As it was, she had taken a big risk by stepping into her landscape. Except, she had to try the energy she imprinted into the scene. This panorama of her dream had been her best one of all and also the most draining of her new found powers. She couldn't explain how or why she was able to impregnate her art with the ability to transport into the creation, but whatever allowed it, she felt blessed. And frightened by it.

Merliah had just meant to go into the landscape for a few minutes to check out the passage. The minutes turned into an hour or more. Abby would return to the gallery to pick her up at nine and Merliah was sure it had to be close if not after the hour. She had been ready to leave when she heard footsteps. Someone came around the corner and she froze. The man had been drawn to the field of flowers, the pull of the energy in the painting perhaps but in either case, she realized he saw her. She scurried to hide, but it had been too late. He drew closer and almost touched her and if he had would have been drawn in. *Then what would I have done to explain how he landed inside a piece of art? He'd freak out, no doubt. I did the first time and I created the painting.*

Fortunately, Mr. Rousseau showed up in time. Glad to see him, she insisted on marking an area just out of arm's reach to restrict the public from getting too close and inadvertently touch the canvas. Bringing this particular painting for the exhibition had been a risk, but something inside her told her to create and show it. The other pieces mesmerized the viewer and even gave the observer a sensation as if the painting called them. This one could literally pull the admirers in. A few more smaller watercolors were back at the institute and she had been experimenting with the energy and invoked them the same way, but after seeing the Sorin look-alike, she changed her mind. The transformation would be too dangerous.

If anyone found out...

No, she didn't even want to think about the consequences of such recklessness. At this moment, she put thoughts into how to get out of the woods unseen. She ran for the exit without another thought and leapt blindly through the portal.

The landing on a hard and unforgiving terrazzo floor when she already had problems with walking wasn't exactly the best way to escape the confines of the painting, but she had no choice.

"Oh, that's going to hurt like hell." She changed positions slowly, from flat on her stomach to a roll onto her side and then a seated position. With the palms of her hands, she began to rub both her knees. Tears began to form, not so much for the pain with her body, but for the fact she might have seen Sorin.

She really saw him. Did he hear her call to him after all? How was it possible a dream could turn real? Maybe the man appeared like her dream lover and in fact wasn't him. Like the myth everyone has a twin somewhere in the world. This person was Sorin's. She'd fantasized a tall, dark and handsome man all her life and even in her coma she conjured up a facsimile of one. The fact a man sort of fitting the description happened to show up the night before her exhibition was totally coincidental.

"Merliah! Are you all right?" Abby called out as she rounded the corner to the room.

"Abby, I...I fell. I'm okay, but can you get my cane by the wall over there?" Merliah motioned in the direction of the wall behind Abby. "I...I tried to walk without it and slipped."

"Well, here." Abby reached around Merliah with both arms and pulled up, lifting to her feet. "Let's get you standing and off the cold floor."

"Thanks."

"Are you sure you're okay?"

"Yes, I'm fine."

"Oh, *mon Dieu!* You found her. What happened?" Antoine asked in a frantic tone.

"I found her on the floor, but she's fine."

Merliah turned away from the owner. In all the chaotic activity, she'd forgotten about losing her veil to obscure her appearance. Glancing frantically around the area, she didn't see it, and then she remembered. *I left it in the woods. Oh no!*

"Merliah? What's the matter?" Abby asked. She slipped an arm around her shoulder and leaned closer.

"My veil. I can't let him see me like this," Merliah whispered and raised her hand to conceal her face.

"You stay here. I won't let him see you. Where did you leave it?"

"I...I don't know. Abby, just get me out of here, please."

"Don't worry. I'll take care of everything." Abby turned away. "Merliah is upset, Antoine. Would you mind if I take her out the back entrance? She wants her privacy."

"No problem, no problem. I also think I have something in my office she can borrow to cover her face."

"What do you think, Merliah? If he has a scarf to cover you, then you won't have to wait for me to bring the car around."

She kept her head down and pulled the collar of her shirt up, attempting to conceal as much of her face as possible. "Okay."

After a half-hour, Merliah and Abby were on their way back to the Berger Institute. Another thirty minutes and she would feel more comfortable. Exposed to the world, stripped of any remaining dignity, retreating back to the sanctuary of the private facility had her craving for the time to pass quickly. The crowded streets thinned and the lights of the city began to wink in the distance. She noticed glancing out the window thinking about how bizarre the night ended up. The drive into the outskirts of Miami traveled along a path of darkness.

"I'm sorry I couldn't be with you tonight to help with the last minute details, Merliah. The art class downtown ran a little longer than I expected. If I hadn't been delayed, I would have been there at the gallery and maybe you wouldn't have fallen. I'm so sorry."

"Don't worry about me, Abby. I'm really fine. It was a small fall. I'll be as good as new after a good night's sleep. You'll see."

"Well, I'm still sorry. I should have been there for you." A moment or two of silence passed. "So did you and Antoine get everything finished for tomorrow night? All the paintings ready to display and the promotional materials?"

"Yes, we're ready." Merliah answered into the glass, as she continued to stare out the window.

"Oh, and guess what? Antoine told me there is already some interest in one of your pieces. The buyer came in tonight he said. Isn't that exciting?"

Merliah didn't answer, lost in her thoughts.

"Merliah, did you hear me?" Abby touched her on the arm, startling her out of the daydream.

"Huh, what? I'm sorry. What did you say?"

"Where were you just now?"

"Um, nothing. Just thinking."

"You've been doing a lot of thinking lately." Her friend grinned. "Are you worried about tomorrow?"

No, she wasn't and laughed inwardly at the suggestion. How could she explain her dreams about a stranger she was not only attracted to, but had imaginary sex with? Many times, no less. And tonight, she may have seen him in person. Nervous? More like anxious to find out if the man at the gallery really was her dream lover. *But, how can I find out? He wouldn't recognize me. Not like this, not with my disfigured body. He'd run away and I'd never see him again if he discovered the real me.*

"Yes. What if people don't like my art, Abby? I saw some of the other artists' pieces and they are very good. Mine aren't great. Okay, maybe but not great."

"No, I think more than just okay. If you have someone already interested, I'd say that's a super indication you are good. You'll do fine. You just concentrate on being accessible to talk if someone has questions. Leave everything else to Antoine and me."

"Stick me in a corner and let me watch. I can't talk to anyone, Abby. Look at me. I'd scare any potential buyer away."

"Oh, Merliah. You are beautiful, sweetie. Don't let anyone tell you otherwise. If anyone hurts you, they'll have to deal with me."

Merliah giggled. She loved Abby. The woman always made her laugh when she felt bad. The reality of the exhibition tomorrow night hit her more than she had imagined. For the first time since awakening from the coma, she would have to socialize with people outside the safety and security of the institute. Why did Abby have to bring it up? Now she was a lot more than nervous, she was frightened to death.

"I don't feel beautiful because I'm not. Robbie, my ex-boyfriend freaked out when he came to visit me after I came out of the coma. It didn't matter anyway, he'd moved on after I didn't wake up right away. I heard he's engaged to be married now. My parents, when they visit, barely look at me. I can see tears in Mom's eyes and Dad stares past me. If my family can't stand the sight of me, how will strangers."

"People can be cruel, Merliah, but I've spoken with your mom and dad. They love you. You're a strong young woman. Look at all you've accomplished in a short period of time. I admire and believe in you. I'm helping get your new career off the ground because you deserve the recognition."

"Really? Thank you, Abby." She really did mean the compliment. Abby had become more than an art instructor, she was a friend and Merliah didn't have many friends.

"You're welcome and I do believe we're here." Abby pulled up to the front entrance of the Berger Institute. "Do you want me to walk you in?"

"No, I should be fine. Will you pick me up tomorrow?" She asked as the door handle released from her grip and opened slightly.

"Yes and I'll have a surprise for you."

Merliah stopped midway from stepping out of the car and turned back to Abby. She stared without saying a word.

"Don't look at me like I'm doing something weird. You'll enjoy the surprise and I'm not telling you anything else. Go get a good night's sleep and I'll see you tomorrow." Abby smiled.

"Okay, but the surprise better be a good one." Merliah exited the car and slowly walked into the sanctuary she now called home.

Within the hour, she took a shower, wrote in her journal and was in bed hoping to fall asleep quickly to dream about Sorin.

Chapter Eleven

The Dreamer Comes Alive in the Light of Day

"Okay, Sorin. Tell me her name again," Alex said as she had her fingers poised above the keyboard.

"Merliah, she said. Now I can't verify Merliah is her real name, but at this point I have no reason to doubt her."

"Got it. With a name like that I think we should have an easy hit as long as she has enough entries in the database. Now, what else can you tell me? Any small piece of information could be helpful."

"She said something about being at an institute. No name though. You want a physical description too?"

"Wouldn't hurt. I can plug in her stats and hopefully they will throw out any hits that don't match."

Sorin sat on the edge of the desk and rested a hand on the opposite thigh. "Okay, I'd say she comes to about here on me." He raised a hand to his collar bone. "And she has flowing blonde hair, crystal blue eyes with the longest lashes, fair skin as soft as silk, and has a sweet, melodic voice."

Alex glanced over at Stefan, who was seated in the occasional chair in the corner, and grinned. "Oh, that's real descriptive, Sorin. Very basic. Thanks."

"What? Did I say something wrong?"

"No, man. You nailed it. Are you sure this isn't just wishful thinking on your part to find this woman?"

"What are you talking about? I told you, Merliah is real, and I sense her. I've seen and touched her."

"In your dreams which vamps don't have, you mean. Of course, I guess for lack of any other explanation she is real, right?"

"Yes, it does and you're making fun of me. May I remind you who is older here?"

"You can, but it won't make a difference. You've got it bad for this woman, whether she's real or not."

Ignoring his friend's comments, Sorin turned his attention back to Alex. "Does this computer of yours have anything yet?"

"Patience, Sorin. I didn't say it would be easy, although with the unusual name there can't be many women with it in South Florida, maybe we'll have an answer shortly."

Sorin?

The woman's voice called to him in his mind. At first, he couldn't make out if the cry matched the one he remembered from all the other times or if he imagined the sound. Then she whispered again begging for a response. She pushed hard against the complex of mental safeguards he maintained. At this point of the evening, he wasn't ready to let her in, at least not with an audience.

Not that he didn't care about others standing around and observing his sexual exploits, but something about Merliah brought out the protector in him. Call him selfish, but he didn't want to share her, even if she existed only in his head. Even as a dream, others there seemed inappropriate, which was strange. He'd never had that feeling with another. A wave of protectiveness washed over him hearing the begging voice.

He began to resent her ability to tap into his thoughts and emotions so easily. The cries weakened him on many levels a couple of which he perceived as impotence and vulnerability. A human female reducing him to a man driven to come halfway around the world to find her had to be dealt with. He didn't know how the encounters happened, but he would get to the source of her powers. No one, especially a human female, denied his dominance or the ability to influence his existence. He would not let her get away with it.

The waiting for the answers from Alex's database tortured him. He had to know, did she exist or not, the question tumbled over again in his mind. His body thrummed with anticipation at what he might do to her once he let down the barriers in his mind. He did his best to relax and be patient, but there was no way to know how long the search would take and the semi-erection pressing against his zipper didn't help matters.

Shit! I need to find her.

"Sorin? Earth to Sorin, did you hear me?" Alex asked.

"I think he zoned out on us," Stefan added.

"What? Did I miss something?"

"Yeah, I've been telling you I got a hit on your woman."

"Sorry, I didn't hear you. What did you find?" He moved behind Alex seated at the computer desk and looked over her shoulder at the screen.

"I widened the search parameters and this popped up. There is a Merliah Travers at the Berger Institute. The facility is a rehabilitation center about thirty-five, forty minutes from here, depending on traffic."

"Is there a picture?"

"No, just basic information. See here, she's a patient. Been there for over four years. Sounds to me like she has some serious medical problems."

"Over four years. What kind of institution is this again?"

"Let me see if I can pull up more stats. Hold on." With a few strokes of the keyboard and a few seconds loading the file, she gleaned through the pages and stopped on the main page. "There you go, have a seat and read for yourself." She rose from the swivel chair and moved across the room to stand by Stefan.

Sorin read the details about the Berger Institute. The facility catered to patients with complex medical conditions, physical and psychological. They boasted about the different therapies available to strengthen the mind, body and soul of all who passed through their doors. To Sorin, the literature sounded more fluff and showed him nothing of the patients. He had to find out if this Merliah Travers was the angel of his dreams.

"Do you know where this place is? Can I get there easily?"

"Like I said a few minutes ago, maybe about thirty-five, forty minutes. Are you planning on going there now? I don't think they'd let you in this late at night. The best you could do is go early evening, you know, right after you awaken."

"Not good. I have to go now. I have to know for sure if this is her or someone else. If this Merliah Travers isn't the one, I'll know to look elsewhere. Did anyone else show up in your database?"

"Nope. She was the only one. If she's been there for over four years, I'd say she's a chronic patient and maybe you don't want to see her. People don't normally stay in those facilities long-term unless they have serious problems."

"I don't care, Alex. I have to find out. Can I borrow your vehicle, Stefan?"

"You're going to let him go alone, in a strange place?" Alex asked of his friend.

Stefan arched a brow. "*Prinţesa*, I wouldn't go unless you were good with it." Then, he glanced at Sorin. "I can take you if you want, brother."

"No, I can manage without you. This is my journey, not yours" Sorin peered over the computer screen to Alex and Stefan. "I appreciate your offer though. You stay with your woman. I'll be fine."

"You sure? You don't know this city," Stefan said.

"Do you have one of the electronic gadgets for finding your way around? All I have to do is input this address, right?" Sorin held up a scrap piece of paper he'd written the address of the Berger Institute on.

Alex giggled. "Yes, there is an electronic gadget. She'll get you there."

"Perfect. I should be able to find it with no problem. Wish me luck."

Sorin needed more than good fortune this time. The trip took longer than the thirty-five minutes the GPS indicated. Mainly because he took the wrong exit and got turned around in the opposite direction and travelled a good five miles before he could find a place to turn back. He reached the facility around one in the morning. The entrance gate housed a security guard so he had to circumvent the grounds and gain access by other means. The gated community proved no match for someone with his skills, but getting into the main building and finding Merliah Travers turned out to be more difficult. *I will not be deterred.*

The melodic voice had ceased after he began the trip. Although the temptation to let down his mind barriers tugged at his willpower to resist, he came close several times when she didn't call out.

Sorin drove past the guard shack of the Berger Institute several times to case out the points of possible entry. No doubt security cameras were perched nearby and would record his visit, so he proceeded further down the street. He cut the SUV's engine and stepped onto the paved street on the opposite side. He breathed deeply, his lungs filling with night mist beginning to settle on the dew-covered grass. The amber glow of a full moon illuminated the building on the other side of the eight-foot black ornamental fence surrounding his final destination. Anticipation of finding Merliah rushed through his veins.

After scoping out the immediate area, he scaled the fence with ease. Taking off in a sprint, he surmised if any surveillance cameras caught his image, all they'd see would be a blur.

Within minutes he stood at a set of sliding glass doors etched with the name Berger Institute on the surface. Figuring out how to gain access with the locks in place took a little time, but his strength surpassed the weak locking mechanism. Upon entering, he searched for the administrative offices. The legend on the wall directly off the lobby indicated they were down the hall to the left. With great strides he tracked toward them.

"Excuse me, sir. What are you doing here?" The woman's voice demanded.

He ignored her and continued his trek toward the offices.

"Look mister, I don't know who you are or what you're doing here at this hour, but I insist you stop, or I'll be forced to call security." Her precise, emphatic words failed to convey the control she so hopelessly projected toward him.

Such a foolish human female. He laughed inwardly as he continued to ignore her.

"Sir, I've warned you. I'm calling security."

Shit! Finding her is taking too much time. Sorin stood in front of the main offices, and then turned to face the annoying woman.

With a paralyzing stare, he tapped into the nurse's mind. She was dressed in what he heard those in the medical profession wore—scrubs. Except the shirt she wore was decorated with cartoonish characters. Did the information he read at Alex's office give an erroneous depiction? Was Merliah Travers not an adult here for rehabilitation of a physical element, but a child with something else wrong? He had no idea, but would soon find out.

"Woman, you will give me access to this room and then find a patient who resides here. Do you understand?" His words compelled her to follow his direction. The cell phone she had opened to call the security she threatened him with moments before dropped to the floor.

Without another word, she walked toward him and stopped within inches. "Very good." Sorin placed a hand on her forehead. "Open this door."

The room was dark, but with excellent night vision he found his way to the administrator's office, dragging the woman by the hand. "Sit, and find Merliah Travers for me."

Modern technology befuddled him and he'd seen no reason in learning all the ins and outs of how to use the blue screen monsters. Even if he knew how, drawing attention to why he searched for Merliah wouldn't work, especially if it turned out this Travers woman wasn't his Merliah. The female assisting him would be just one he'd have to deal with, not an entire group of people if he were discovered. Within a few minutes after all the protocols of the system were satisfied, the patients' files were accessed and then Merliah Travers' appeared on the screen.

"Excellent. Now what room is she in?"

"Room 593, West Wing."

"Take me there and tell anyone we encounter I'm a relative from out of town."

"Yes, I will tell them."

Several twists and turns down dimly lit long hallways, Sorin and the woman under his mesmerizing control found their way onto the West Wing, walked past the nurses' station and to the end of the hall. The nurse moved ahead of him and stopped in front of the last door on the right. Room 593.

Sorin held her gaze and instructed her to leave him, not to remember anything she'd done to lead him to Merliah Travers' room. She blinked, muttered something incoherent, and then walked back down the hallway toward the nurses' station.

With a slight push of the lever, the door opened. The latch gave way too easily he thought, but brushed the peculiarity aside. The room was dark except for shadows cast across the room from moonlight slivering through the mini-blinds at the window on the opposite side of the room. With the stealth of a predatory wild cat, Sorin took several strides toward the bed. He sensed something amiss.

In fact, he sensed nothing.

Without hesitation, he touched the crumpled bed coverings and his hand collapsed the linens to the mattress. Glancing around the small room, he sensed no one in the room. Then, he turned his head toward the other door and saw no light illuminating from under. *No one in the bathroom either. Where is this Merliah Travers?*

He spun around, aggravation built inside him. All the time spent finding the facility and to get to the room and discover the woman, his possible dream angel, missing. *Fuck, now what?*

Nothing, but leave the premises, then he did, getting no further than outside the room.

No sooner had he departed, and he was cornered by another nurse on duty.

"Who are you and what were you doing in Miss Travers room at this hour?" The portly woman demanded, and not in a quiet voice. She pushed her way past him and opened the door he just exited.

Taking the opportunity while she turned attention away, he walked fast through the hallway. Before he reached the nurse's station, he heard the nurse yelling after him.

"Stop him! That man has done something with Merliah. Stop him!"

Sorin glanced around for the quickest way to leave the premises without drawing more attention. To glamour more than one human at a time wasn't the easiest of tasks to perform. He rushed with quicker speed toward the way he came in. Pushing through the electronic double doors, he dashed out into the night, across the ground fogged lawn and over the fence. Exterior lights flashed on just as he landed on the other side of the barrier. The security guard at the gate alerted and pointed a flashlight beam in his direction, but the shaft of light passed harmlessly behind as he trotted toward the parked SUV.

After keying the address for Stefan's penthouse into the navigational system, he started the engine and drove away. The night turned into a bust. With only a few more hours of night remaining and no sensing of Merliah attempting to contact him again, he wondered if he'd begun the descent into madness. The years spent as a vampire were catching up to him. He'd heard rumors these types of things happened to older ones. Was he approaching the age of paranoia, losing his mind? Vampire dementia? Would he be forced to end his existence, because if he turned into a maniacal lunatic like Dragos, better to go out now with honor than succumb to the fate his sire met.

A loud growl pierced the silence within the vehicle, overshadowing the sound of the roaring engine and annoying voice on the electronic gadget that he couldn't figure out how to shut off. The lights of Miami illuminated the distance and he careened down the road toward Stefan's penthouse.

Chapter Twelve

Just One More Canvas

With all the tossing and turning, she realized what kept her from falling asleep—the compelling desire to create another canvas ran on a continuous loop through her mind. The haunting dark eyes. Those piercing eyes gazed at hers in the deepest recesses of the dream, and compelled her to leave her room at one thirty in the morning. The dreams were driving her insane. The energy coursing through her hands to the paintings began to frighten her, but not as much as the exhibition this evening.

Sorin. She'd called out for him several times, but he didn't answer her pleas tonight. She needed him and he didn't fill her dreams, contributing to the restlessness. The mysterious man at the gallery was real and looked like Sorin. In the flesh, he was as handsome, as intriguing, as beguiling as in her imagination. She wasn't severely brain damaged to the point not to realize he was the trigger for this latest surge to paint. And paint she did.

Merliah inched back from the easel. As she studied the almost-finished picture of a castle in the mountains, a scene totally imagined, but somehow familiar. In the foreground, a small field of wildflowers similar to the other work hanging in the gallery boasted more lush colors—greens, yellows, purples of varying hues. Something wasn't quite right though. The castle, or what she thought depicted one from a fairytale, looked lifeless, cold and dark. Yes, the piece needed a few more details, but her energy level began to wane. Being in the studio this late had been like a compulsion, to put on canvas what she'd seen in her mind's eye, felt in her heart.

A drop of perspiration trickled down Merliah's brow. She'd worked frantically, putting stroke after stroke on the canvas trying to forget him. A man like him would never look twice at her, only run in the opposite direction. Her hideous appearance would frighten, not attract. Absently she swiped the bead away with the back of her hand. The sable-tipped brush in her hand felt like a lead balloon as she finished the last touch. She was too tired to add one more stroke. Tonight's event would come early if she didn't get any rest, so she decided the special touch she'd add later in the day. After cleaning the brushes, she covered the image with a sheet and left the studio.

Merliah returned to her room about four o'clock in the morning and found the nurses fussing about. *What on earth is going on?*

"Miss Travers! Where have you been?" The head nurse, Miss Jenkins, exclaimed as she rushed toward her practically knocking her down in the process.

"Huh? I was in the art studio painting. What's going on?"

"Oh, my Lord, we've been on lock-down for an hour because a stranger was seen leaving your room. You weren't in your bed. Well, we called the police and everything. They're in your room now collecting evidence."

"Ohmigod, you're kidding? I'm sorry I've worried everyone."

Another nurse and Dr. Wright appeared around the corner. The nurse seemed pleased to see Merliah, but the doctor had an expression of displeasure on his face. Merliah all of a sudden felt sick. All she did was go to the art studio and all this confusion erupted from leaving her room without telling anyone? Then, she realized Nurse Jenkins said a stranger was in her room. *Who?*

"Merliah, you're all right. Nothing happened to you?" Dr. Wright questioned as he approached.

"Yes, I'm fine but tired. I want to go to sleep."

"She said she was in the art studio, Doctor," Miss Jenkins said.

"The art studio? At this hour? What in the world were you doing there, Merliah?" Dr. Wright asked.

"Painting. I wasn't able to sleep. One more picture kept running through my mind. I had to get up and do it."

"Well, my dear, you should have told one of the nurses. We were all worried, especially when we heard a strange man came out of your room."

"I'm sorry." She really did mean it. "What man?" Why everyone fussed over her was confusing. She thought the studio would've been the first place anyone would have searched for her.

For the past several months, she practically lived in the south wing of the building. With the exhibition happening in over twelve hours everyone should have known. *If Abby had been here, she would have found me right away. I just know it.*

"Oh, don't worry. He's gone now. The police will take care of tracking him down."

She stifled a yawn. "Can I go to my room now?" With every passing minute she stood listening to another comment about how everyone was happy to see her, she wanted to strangle them. Didn't they understand how tired she was? Her solitary bed called to her.

"Yes, I'll take you. The police are still in your room and I'll explain what happened."

"Thank you, Doctor Wright."

After a long explanation to the detectives, as well as some of the medical staff, Merliah settled into bed exhausted beyond thinking straight. Before closing her eyes, she thought about who would've come into her room late at night. *Could the man have been Sorin?* The wishful thinking teetered on the edge of her consciousness as she quickly slipped into a dream about the man in the gallery.

She called to him within the darkness, and he came to her in the field of wildflowers. The warmth of the sun bathed their skin. As she gazed upon his handsome face, he reached for her and cupped her face in his two big hands. She had an overwhelming urge to touch him, to see if he were as real as he appeared, not a part of her imagination.

"Sorin, are you real? Tell me you are." She was all for making up for lost time. They had many meetings in her dreams, but each time seemed like the first. She was addicted to him and the last time they were interrupted, leaving her unsatisfied and confused. Starting to doubt her sanity about him being real or her imagination, tonight she'd pretend he was real and experience everything about him. All she intended to do was make love to Sorin as if she'd never see him again.

Without a word uttered, he slowly lowered his head, and then gently pressed his lips to hers. They were warm and soft, yet firm under hers. Without resistance, she leaned against him, reached up to hold onto his shoulders and deepened the kiss. Her lips parted and she flicked her tongue against his, begging for more of him, and he responded to the plea. His tongue tangled with hers in a passionate and wanton way.

He groaned and pulled her body tightly against him. His chest was like a wall of solid granite, yet it gave off enough heat to sear her flesh. His kisses had become addictive and intoxicating as her favorite chocolate.

Wanting more, much more for so long, the loneliness of years flooded her mind and body. She pressed against his chest, rubbing her aching breasts until the nipples hardened into little points responding to his warmth. The fire coursing through her veins almost had her fighting to climb inside his skin, to become united as one with him.

Finally they broke apart. His heavy-lidded dark chocolate eyes possessed an almost animalistic quality, not feral but rather they burned with such an intensity she swore red ringed the iris. "I've been searching for you, angel. This time I want to know more so I can make this a reality."

"I want the same. What do you need?" She ran her fingers over his taut abdomen, then fluttered light kisses on his skin.

"Oh, angel, what you do to me. I searched for you and couldn't find you. Now, you're here." He moaned his delight then gently pushed her away from him. "It was over before anything began last time. On this occasion, I want to take it slowly." Within a few moments, he pushed his hands under her T-shirt and ran his palms over her stomach. He tugged at the hem and pulled the fabric over her head, revealing her upper body nakedness. He offered her a knowing grin. "Your breasts are so lovely. I just have to taste them."

Then he gave her right nipple a flick and she jumped in response. Making a pleased sound at the back of his throat, he bent down and lifted her breasts, cupping them in his hands. The hot brush of his lips against her nipple had her clutching the back of his head. When he sucked the stiff peak into his hot mouth, she nearly screamed. He sank to his knees, tugging her against him as he kissed and licked his way across her breasts then trailed a line of damp kisses to her navel. He stopped and fumbled briefly with the ribbon tied at the waist of her pants bottoms.

With a quick tug, the bow-tied ribbon gave way and he pulled the garment down over her hips and then ankles. She stepped out of them and he returned to nibbling around her bellybutton for a while before continuing downward. Pressing forward, she made a guttural sound deep in her throat as he took the edge of her lacy bikini panties and pulled it up tight, pushing the cloth against her aching pussy and tender clit. He lowered his mouth and sucked her aching nub.

The sudden maneuver shocked her, but oh, it felt so good. He moved quickly, with no pretense, and no build-up. He just took her. She stared down at him, fully aware of this being a dream, but she thought she was in control, not the dream, not Sorin. The sensation was intense with his tongue rasping back and forth, twirling and sucking over the tiny button, and her entire body was melting and quivering under the scorching heat of his touch. Cream flooded, trickling down her inner thighs.

Sorin pushed her legs wider apart and he took a deep breath. "I can smell your arousal." Smiling up at her, he licked up and down her slit, lapping up her juices. As fast as he licked them, she made more. Using two fingers, he slipped them deep inside Merliah's sheath and began to slowly push in and out, searching for her G-spot. He flicked his tongue once over her clit and she jerked beneath him.

Merliah shivered as her pussy clenched tighter.

His tongue worked magic on her sensitive clit, faster, harder, applying the right amount of pressure as he rocked his hand against her pelvis, then he slipped another finger inside slamming in and out of her wetness. She whimpered as the tension built.

He sank lower on his heels, and licked the length of her swollen pussy lips with long and languid strokes, drawing the impending climax from her. She was close to release and squeezed her inner muscles around his invading digits. Sorin tugged and sucked on her clit as he continued to fuck her with his fingers.

She fisted her hands in his ebony hair, moaning with every flick of his tongue. She was on the verge of screaming in ecstasy when he drew away from her and pulled her to her knees. She moaned in dismay.

He captured her mouth in a savage kiss. She tasted herself on him, strange but not repulsive. Quite a different experience she'd never had. *Eagerly she leaned in to kiss him deeper, flicking her tongue into his mouth to savor the taste of female essence on him.*

Their tongues intertwined and danced, thrusting in and withdrawing for long moments before he broke off the kiss so he could lower them down to the ground and wildflowers. He rolled her onto her back as he hovered above her placing his weight on his elbows.

"You want to come, don't you angel?"

She nodded.

"Tell me. Say it aloud, angel."

"Yes, I want to come."

Leaning forward, he caught her swollen bud between his teeth, and stroked the bundle of nerves with his tongue over and over. Inserting two fingers again, he pumped them in faster and deeper and continued to suck hard on her clit. The explosive climax hit within seconds and she screamed his name several times as he slowly let her down with long, slow licks and easy pumps of his fingers until she moaned. He withdrew his fingers and sucked them into his mouth as she watched.

The erotic vision was too much and she reached up and began to unbutton his shirt. More than anything she wanted to run her palms over his solid chest, to feel his heat. His skin to her skin. With quivering hands, she reached down his abdomen to stroke over the taut muscles—and his engorged cock. Her insides tensed with anticipation. She couldn't deny the desire to have his hard shaft embedded deep inside her.

He helped her by unfastening the top buttons while she undid the lower ones then she lifted and freed the hem. At last the shirt dropped to the ground and she could see him. Even with her little experience, she recognized a well-toned body. Ohmigod, this man never ceases to send shivers through me! He isn't real, only my idea of a god on earth.

Except for the deep scar which ran from his right eye and across his cheek, his face was flawlessly handsome. His torso was sculpted and defined, truly a delight for her eyes. While his handsome features and brawny build were visually appealing, it was the curling wisps of hair blanketing his upper torso drawing her attention. They looked soft and downy.

Gingerly, she ran her hands over his chest, loving his heat and the way his muscles responded to her touch. With more exploration, she stroked his back, feeling his spine and his shoulder blades then slid her hands lower inside his trousers to cup his taut, rounded ass.

Her gaze slid lower, following the dark trail of hair below his navel and down to his groin. When her inspection led her to the erect form of his huge member, she gasped. He seemed bigger than she remembered from their previous encounters.

Moving between her legs, he spread her thighs wider. "I think this wet little pussy wants more, it wants this cock, doesn't it?" He was toying with her, talking dirty like none of her boyfriend's ever did and she loved it.

"Yes," she whispered.

He shoved two fingers inside her and thumbed her clit as he moved them to the hilt with each plunge into her moist hotness. Merliah moaned and arched her back, spreading her thighs wider.

"Say it louder, angel," he said repositioning himself for a better entry.

Because her whole body felt as if it were on fire, she was stunned when she replied as he asked. "Yes, I want your cock. Now!"

"Fuck, angel. You're beautiful when you beg." With a single seamless thrust, he pushed into her. His hands gripped her hips and began to move inside of her, developing a rhythm.

Merliah wrapped her arms around his shoulders, letting him rock her back and forth. Her breasts rubbed back and forth against his chest, hardening her sensitive nipples. He reached between their bodies, feeling his way to her clit and rubbed the hypersensitive nub as he continued to thrust deep into her.

Merliah moaned as Sorin fucked her senseless with his huge cock. The heat built as his fingers coaxed her clit toward release.

"Ohmigod, please," she begged, but wasn't exactly sure what she was asking.

"Tell me, angel. What do you want?" He pushed harder into her. "Tell me what you want. Tell me to fuck you harder."

Merliah groaned. This dream was so much more intense than any before. Sorin was like an animal, claiming his mate for the first time. She'd never imagined how much his dominance turned her on.

"Yes! Sorin, I want you to fuck me. Hard. Fast." She lifted her hips to match his rhythm, thrusting back hard.

He drove into her with a greater force, the earth beneath them seemed to move.

She closed her eyes, drawing in a deep breath, and hung suspended for one endless moment. "Ohmigod," she screamed, crying out as the orgasm fast approached, and clawed at his bare back as her hungry pussy fluttered and clenched around him.

He intensified the swirling of her clit and thrusting hard. She shuddered and bucked underneath him as her pussy began to spasm around his cock.

"No," he growled.

She opened her eyes to see his image almost transparent.

"No, not again. Sorin, please don't leave me. You can't." She cried out, louder and louder.

Within a few seconds, his specter completely faded.

"No, Sorin. Come back to me."

Merliah bolted upright. A cold sweat swept over her, and her chest heaved with labored breathing. Tears burned her eyes. *Why does this keep happening? I can't finish the dreams like before. I don't understand.*

Gradually, her eyes began to close. The hour was late and she dusted off the dream as another example of her imagination conjuring up a man to satisfy unrequited sexual fantasies. As she turned these thoughts over, the soft sounds of a gentle breeze rustling the palm trees outside her window lulled her back into the black unconscious world of slumber.

Merliah awakened with the sun streaming brightly onto her face. Loud bustling noises penetrated her consciousness. Blinking her eyes several times before opening them completely, she then rolled onto her side. She stretched and yawned before eyeing the alarm clock. "Ohmigod! Three-forty?"

She turned on her back, the jolted upright. "No, no, no. Mom and Dad will be here any minute. I've slept the entire day away." Kicking the covers back, she darted off the mattress and stumbled to the floor. Her legs gave out under her, stiff like they always were when first rising in the morning. Only now, it was the afternoon and she ran late. Her mind totally forgot in the moment of panic she needed to stretch before leaving the confines of a bed.

Umph!

"Ow! Where's my cane?" Her eyes darted from one side of the room to the other. The last she remembered having the walking stick was in the bathroom, washing her face before bed. *Did I leave it there? How'd I manage getting across the room without it?*

A tap on the door startled her and she whipped her head around in the direction of the knock.

The latch clicked, and the door opened slightly.

"Liah? It's Mom and Dad. Can we come in, sweetie?"

"Uh, Mom—"

"Liah! Are you all right? What happened?"

Unfortunately, she was flat on her stomach as her parents entered.

Before she could utter another word, Merliah moved to her hands and knees. Now, her parents would think she wasn't capable of taking care of herself. Merliah had spent the last couple months learning to speak without stuttering and walking without falling. Gaining her independence again had been the goal. The exhibition was supposed to be her stepping stone to achieving the final piece to the emancipation. Her parents had insisted she leave Berger and come home with them, the suggestion she totally disagreed with.

She quickly scrambled pushing onto her feet, wobbly at first but she braced against the bed.

"Mom, Dad. I'm fine, just looking for something I dropped on the floor." She put on a smile to emphasize her point of being okay.

"You're still in your pajamas, sweetie. Have you been sleeping all day? Are you up for this tonight?" Her mother asked as she patted her daughter on the arm. "Are you sure?"

"Yes, Mom. I'm fine. I slept a little late today because I knew I'd be up late tonight." She lied. She seemed to be doing a lot of sleeping lately and that was something she didn't normally do.

"Well then, we have to get you ready. Abby said she'd be here around five to pick you up. Dad and I are driving separately." Her mother turned attention to her father, motioning a hand at him.

"George, hang Liah's dress in the closet before it gets all wrinkled. I don't have time to press it again."

Merliah smiled inwardly. Her mom always pinged on her poor dad. How he put up with her mother's bossiness was beyond Merliah's comprehension. *Will I treat the man I marry like Mom treats Dad?* Would her husband put up with it? *Who am I kidding? I'll never find a man to love me, let alone marry. Not the way I look. Robbie abandoned me.*

"Yes, I know, *Michelle*," Merliah's father answered.

Well daddy has grown a set of balls over the last couple years. Good for him.

"Why don't you two go to the dining hall and let me take my shower. I'll meet you there when I'm finished," Merliah suggested.

"I think that's a good idea. C'mon Michelle. I'm hungry. The lunch you made wasn't enough to keep a bird alive." George walked up to his daughter and gave her a peck on the cheek. "We'll see you in a little while."

"George, you're always starving. What about your heart. You know what the doctor said."

"Mother, let's go." He turned and took several strides toward the door, then turned. "I said I want to eat. Now, let's go."

Merliah rushed to shower, and when finished dressed in jeans and a T-shirt. A half-hour later she made her way to the dining hall. Stepping just inside the large room, she paused and glanced around the crowded space, peering over the early dinner seating group to find her parents. She preferred the second time an hour later to avoid the crowds. She liked, and always did, eating any time after six-thirty, especially before the sun went down. Sleeping late tended to skew her timetable for a lot of things in her life. *Like staying up late to paint and sleep until three in the afternoon.*

As she limped into the large hall, she glanced around the room to find her parents. They were sitting at a small table by the window wall. She waved when they looked in her direction and sucked in a deep breath. *Here we go.* Walking slow because she left the cane behind, she moved through the room weaving between the tables and using them as support.

"Mom, Dad." She nodded to each. "Did you get something to eat?"

"Yes, sweetie. Abby's here. She's getting a cup of coffee. I think she's more excited than you are. She said she couldn't wait." Her mom frowned. "You need to eat something. Can't have you going to your show on an empty stomach."

"A salad maybe."

"You need more than that. You are as skinny as a rail. How about meatloaf. Mine is exceptionally good. Although not as good as mine, but decent. You need your strength so you can come home with us."

"Michelle, leave the girl alone. She's fine." He placed a hand over Merliah's and smiled. "I'll get that salad for you, honey," her father said. "What kind of dressing do you want?"

"Ranch and thanks, Dad."

He rose from the table, taking one more sip of coffee. "Be right back, ladies."

"So, Mom. Have you seen or heard about Robbie?"

Her mother's eyes widened. "Liah? What brought him up?"

"Hmm, I don't know. It's just...I don't know. I've wondered why he never really came to see me after the one time when I first awakened."

The diminutive woman placed a hand over Merliah's. "Sweetie...he couldn't bear to see you in pain. Besides, he's engaged now."

"I know, you told me."

"I, yes, I did. I forgot."

"I'm happy for him. I...I'm never going to have a man in my life again am I, Mom?"

"Sweetie, you'll have lots of men in your life. You'll see. When you get better and make it big with your painting, you'll have the most handsome and loving man falling head over heels in love with you."

"*Mom*...you're just saying nice things to make me feel better. Look at me. I'm...I'm ugly. I've been thinking about this so much I've imagined a man in my dreams. I think I'm going whacky in the head." Merliah lowered her head.

"Liah, you're not losing your mind."

"I am. I've created a place where I can meet him and I'm beautiful there, at least I think I am. I feel beautiful because he seems like he wants me." She raised her eyes, and then bit her bottom lip. "I created him, but yesterday I think I saw him. Alive, at the gallery. I really think I'm going crazy." Tears burned at the back of her eyes.

"Here you go, Liah. This was the only size of salad they had. Hope you like it." Her father placed the small bowl on the table in front of her.

"Liah? What's the matter?" the voice of her best friend came from above her.

Merliah raised her head and wiped the fallen tears from her cheeks with the back of her hand. "Abby, um, I'm scared. The party tonight, I'm afraid to show up and people see me, and then not like my paintings." She lied, kind of. The emotional mess mounted within her. *How am I to survive tonight?*

"There's nothing to be afraid of. Your work is phenomenal, your mom made a beautiful veil for you to wear so no one will see you, and we'll be there for support."

"Sweetie, I promise we'll keep you protected. No one will talk to you unless you want and I'm sure Mr. Rousseau has an office somewhere you can stay in if you wish to avoid the guests. Right, Abby?"

"Mom, I can't avoid everyone, but if someone stays with me, I think I'll be okay."

"Of course, sweetie. We won't leave you alone."

"Then, let's get ready. I want to get this over with as soon as I can."

"Not until you finish eating, young lady. I don't want you fainting from lack of food."

"Fine." That was the fastest Merliah ever ate dinner.

What have I gotten myself into?

Chapter Thirteen

The Really Big Show

Instant joy put a smile on Merliah's face from the surprise limousine Antoine Rousseau arranged to take her to the show. Abby told her the gallery owner didn't want her uncomfortable on this of all nights. Abby said he wanted to treat his up-and-coming artist to the beginning of a great career. Merliah settled into the backseat of the luxury sedan, wide-eyed and trying to absorb the magnitude of the night. The last time she rode in a limousine had been during senior prom in high school. Too many years and too many unhappy days faded into dark memories to remember that time. Tonight though, new memorable recollections were to be made.

"I can't believe you painted one more, Merliah. It really wasn't necessary, you know," Abby said.

"I do realize I didn't have to, but I did. It called to me late last night." She adjusted on the seat, tugging the short black chemise down over her thighs. "Do you think Mister Rousseau will like one more and put it in the gallery even though the program is already printed?"

"Oh, I think it's okay. Last minute changes always happen. He'll be pissed, for a few minutes, and then he'll see this and fall all over himself to find a place to display it."

"Well, if you say so. This one is a little different from the others. If it doesn't draw interest, I'll keep it in my room." She scratched her head. The wig her mother brought for her to wear was not what she had in mind for covering her head. She thought a nice sheer scarf would have been sufficient. The night was warm and a wig plus the small lace veil fastened with a ribbon tied in the back covered her face. The itchy fabric became more irritating the longer she wore it.

Merliah scrutinized Abby studying the three-by-two-foot canvas. It was a larger piece than she used for the others in the show. Her inner muse demanded to try creating a different painting for the final one. She chuckled to herself knowing in actuality the canvas was the only one prepared and available at the studio, but the other reason sounded artsy. She held her breath, waiting for Abby's opinion. "This will be the main showcased piece, if I can convince Antoine to put it in the show last minute," Abby declared at last.

"Really? Are you sure it's the best one?"

"If you can create this overnight, than yes, Merliah, it's good enough. At this rate, I have a feeling you're absolutely on your way to a one-woman show in the very near future."

"We've talked about my talent before, Abby. I'm not good. I'm just dabbling at painting. Maybe after years I'll be good enough, but not after a few months. I can't believe Antoine agreed to do this. I'm no way in the same league as the other artists. I don't even have many pieces. I bet what they have on display is their best of many. The ones I have are all there is."

Abby turned to her with narrowed eyes. "I've been in the art business for over fifteen years, and five of them teaching at the institute. When I interned in New York, I saw some of the best in the country. Hell, make that the world. Trust me, Merliah. Your work is as good if not better than any I've seen before. There's something magical about these paintings, and I know, no make that, guarantee the public tonight will recognize what I see. And what Antoine sees. Sweetie, you have such a natural talent for someone who just survived a horrific accident, leaving you in a coma for years, and came out of it doing this. I'm in awe." She glanced back at the painting. "Especially this one. So unusual and it's like I'm literally there." She stared without blinking once.

There was a peculiar tone to her voice Merliah couldn't decipher. Did she suspect the energy she impregnated into the painting? She thought she was the only one who felt it, who could transport into the dream-like scene. If not, if others could as well, then she was thankful she insisted on keeping the public back at least arm's length from any of her pieces.

"I have grown attached to this one the more I look at it. How about I just display this one with a *Not for Sale* sign? If it is as great as you say, people will want the others and I can eventually keep this."

"What a good idea, Merliah. But, if the right offer comes along, wouldn't you sell?"

"I don't think—"

Abby rode right over Merliah's objection. "This is your best work and needs to be recognized. What better way than to sell it to a collector, a wealthy collector willing to pay you for your talent. Trust me, sweetie. This will help establish you in the art world and help you earn your independence."

"I don't think…" Merliah paused expecting Abby to interrupt again, but she didn't. "I don't think I'm quite ready to leave the Institute yet. Maybe in a few more months."

"I didn't mean you'd be declaring your independence tonight." A small half-hearted laugh followed by a pat on the hand brought Merliah's attention back. "Doctor Wright told me last week your progress is moving along at a fast pace and highly expects you to move into a transitional home soon. You won't need twenty-four hour care anymore. Personally, I think you're good to go now. Your mobility has improved, your speech, and good grief, your painting is bringing in money. Antoine said the transaction for the sale on the *Wildflowers* painting was completed. The buyer wired the money this afternoon."

"Really? I sold that one?"

"Antoine wouldn't joke about selling art pieces to a buyer if he didn't. He wanted to surprise you with a check tonight, but I'm so excited for you, I couldn't help telling you now. Just act surprised when he gives the check to you later."

"Okay, but one painting sale doesn't make me independently wealthy, Abby."

"No, but it's a start."

Merliah glanced out the window. The lights of the big city began to wink at her. The sun had sunk to the horizon, the day sky was now showing its flourish of violets, reds and yellows. Soon she'd be conversing with an elite crowd of people who were foreign to her. Making small talk never interested her, not even before the accident. Give her an intimate group of friends and she'd be content, but talking about her art, her very soul when she thought about it, was not in her comfort zone. Living in a coma-like state for four plus years and in rehabilitation for over six months didn't exactly prepare one for the onslaught of questions she'd have to answer. The stares and whispers about her by strangers scared her the most. She wasn't prepared for whispers behind her back and her heartbeat sped up. *How am I to survive the night? If only my dream lover were real, he'd protect me. He saved me once. Maybe he can do it again.*

She drew a sharp breath. He wasn't real, only a figment of her over-active imagination. No, she'd have to lean on her family and Abby to get her through the event, then back to the sanctuary of the institute. In time, she'd venture out and if Abby was correct about selling her art, enough to make a decent living, then she could leave Berger and find a small apartment and be on her own. *Life wouldn't be so bad out on my own. I was living alone before the accident, had a good job, family and a boyfriend.*

A boyfriend. Robbie. Those days seemed so long ago. With a deep drag of air, she let the breath out swiftly, slightly shaking her head. Getting back some semblance of a life again was attainable. The boyfriend part, not so much. With the disfigurement and other physical disabilities, she doubted a man would ever look at her in a romantic way again. A tear slipped from the edge. *Only in my dreams. I'll never find love in real life.*

The limousine came to a slow stop in front of the Rousseau Gallery. A large group of casually dressed men and women were entering the warehouse building. The entire district of this part of town housed various storefronts of galleries, stores, and restaurants. Just on the outskirts of the area Merliah remarked every time to Abby what a difference a couple of blocks can make.

"We're here. You ready to wow the public, Merliah?"

"Yeah." The reply bordered on boredom.

"Merliah. C'mon this will be fun, I promise."

The driver opened the door and Abby exited, then turned and peered back in. "You want to hand me the new painting."

After Merliah gave the piece to Abby, she adjusted the lace veil over her face, tugging on the hem of the dress to cover as much of her thighs as it could. She scooted across the seat and leaned on the cane. The driver extended a hand to assist her. Taking a deep breath, she pulled up and out of the door. *Okay, step one. Only a few more to go.*

Abby had gone ahead at a quicker pace, leaving Merliah to maneuver the crowd on her own. She glanced around the outside for her parents, but they were nowhere she could see, so she thought they might already be inside.

No such luck.

The gallery was abuzz with a flurry of people. Too many for Merliah's comfort. She swore all eyes fell on her as she entered. A well-cut young man in black pants, white long-sleeved shirt and skinny black tie stood at the entrance with a tray. Crystal flutes half-filled with champagne set atop the silver round platter.

"Champagne, miss?" he asked.

She shook her head, too scared to utter one word. *Ohmigod! I really don't want to be here. I have to find Abby.*

Moving slowly into the room, the discomfort Merliah experienced almost became unbearable. The menagerie of hot bodies, temperature and physiques, didn't help much either. The damned wig made her head itch wildly. The short, tight dress her mother brought made her self-conscious and the lace veil had too many swirls in the pattern she couldn't see straight. Plus, it didn't help the damned thing kept sticking to the lip gloss. *A bright blood red on top of everything else overwhelms my skin tone.* She told Abby it could be seen through the cover and added to the mystery Antoine said it would help sell her image, and art pieces. *Ha! If people only knew what lay behind the black shroud covering my face, they'd freak.*

At this point, she strongly contemplated taking the nice man at the door up on his offer of champagne. Maybe if she got a little drunk, she'd relax and forget her insecurities.

Or, maybe not. Nothing would cure her problems.

"Merliah, I love the new piece. I've displayed it on an easel instead of hanging. Not enough time. Come. Let me show you before I announce the official welcome and introductions." Antoine curled his meticulously manicured fingers around her forearm. "You want some champagne, darling? Sure you do, let me get you a glass." He stopped and glanced around the room, then motioned to a server a few feet away serving other guests.

"No really, I don't need a drink."

"But of course you do. We have to celebrate. I have a wonderful surprise for you, darling."

"Thank you, darling." Antoine lifted two flutes from the tray the server presented. "Here you go." He clinked the glasses as soon as she took hold of the stem. "Cheers."

"Cheers," she said softly. *Really?* Did he read her mind about getting drunk? She lifted the glass to her lips behind the veil.

"Come to my office when this soiree is over. I have something to give you." He winked and gave a little grin.

If she didn't know better, she would have been offended by his little innuendo, but he was innocent and non-threatening. Then, her suspicions were confirmed, the man she caught a glimpse of across the room, with eye make-up wearing tight khakis and a tropical shirt opened to his navel, sauntered toward them.

"Baby, kiss, kiss. This is a marvelous par-*tay*. You've outdone yourself as usual, Antoine. The artists are fantastic. I can't wait to see the backrooms if what is displayed here is any indication." He turned attention to Merliah. "Oh, and who do we have here. The mystery woman?"

"Sorry for my bad manners. Yes, this is…is Phoenix. She's the artist of the landscape watercolors."

"Ah, very nice."

"Thank you."

"Antoine, I need to talk to you…in private. Excuse us, will you, Miss Phoenix?"

Antoine turned back and addressed her, "Darling, if you want to sneak into the other room and check out your new piece displayed, you can. I won't raise the ropes for at least another ten or fifteen minutes."

Merliah nodded as she watched the two men walk toward a group about ten feet away. The opportunity to get away from the claustrophobic wall of people elated her. She smiled at the older man who moved closer. He seemed too interested in asking her about her veil. She turned slowly to balance on the cane. Weaving between the mingling guests, she finally made her way through the room, down a short hallway and turned the corner into the small area designated as her mini-gallery. As she approached the solid white room, floor to ceiling, she delighted in the appearance. Her paintings looked beautiful against the starkness of the area. The last piece sat upon an easel, just as Antoine said he'd done.

The silence in the room brought her peace, much like the paintings themselves. She shuffled to the castle portrait. Fortunately, she didn't put the complete energy force into the piece at the studio. If Abby had been drawn into the landscape while she examined it or even Antoine putting the new piece on display, how disastrous someone inadvertently touching the piece would have been. She stood before the piece contemplating to add the final touch, *or* not.

Stepping closer, moving the red velvet rope stanchion for everyone else not to cross. Only inches away, she reached out with both hands, closed her eyes and placed her palms on the surface. After a few minutes, she lowered her arms. To her eye, the glow radiating from the landscape shone bright indicating the completeness she wanted.

The lace veil caught again on the lip gloss and in frustration, she ripped the fabric from her head. Merliah remembered the lost scarf from yesterday and stepped over to the centerpiece painting. "I left it there, I'm sure." She partially turned toward the entrance into the room. No one was near. The room fell ominously silent as she tuned out the distant sound of soft instrumental music reverberating through the wall speakers and the din of voices continued to fade into nothingness. She took a deep breath and reached toward the wildflowers and then she was there, in the sunlit field.

With a quick glance over her shoulder, in the distance behind she viewed the pendant lights of the gallery, and turning her attention inward she spied the distant woods, where the scarf had to be. She took off in a sprint toward the dark woods in search of the lost sheer camouflage. *Freedom!*

As she reached the edge of the woods, she slowed her gait and walked tentatively into the dense brush and woods. Retracing her steps from yesterday, she traipsed over the ground with ease. She had sought solace within the realm of her paintings many times. Running and frolicking, breathing in the fresh air, soaking up the sun as the rays warmed her skin, all things she was unable to do in the world of reality. Here, she could be and do anything or everything she had lost since the accident. Better than dreams, here she felt alive, vital and happy in the conscious world. The pain disappeared, her hair was full, long and curled loosely down her back, and the scars were gone. Only here she could be the way she was before the collision changed her life almost five years ago.

"Ah, there you are." She found the allusive scarf a few feet in front of her, lying on the ground by the tree she hid behind when the mysterious man peered into the painting. In the panic of hiding from him, it had slipped from her hand. She knelt and dislodged the red veil and shook the leaves off.

Oomph!

As she turned to leave, a hard wall blocked her path. A broad-shouldered wall of flesh to be exact. Slowly raising her head, she recognized the familiar eyes, the knowing touch, and the recognizable scent. Her heart beat hard against her ribs. "So...rin?" She took a few steps backward.

Chapter Fourteen

The Angel of My Dreams is Real?

Sorin gulped the cheap champagne and hissed as the bitter alcohol burned all the way down to his stomach. He'd come to the exhibition for his friend and to investigate the painting from the night before, not mingle with pretentious humans. An attitude driven by the arrogance of new found wealth by these elitists burned his insides as much if not more than the alcohol. He hung around out of respect for his friend, but he needed to get some air.

As Sorin contemplated how he'd steal away from the party for a few minutes, he suddenly became distracted by the vision of a mysterious beauty. A veil covered her face and a long fall of blonde hair. She walked with a slight limp toward another room. The woman had curves in all the right places, filling out the black sheath dress to perfection. Something familiar tugged at the back of his mind as well as a stirring in his pants. He watched her move across the room and focused in on her scent. The exotic perfume she wore wafted through his nostrils. He wanted her and no longer felt the need to depart so quickly.

Quickly putting his glass down on a small cloth covered table, he threaded his way through the crowd following her, staying a respectable distance. He walked down a hallway to another room. Could she be the artist named Phoenix? The one who painted the landscape he purchased. *Antoine said she was a mysterious woman.* He caught a glimpse of her and hurried ahead. As he turned the corner, she disappeared into the painting. *What the fuck?*

With quick strides, he stopped short of the displayed canvas in the center of the wall. Then he touched the painting, and the momentary dizziness put his vampire senses on alert. The ground shifted under his feet, his eyes were briefly blinded by the bright light and the feeling of home, of rightness astounded him. Then, he saw the woman running through the field ahead of him and followed. Little did he know at the time, but the world he had known for over seven hundred years would take a change for the weird. He was vampire, and nothing should shock him, but the past six months, especially six weeks, tested his resolve to the limits of belief.

"Angel?" His low, velvety voice sent tingles up and down her spine. He reached out, but she took a step back. He lifted his eyebrows in question.

The intensity of her eyes had such passion, he forgot to breathe.

"This can't be real. You're the man from yesterday…and…and the man in my dreams." She took another step back. "You're Sorin? You're real, not my imagination?"

Not uttering a word, he moved toward her. Merliah held her hands out and took another step back. "Wait. I don't understand how you're here. I didn't paint you in this scene. None of this is—"

"Real?" He blocked her retreat with a hand on the tree next to her cheek. "Touch me, Merliah. Then tell me if I'm real or not."

Merliah cut her eyes to the large hand resting on the tree next to her face. "How did you find me in here? I made sure no one saw me."

His palm cupped her cheek, nudging her face upward a bit. "I saw you disappear into the painting, touched it and found myself in a field and a woman running ahead. I followed, not knowing the woman was you. Until now."

He reached down and gripped her hand tightly in his. "You know who I am, my angel."

Her huff of breath, the tears glistening in her eyes challenged hundreds of thoughts reeling in his head. He could tell she had similar ideas, conflicting ones. Not that he could read her mind, which continued to confound him, but the expression across her face spoke volumes.

"This is impossible. I made you up. You can't be real." She jerked and twisted her hands to release his embrace.

He tightened his grip. The intensity of his gaze must have calmed her, because she stopped struggling.

"I thought I dreamt you as well and didn't know if you were real either. Until now, here in this place." He lifted his head and peered around then brought his attention back to her. "By the way, where are we? I was in the gallery one minute staring at a painting by someone named Phoenix and then I saw you running into these woods. Where am I?"

A soft smile lifted the corners of her mouth as she slowly pulled her hand from his. "You don't know? I'm Phoenix, like the creature rising from the ashes, just as I did. You're in my painting. My make-believe creation."

What the hell did she say?

"Well, I can assure you I'm not make-believe and you don't feel like my imagination, so how is it possible to transport into this painting? I believe in a lot of things, but this seems impossible."

"I…I can't explain how. Suffice it to say, I created this through my brushes and my hands. Something inside me radiates from me when I paint. I can't explain how I do it."

Voices in the distance drew their attention.

"Hide. No one can see us in here, Sorin. It's bad enough you followed me in. I never wanted anyone to find out about this." She crouched low and took a few steps deeper into the trees. He followed, glancing over his shoulder toward the field and the bright light beyond.

"Where are those voices coming—"

"Shhh, they'll hear you."

"Who?"

"Them." She pointed across the field. The faces of strangers came into view through the portal. The vision of a bright white wall had been replaced by giant bodies, faces and booming voices.

"We're in the painting, small and insignificant to their real-life size. Fuck. This isn't good."

"Shhh." She covered his mouth. He wanted to cover her body. Their close proximity had his heart beating fast. His dick jumped to life. *God, what she does to me.*

Instead, he covered her hand with his, and then kissed the tips of her fingers. Her eyes widened. The beautiful crystal blue ones he became lost in every time he was with her. The seconds ticked by, and then she pulled her hand back. "Stop, we can't do this now. Please be quiet."

He couldn't. The beautiful woman captivated him, much as she did in his dreams. But, they weren't dreams, exactly.

"Why are you looking at me like that?" she demanded.

"Thinking about how beautiful you are and how I want to make love to you."

She snorted and rolled her eyes. "Yeah, right. I'm not beautiful."

"Really, angel? You're ignoring what I said about making love to you and focusing in on whether or not you are a beautiful woman or not. I want to be with you, *in* you right now just as I have taken you almost every night for the last six weeks."

"Stop it. I thought I was dreaming. Fantasizing. Hallucinating for God's sake and even to the point I thought I was insane. I didn't know you were real. I wanted you to be flesh and blood, but that's beside the point."

"Is it? You have haunted me for months, in dreams, in reality, I don't care which. I came here searching for you and I found you at last, my beautiful angel. I'm not letting you go. Ever."

She stood and turned away. With a whisper she said, "I'm not beautiful *or* an angel. You don't know the real me, Sorin. The scars and the pain…"

He slowly rose to his feet, taking care not to be seen from the other side. "Merliah, scars and pain can make someone beautiful just as much as a pretty face or body. I have wounds and hurts from my past, but I've overcome the ugliness and moved forward to experience a life of fulfillment."

"Scars." She extended her hand to his cheek. "You had a scar in my dreams, but it's gone."

Looking at her quizzically, he reached up and touched his cheek, running his fingers along the skin where he knew the mark disfigured his face. The permanent reminder of a sword battle with another warrior shortly after his transition wasn't there. "My old wound is gone. What magic is this?"

"I don't know. I really don't, but I like you with or without." She grinned.

"Well, I like you with or without scars too. I've known you in my mind for what seems like an eternity. I too thought you were a dream. I believed I was on the verge of insanity, but whatever this is, this world you've created, I've never felt more alive than I do right now. You've brought immense joy and pleasure, angel. Your magnificence can be seen all around us and evidently erase our damaged lives."

"Ah, such poetic words. But, I can tell you love the beauty of what you see, not what you know."

"How wrong you are, angel. I—"

"Stop! You don't have any idea what I've created through the pain and anguish I've endured. I don't have any clue as to why this has happened to me or how. I'm alive, but at what price, Sorin? Until now, no one saw me like this, except you and I thought I made you up." A nervous laugh trailed off in her voice.

"Angel, you need to calm down and explain what you mean."

"I am calm *and* sane…and confused. You saved me from the darkness, but I thought my mind created you so I'd keep from falling over the edge into insanity. We made love and I fulfilled fantasies I never dreamed of doing in real life. Now…now I find out you are real flesh and blood."

Fuck! Blood? I have no desire for blood! What is happening to me in here?

She twined her fingers through her hair, pulling the tresses into a tight ponytail, and then let them drop out at the ends. Turning away again, she stumbled over her words. "I can't do this. I wanted to be with you for so long and now that you are, I don't know how to handle this. You have to go when the room is clear."

"And what about you? You're going with me. Now I know you exist, there's no way I'm letting you out of my sight."

"I…we can't be seen leaving together. It's too dangerous."

"Then we stay here, together. You can tell me about these fantasies." He scraped his fingertips along her bare arms, pleased she didn't flinch or pull back. Leaning into her, he cupped his palms along her jawline and placed a soft, sensuous kiss on her lips, barely touching the moist plump flesh. *This is real. My angel is alive and mine. All mine.*

Her body yielded to his dominance. Sorin knew without a doubt the woman he caressed was his. This strange world, the creation of her paint brush she said, amused and confused. He didn't experience the ache in his body and specifically his vampiric teeth trying to elongate. In fact, the urge to bite or the rush of energy sweeping over him as he was about to attack prey didn't rise up and overwhelm his senses.

His thoughts were interrupted as a squeal from a woman outside drew his attention.

"Did you see him?" The woman asked of another.

The high-pitch brought both he and Merliah to an instant freeze of any motion. Then in one swift movement, Sorin toppled her backward onto the ground, following her down and blanketing her with his body.

"Who?" The other half of the couple standing in front of the painting asked.

"I swear I just saw a rat run behind the corner. Eew! Let's get out of here, Todd." The clicking of heels on the terrazzo floor faded away in the distance, as the chatter and protest from both people echoed back into the painting.

The realization they weren't seen sunk in but he wanted the moment between them to last. His face rested within inches of hers, the heat of her skin warmed him. The sensation was intoxicating. The crystal blue of her eyes sparkled in the dim light of the forest and the delight of swimming in their coolness ignited his blood. He captured her mouth with his, his lips punishing and hard. As her lips parted to allow his tongue to thrust into her mouth, his knee spread her thighs wider and his groin ground into the juncture of her thighs, and all he could think about were his own selfish needs.

"This is so wrong. I'm not good enough for you. Please, you have to stop." Her voice had lowered to just above a whisper.

Confusion muddled his mind. Why was she resisting the attraction between them? He ignored her protest and closed his fingers around her shoulders. "Merliah, what we've shared for several months is special. It doesn't matter how we ended up here today. We're together and there's nothing wrong. You want this between us because I hear the pounding of your heart, the sound of your breathing, and I see the glistening in your eyes. What do you really want, Merliah?"

She lowered her gaze to his chest where she splayed her fingers over his shirt. From their times together, he knew she liked touching his chest. Other places as well, but especially caressing the taut planes of his abs. He waited for a verbal response, expecting more of an answer than a graze of hands. Since they were in an invented realm made by her rules, his mind touches didn't work, just like the hunger for blood disappeared. She'd have to verbally communicate for him to understand her thoughts. For him, the silence was an unusual and new experience.

With her chin lifted, she gazed into his eyes. A smile curved the corner of her lips. "Dare I guess what you want?"

"We're not discussing me, angel."

"No, we're not."

"So, I'll ask again. Tell me, what do you want, angel?" He asked this time with a huskier voice.

"I–I want you. Don't tease me. I need you to love me like you mean it."

He tightened the hold on her shoulders. "I'm not playing games, Merliah. This is real, not a dream." In a flash, he pulled her arms over her head with one hand and cupped her chin with the other. "Now since I've found you, if I take what I want, will you take what you want?" His body pressed harder into hers, and then he lowered his head, his lips just inches from hers. Each breath she took scraped her breasts against his chest, and even though layers of clothing separated them, electricity arced between their bodies.

"Oh God. Kiss me, Sorin. Take me in a slow, tantalizing and seductively masterful way. Make this time last until the end. That's my fantasy." The silky tone of her voice flowed wantonly like a gentle teasing breeze over his inflamed skin.

With her making the assertive move, his experience suggested he had the answer. His angel wanted him as much as he did her. All he ever desired was to hear the acceptance from her. Here in this make-believe world, they both lived unencumbered by the outside forces which could keep them apart. They were free to love each other without the confines of pain or remorse, and he without the beast within begging for release. She suffered an unknown fear he was bound and determined to find out more about.

He licked the dryness from his lips with the tip of his tongue. Before she could thwart his attempt, Sorin's lips captured hers in a powerful kiss. Her arms wrapped around his neck, pulling him closer and he willingly let her. His body tingled as he remembered gliding his hands over her smooth skin in the dream from the night before. Her back arched upward to meet him. Despite his long practiced self-control, Sorin felt his body come alive. The sensation more intense than any he'd had in years. The freedom to let go without maintaining control enlivened every nerve in his body. Fire coursed through him, sending its heat to his burgeoning erection. The kiss was heavenly just like her, but he needed more. He broke the embrace and inched the fabric of her dress up over her thighs.

"Oh yes, Sorin. Touch me. Make love to me."

"Pretend I'm part of your fantasy. Tell me what you want. We won't be interrupted this time, not like last night."

She blushed. "Interrupted? The dream last night wasn't…I mean you were there, in my head. I wasn't dreaming?"

The red glow on her face endeared him. She would learn to trust him to give her what she desired, what she craved. His gaze focused on her full lips. "No you weren't, I came to you. If what we shared was a dream or our minds interconnected somehow, I don't know, but does any of that matter now? Tell me," he asked, through gritted teeth. "Do you want me to kiss you like this?" Slowly and deliberately, he kissed across her cheek toward the throbbing vein below her ear. He suckled the gentle skin and heard the rush of her breath past his ear, but the sound of her blood didn't echo in his head. For the first time in centuries, the urge to bite vanished. "Or harder?" The nibbles along the column of her neck he found just as rewarding, just as intoxicating.

"Please, Sorin. Should we be—"

He silenced her with a crushing kiss. He deepened it, and she made a whimpering sound. Stroking and suckling, he teased her lips apart. Their tongues intertwined and danced, thrusting in and withdrawing for long moments. She moaned in delight. He kept the pressure on her mouth as his right hand slid over her hip. After he released her arms above her head, she wiggled her hands up under his tight black T-shirt which stretched across his bulging pecs and flat abs. His breath hitched at the unexpected shock of a fingernail flicking and swirling over his nipples, teasing each erect. *Mmm, I think she likes it hard and rough.*

"Fuck! This isn't working well. Clothes have to go."

He stood up and pulled her to her feet at the same time. Merliah's gaze dropped to the waistband of his black trousers, and then to the bulge at his groin, and with her eyes burning with intensity, he realized her highly aroused state. He didn't need to use his vampire skills. Their times together in the dreams made him keenly aware of her preferences and desires. His stomach knotted with instant need with the knowledge, causing his cock to press harder on the zipper of his trousers, causing some discomfort. He enjoyed the new pleasure of reading her body instead of using his senses as a vampire to recognize them. His heart raced in anticipation of discovering the nuances of her body from this new perspective. *Like exploring virgin territory.*

"Do you think anyone will see us?"

"No, I believe the trees are thick enough where we are. We should be hidden. I can barely see the light on the other side." His tongue slid along a full bottom lip. "Now, let me undress you."

As he steadied her, he reached around her back and slowly drew down the zipper. He smiled as the dress slipped from her shoulders and down her body, landing in a puddle on the ground. She stood before him in matching black bra and panties. "I want to see every inch of your skin, to touch you all over. Experience you like this is our first time." Then he slipped one digit under the strap of her bra and gently nudged it off her shoulder. Reaching around, he unclipped the fastener and the delicate lacy fabric fell to the ground. Cupping the lush flesh of her breasts, he kneaded the generous orbs until she leaned forward against him.

"Oh, don't stop, Sorin," she pleaded softly.

His fingers gently traced the contours of her brow, her cheek, her jaw, slowly moving toward the curve of her throat. Bending his head forward, he brushed his mouth across the tingling skin, trailing tiny kisses down her neck.

"Oh yes, I want that too. Please…" Her voice trailed off.

Sorin's grin widened. "But first, I want to taste you." He dropped to his knees between her legs and brushed his hand across the skin of her thigh. "Spread your legs for me, angel."

Without hesitation, she did as he demanded. Using one finger, he hooked it around the elastic and tugged the slight slip of lacy fabric down over her hips, then tore them away from her body, growling his pleasure.

"Hey, those were my nicest pair."

"I'll get you another." One hand held her hip and the other palmed her mound. He glanced up at her and licked his lips, then slipped his tongue between her tender folds, tasting her with a groan of what sounded like relief.

She threw her head back with a hiss, "Oh God yes!"

He sucked and licked, urged on as her cries and pants got more urgent. Pressing closer and teasing her pussy with his tongue, he then slipped a finger into her heat and groaned as he flicked more forcefully. She squirmed under his ministrations and arched her body into his mouth as she opened wider for him. He spread the swollen lips and ran his tongue from the bottom to the top but stopped just short of touching her clit. She moaned and whimpered, seeming to want to be licked senselessly. Taking the suggestion with determination, he licked and tugged all around the sensitive nubbin, resisting the little nudges she kept making to push him to the point of pleasure.

Finally, she grabbed his hair. "You're teasing me. Touch me there," she demanded.

A soft growl vibrated in the back of his throat and he chuckled inwardly. His angel was taking control and he'd have none of that. Bringing her to submission was his primary goal and he'd provide the incentive for her to succumb to his dominance. The more his lips touched hers, the more he insinuated his control over her. As soon as she let go of his hair, he sucked the waiting clit inside his mouth and flicked his tongue over and over until she screamed.

"Shh, angel. You'll draw attention to us." He stopped and waited for her to catch her breath then started licking and sucking again. Just when he sensed she was about to climax again, he stopped and stood up.

"On your hands and knees, angel." As she complied with his demand, he divested the remainder of his clothing. He dropped to his knees and positioned his long and thick cock at her entrance. "You're so wet and ready for me." Then he ran his cockhead along her swollen folds, lubricating the tip with her juices, and with one thrust he pushed inside her hot sheath. She groaned and pushed back against him until he entered her just a few inches. He stopped and pulled out and repeated again. The soft mewing noises she made indicated her need for more, and still he stopped just short of fully entering her. He wanted her begging and he didn't have to wait long. His angel was a quick learner.

"Please," Merliah cried.

"Please what?"

"Make love to me. I can't stand it anymore. I need you inside, Sorin."

Obliged to please, he plunged his rock-hard cock deep into her moist heat. As her wet sheath gripped him, he roared his pleasure, which echoed through the forest of her creation. Her internal muscles contracted around his shaft, wringing another moan from both of them. She met his rhythm, urging him on. The need to feel her milk him to completion pulsed through his body. "So tight and wet." He leaned over and growled into her ear.

Merliah tilted her head to the side, exposing the smooth, pale skin of her throat. The desire to bite her burned inside him, but his fangs did not descend. The beast within didn't claw at his chest. A pleasurable cry tore from her as her pussy grasped him in her release. She was so beautiful, eyes closed, her flesh slapping against his as she rode wave after wave of desire. His body tightened with each contraction, thrusting deeper and faster. As he followed her over the edge of release, he shuddered and panted while his hands held her still under him. They ended up collapsing down to the earth, both physically and metaphysically from the high of their shared orgasm. He pulled out of her slowly and flipped her to her back. Smiling, he kissed and nuzzled her on the neck. They lay on the ground trying to catch their breaths before he stood and retrieved his leather long coat and flattened it out to lie upon.

Scooping her up into his arms, he placed her on the makeshift blanket then moved beside her, spooning against her back. He caressed her hair, smoothing it gently and reveling in the bliss he felt. He'd taken her body, but he hoped he'd capture her heart as well. Within a few minutes, he heard the soft breathing shift realizing she fell asleep. Sleep crept up on him slowly despite his fighting the urge. As if taunting him, forcing him to acknowledge the peace in his existence since he found Merliah, sleep finally claimed him. The dreams could come and he'd be content, and then he slipped into an unconscious state, the first in many months.

Love had snuck up on him and filled his heart without warning. The dreams had become reality.

Chapter Fifteen

Rebirth of a Vampire

Sorin's eyes popped open, his heart thundering in his chest. How many times since his transition over seven hundred years ago had he awakened with the uncontrollable urge to devour the flesh and blood of an unsuspecting prey and sate his hunger. He'd grown accustomed to the hard realization his desire to feed first overwhelmed his mind and body. No coherent thoughts or actions could stop his quest until he did so.

He despised the ache coursing through his veins every night until the beast within received satisfaction. A few deep breaths calmed his heart. He lay still, taking stock. A forest. On the ground. In the arms of another. A heart beat beneath his flattened hands placed on her breast.

Momentarily, confusion furrowed across his brow. *Angel?* This wasn't another of the haunting dreams. He lay there in an imaginary world created by his dream angel. She was real, not his imagination. *But...how?* He smiled aware the urge within to take her blood didn't exist within the picture. God, what salvation had been placed upon him to find such a beautiful woman who could grant him a brief respite from his dark existence.

His breath caught as he gazed upon the woman he embraced within the curve of his body and arms. Her quiet beauty and the perfect glow to her skin amazed him. The mysterious woman still had a few secrets he had to tap into, like how she was able to eradicate his hunger for blood and made the facial scar disappear. Fascination didn't exactly define his curiosity for the ability she possessed to transport them into a watercolor fantasy world. *What other magical powers does this woman possess? What am I thinking about? Magic is sleight of hand and special effects, not anything like this. Maybe I'm really dreaming, after all.*

With a gentle skim over her breast with his fingertips, the only consuming need tugging at his body was the thought to slip inside her warmth. This little submissive morsel exuded sensuality like he'd never encountered. She had a fire which lay under the light surrounding her. The aura shone from every pore on her skin. He fell under the spell of her magic, falling headfirst into her seduction. *What has she done to me? Is this love or something else?*

Under the influence of this fantasy world, he also had no concept of time. How long had he been there? On the outside, silence fell. The lights were dimmed, but inside the landscape the sun shone. *The sun?* The concept still confounded him. He hadn't seen the light of day in ages and wasn't sure if the bright illumination at the perimeter of the forest was in fact due to the sun or the suspended lights inside the gallery.

Already used to sleeping with her in his dreams, the feel of her soft skin close to him was something he never experienced with any other women. He thought of all the little things he'd taken for granted when with a woman he loved. Anya seemed like eons ago. The extent of his sexual dalliances revolved around his business and nothing more. He used women for personal pleasure, and never settled with one for a long-term relationship. With Merliah, his mind reeled about those romantic and comforting nuances of a bond, like taking long walks on his estate, sitting in the library on a cold winter night snuggled on the sofa in front of the fireplace talking about everything or nothing in particular. After, they'd make love the remainder of the night. He closed his eyes and sucked in a deep breath. *I love her.*

The sun slivered through the trees and glistened off Merliah's golden hair, creating a halo around her head. The episode disrupted his thoughts. *She is my angel. Could she really be one and this place she's created is paradise?*

The beauty stirred from sleep.

Rolling onto his side, he propped himself on an open hand, his elbow beneath him. Brushing his fingers along her arm with a free hand, he relished the feel of her skin beneath his and nudged her awake. "Angel, wake up. We need to go, love. My friends are probably wondering what happened to me," he whispered close to her ear.

A whimper slipped from her mouth and she turned in his arms. She smiled up at him and his heart skipped a beat. "Did I nod off?"

He returned the smile. "Yes, you did."

She cupped her hand on his cheek. "Oh Sorin, you make me so happy. For the past several months since recovering from the accident, I've had to live with such pain. You saved me and I've spent the last several weeks desperately trying to find you again in my dreams. I don't know how or why, but you were my salvation. Now, I can endure anything with you in my life." She broke off, and ducked her head down resting against his chest. "I just want all the pain to be gone, forget the darkness that trapped me in a living hell. Love me, Sorin." She took a deep breath and let it out as he wrapped his arm around her shoulder. "I feel like I've been born again within our dreams. You saved me and I wanted you to know how I feel."

He exhaled noisily and took her chin in his hand, lifting her face to his scrutiny. The corners of his mouth turned up and then licked his bottom lip, drawing her attention there. "I feel the same, angel." Their lips met, the natural static in the air crackled around them, sealing their bond. She pulled back and smiled at him again, her eyes were heavy with tears. "Thank you."

"You're welcome." He held her tight. A light breeze circled around them cooling his skin. The sensation made him shiver, a sensation he hadn't felt in a long time.

"Angel, I would love to spend all night here with you, but I think we need to leave," he spoke with a heavily accented voice, velvety and soft.

"Do we have to?" She pouted and touched his cheek. "I don't ever want to leave."

His eyes closed for a split second, he didn't want to leave either, but Stefan and Alex had to be wondering what happened. "Yes, we do even though I want to stay here forever as well." He gave a light smack on her ass cheek, and then he lowered his head and captured her lips, a soft yet passionate kiss. He released her lips and licked his way down her throat, across her collarbone, trailing fiery kisses down her skin until he reached her breast. The woman was like a drug to him, more so than any other in his lengthy existence. The simple intimacy they shared in this sanctuary was one he didn't wish to leave, but there was the conundrum he faced. *Here*, he wasn't vampire, except he was vampire and *that* was the reality. Eventually, he'd return to the darkness of the real world. "Angel, I'm falling in love with you."

With a gasp, she pulled back. "Oh don't say that. I mean I'm not good enough for you, or anyone. We have no future beyond this." She waved her hand in the air.

"Angel, you're perfect for me and mean more to me than I ever thought possible. We met under strange circumstances, but now that I've found you, I don't want to let you go."

She shook her head. "No, I'm not perfect. You don't know the real me."

"I know enough and I'll show you how ideal you are." As his body over-rode his logical thoughts to leave the magical place and her, he swirled his tongue across her nipple and she moaned. She arched her back, pressing against his mouth, encouraging him, and then, when he continued lower, she pushed back unexpectedly.

"Sorin! We need to stop. I don't know how long we've been here, but my parents and friend are waiting for me."

"Yes, mine too." He paused and stared for a moment.

"Your parents are here?"

He chuckled. "No, my parents are dead. My friend is here and he no doubt wonders where I disappeared to." He cupped her breast, his hand massaging her flesh. "I guess we can continue this later."

"Where are my clothes?"

As Sorin gathered their clothes and they dressed, his deep desire was to stay and never leave, but the option wasn't on the table. Logistically speaking, living inside a painting didn't make sense, especially for a vampire. Eventually he figured the beast would raise his ugly head and demand release to satiate the bloodlust. Losing his angel wasn't an option either, not when she became his salvation. To give her up now would be impossible. In his gut, visiting the landscape again was a temptation. Indulging in fantasy no matter how intoxicating, the place spelled suicide for him. For the time he had been inside, he felt powerless and after seven hundred years, he didn't know if giving up the beast was worth the trade-off for the sunshine and the bloodlust. Now that he'd purchased it, he had to figure out how to get her to come with him and test the idea.

"Are you ready?" The last thing he grabbed was the leather coat. He shook the leaves and grass off and folded it over his forearm.

"Yes, let's go."

They walked leisurely out of the woods and into the field toward the outside, with a white blank wall in front of them.

"So, you want to explain how we get out of here? Do I do the same thing by touching the edge and then..."

"Actually, the only way I've found is you kind of jump through and hope you land on both feet on the other side. If not, it can be a bit bumpy on the landing. So, can you go first and help me out? My knees have been hurt enough from doing this a couple times already."

With a narrowed glance over his shoulder, Sorin gave her a mischievous grin. "Hmm, I think I like you on your knees."

"Oh." She blushed.

"Is there something you're not telling me about exiting out of here?"

She cocked her head. "No, I'm telling you the truth. The drop from the height of the picture to the floor is a bit of a distance. For me anyway."

"You have a point." He turned and gave her a quick kiss. "Okay, wish me luck." He took a deep breath and took several quick strides and pushed through the barrier, then landed on the floor of the gallery on the outside. A rush of adrenaline coursed through his body instantly. Within seconds of standing, the beast awakened and the hunger for blood tugged at his body. As he took a few steps toward the painting, he extended a hand, his fingertips within inches of the surface. With the image of Merliah just out of his reach, he smiled and then softly spoke. "You know this is freaking weird, angel."

He heard a low giggle, and then another voice had him spinning around.

"Sorin? Where the hell have you been, man?"

"Stefan." Sorin stepped back to conceal Merliah's image as much as possible. "I've been around. I came in here to see the painting I purchased."

"Really? I checked in here several minutes ago and you weren't anywhere around. What did you do, sneak in the back door?"

A half-hearted laugh preceded his answer. "Yeah, I did. Are you ready to go?"

"Just about. The show has pretty much broken up. A few people are milling around, but I think I'm done for the night." Stefan took a few steps toward him. "Is this the one you're getting?"

Sorin sidestepped to shield the painting. "Yes, I think I'll get it crated up immediately. I'd like to take it back to your place if that's okay with you."

"Sure, but there's no hurry." Stefan paused and narrowed his eyes. "Is there?"

"No. I guess Mister Rousseau can take care of it tomorrow. I might even take the rest of the collection if they're available."

"Oh, and nothing of mine? Thanks a lot, brother."

"No, no. I'm interested, but thought I'd wait and see what happened tonight with the show. You could find it in your generous heart to donate something to *my* collection, you know."

"So, let me see this piece you're enamored with." Stefan leaned around Sorin and spied the painting. "Hmm, interesting, but I don't see anything special."

Sorin turned on his heels, but not fast enough to prevent his friend from viewing Merliah. To his relief, she was nowhere to be seen. *She must have gone back into the woods.* "I like the piece. Something familiar about the subject matter in the piece drew me to it."

"Hey, man, that's what art is all about, all the *in the eye of the beholder* shit, right?"

Sorin cleared his throat. "Yeah, sure." He turned away, and then took a few steps to leave the gallery area. "You ready? Let's go." The sooner he could get out of the room, the better chance Merliah could step out. What lousy timing for his friend to show up when he did. Although better him than a stranger possibly discovering the magical painting.

"What about this one?"

Sorin followed the eyes of his friends resting on the painting situated on the easel. "What about it?"

"Talk about familiar. The scene looks like your manor in the mountains."

Sorin pinched his brow, and then took a few steps toward the watercolor. He hadn't noticed the picture earlier. "What the...no, I can't believe she could have known."

"Sure as hell is or at least a pretty damned good facsimile. Who is the she?"

"Who's the artiste, Stefan?" Rousseau walked into the room and made a few affectations with his arms. "Didn't you meet her on one of your appointments here? Or maybe that was your lovely woman, Mademoiselle Alexandra. Can't remember now. Oh well."

"No, I haven't."

"Well," Rousseau huffed. "Whatever. This is a new one Miss Phoenix brought tonight. What do you think, Mister Bochinsky? Something you would like to add to your collection, perhaps?"

"Mmmm, yes," Sorin replied. "I'd be very interested, but can we discuss this later." He had to move everyone out of the area so Merliah could exit the landscape and a strange sensation began to course through his veins. Turning to his friend, he grimaced. The overwhelming burn hit his body, almost doubling him over in pain. The beast had reared its ugly head and the insatiable hunger returned with a vengeance. Despite the fact he'd fed before arriving tonight, he was surprised the need to feed again came so quickly. *I have to get out of here and fast.*

"You all right, man?" From the look on his face, Sorin felt relief his friend understood his situation. "Let me get Alex and we can go."

"Please." Sorin's insides began to twist and the gnawing pain felt like a freight train had run through them. A fog settled over his body, blinding him to reason and all he could think about was satisfying the bloodlust.

"Antoine, I'll be in touch with you tomorrow. My friend is feeling ill and we have to go." Stefan wrapped his arm around Sorin's shoulders.

"But...but, Stefan. The show is not over. You still have guests viewing your pieces."

"It is over for me. I will speak with you later." Stefan huffed out his response.

Sorin's body tensed, his chest rose and fell quickly as he struggled to maintain control over the beast demanding to be released. His brain strained to comprehend what was happening. If he didn't know better, what he experienced occurred when one turned. He hadn't felt like this in over three hundred years. The last time, he'd been confined by Dragos in a dungeon for six weeks before being rescued. Stefan and a few others tracked him down and the conflict between the two factions of vampires began. Sorin recovered, but the pain from the confinement nearly destroyed him.

The two left the small area, turning their backs to the gallery owner as he continued to stutter over words Sorin heard but didn't care about.

"Alex," Stefan called out. "*Prinţesa*, we're leaving."

Sorin honed in on the human female. His mind recognized her, but he saw the woman as nothing more than fresh, warm blood to ease the pain within. He focused in on the pulsing vein rushing along the column of her exposed neck.

"Shh," Alex covered the cell phone at her ear with her free hand. "I'm talking with my boss." She turned to the side, continuing the conversation with the voice on the phone.

"Hey man, as soon as I can get a word in with Alex, we'll leave. Are you all right? I haven't seen you like this…since I found you in Dragos' castle."

Sorin ignored his friend. The prattle was nothing but white noise at that point. The beast within needed to be satisfied and the red-haired woman standing less than ten feet away called to him. Sorin took a step forward and a strong squeeze to his forearm prevented his forward movement causing him to snap his head to the side. "Let go of me before I rip your heart out." He expelled the sharp words through gritted teeth.

"Okay, that's enough."

"What's wrong with you, Sorin? Why are you looking at me like you want to suck my neck?" Alex asked, taking a step backward.

"He's not feeling well. Alex, I'll see you at the penthouse."

"I don't know when I'll be home. Johnson and I have a new lead on the serial killer case to deal with. He's on his way to pick me up."

"Be careful, love." Stefan placed a kiss on Alex's cheek then turned to Sorin. "C'mon."

Sorin trembled, the pain almost unbearable as his thoughts scrambled to make sense of the way the beast stirred deep in his core like never before. Each breath he took vibrated through his body, every nerve tingled, and his muscles ached from the tension. *What is happening to me? Merliah and her magic painting? I need blood. Now!*

As he turned to leave, a scent caught his attention. *Vampire.* He scanned the room. Across the room, a man dressed in black, eyes dark stared back. "Who's the vamp over there?"

Stefan turned in the direction Sorin gestured. "I don't know. I've never seen him before. I'll deal with him later. Right now I need to help you."

The two vamps left the Rousseau Gallery under the dark veil of the night to satisfy the bloodlust of the beast within.

Chapter Sixteen

A Secret is Revealed to the Monster

"Fuck this shit," Esteban mumbled. "I hate these pretentious parties and people." The incredulous stare of the beast within tugged at his mind. The stench of the humans fondling all over each other and the sickening sweet talk they exuded made his stomach roil. The gasps of disgust for his masterpieces angered him the more he remained in the presence of the despicable creatures.

The crowd thinned out as the evening progressed, calming the monster somewhat. At least long enough to make coherent small talk with the vermin he had to associate with. He blew out a tight breath. "Soon all these assholes will know the real Esteban," he murmured as he alerted to a new scent he didn't register from earlier. Vampire and more than one.

Esteban scanned the gallery. *There they are. Do you see them? Who are they?*

Their eyes met, but he didn't have a chance to find out the answer to his unspoken question, as the two unknown vamps left the building. Ignoring the issue for now, he stepped around the corner to the next exhibitor's section. *Let me out and I'll take care of all of them for you. These disgusting humans and those two evil creatures leaving are no match for me.*

Esteban wrestled to gain control. "No. It's not time yet. Soon, real soon you'll have your revenge, my friend." He pushed his fists into his jacket pockets. No, the beast couldn't be released until the plan had been completed. The purpose became clear—eradicate the refuse trashing and censoring his existence. They were blights on all life and when the time was right, he would set the monster loose and his work would be complete and he'd move on. Maybe New York. Or, Los Angeles. The Midwest held some appeal with a less dense population. *Yeah, maybe Kansas or why not fucking Alaska? You think you can go somewhere isolated and get rid of me? You can't survive without me, Esteban. I'm not finished with you yet. I intend to exact revenge on all of them for you.*

"Shut up. Not here. We'll discuss this later," he muttered and stopped abruptly, moving quickly behind the corner wall. "What the…"

A few blinks of his black eyes, and he bent his head slightly around the corner. A woman. A human female literally just stepped out of the painting hanging on the far wall. He spied her encumbered gait and assessed her dress. A red veil covered her head, the bottom resting just past her shoulders. She walked slowly with a slight limp in her step as her hand slid along the wall for support. With her back turned to him, he comfortably moved into the area and followed her at a distance. He stopped at the landscape and stared at the painting for a moment then continued to keep pace with the woman vanishing around the opposite corner wall back into the main gallery. "Did you see that?"

I did. Go back and see.

Esteban did, not so much from the beast commanding him to do so, but for his own curiosity. Pushing the red velvet rope aside, he stood before the painting, angling his head from one side to the other. Nothing obvious jumped out, like a hidden door or panel. He stared at the landscape and the patterns seemed to move. After a few blinks to clear his vision, assured he had to be seeing things. From the corner of his eye, he caught a glimpse of something lying on the floor. He knelt down and picked up a black lace fabric with a ribbon attached much like a mask. A smear of red lipstick and the scent of an exotic perfume drew his attention.

"Hers?" Lifting the lace to his face, he inhaled deeply and imprinted the scent. He stuffed the fabric in his pocket and resumed his attention to the landscape on the wall. The tree branches swayed slightly. He didn't imagine movement before, and then with a tentative hand, reached closer to the watercolor. With his index finger, he slowly moved closer and then…

The hard ground covered in lush green grass reached up and met him as he plopped through a dark vortex, rolling to his side. The landing wasn't the most graceful and the dizziness soon wore off for him to gain his bearings. He stood and spun around taking in everything. Inhaling the scents around him, Esteban blinked with recognition of wildflowers and the earthiness of the woods filling the air. He stopped at the portal of the entrance and realized the shadowed white wall ahead was the one in the gallery. Glancing down at his hands outstretched in front of him, he turned his palms up and down several times, then tilted his head up and smiled as the warmth of what he presumed was the sun gleaming down warming his face.

"What kind of black magic is this?"

No answer from within his head came. He drew a sharp breath and covered his ears with his hands. "Where are you?" His heart pounded in his head and he tried to lecture himself into calmness, but agitation deepened.

Still, the beast within made no response when he called. *What is going on?* For several long moments, question after question slammed into his mind, wanting to know what the hell was going on. He spun on his heels to face the portal again and took three strides toward the glowing wall. Just as before, he touched his fingers to the undulating film and he fell forward into the spinning blackness. The fall onto the wood laminate floor didn't break his descent into the gallery any better than the grassy earth did the other direction.

Slowly rising to his feet, stunned and panting from the bizarre trip, he gathered his wits about him and glimpsed over his shoulder at the art piece. "What the hell was that?" His astonishment turned to interest in a split second. This was a good thing. What opportunities he'd have to possess this powerful magic.

A sudden rush and piercing pain in the back of his head made his vision blur and he leaned against the wall momentarily.

"Damn, not again." The throbbing settled at his forehead, making him squint and rub his temples, trying to quash the monster struggling to regain control. He groaned and crawled along the wall as the agony thrashed behind his eyes. Then, as quickly as the discomfort gripped him, calm settled over him. For a few seconds, he took deep breaths and let them out to clear his head. An insatiable desire for blood tugged at his core.

Running a hand over his bristled, dark-haired jawline, he tried to grasp what in the hell just happened. A hard landing in a landscape watercolor and then an excruciating shooting pain couldn't begin to explain what he experienced. The woman had to be the answer. The beast roared in his head. *I told you. I'm not going anywhere. Now, find the woman. I want her.*

For once, he had to agree. He shoved his hands in his trouser pockets and paced in the direction he last saw the veiled woman. After turning the far corner, the main gallery came into view. Surveying the room, he caught sight of the red veil. The woman with the blonde tresses falling down her back underneath the crimson sheer drape was surrounded by an older couple and another thirtyish woman. A few incredulous eyes fell upon him from designer dressed and overly tanned humans. As he began to move toward the group, a hand clapped down on his shoulder, followed by the nauseating sound of the gallery owner's voice.

"Esteban, my boy. Where did you disappear to? I have someone I want you to meet." The older man leaned in closer to Esteban's ear. "A buyer for your large piece. He wishes to speak to you about the composition. Isn't that exciting?"

"I'm not interested," he huffed and stayed focused on the red veil and the woman who wore it.

"But, you must. Do you not want to sell your work? We're talking five figures, *mon ami.*"

Esteban crooked his head toward the annoying Antoine. "Who's that woman?" He removed his left hand from his pocket and gestured in the direction of the woman standing with the other humans.

"Who? Ah, you mean Mademoiselle Phoenix?"

"Is Phoenix her first or last name?"

"Just Phoenix. The name she insists to be known by. Why do you ask? Haven't you met her before? She's one of the other artists on exhibit tonight."

"No, I haven't. Why does she cover her face?"

"I don't know. Mademoiselle Mann, her mentor and teacher, says the young woman has a disfigurement and is self-conscious. I guess the reason makes sense, but I can't confirm one way or the other. I've only seen her wearing a veil every time. Would you like to meet her?"

A piercing pain began in his gut, the same uncomfortable feeling he'd experienced years ago when he transitioned into the hideous creature he was tonight. *No, that's impossible. I need to feed, nothing more.* He righted his stance, squaring his shoulders and straightening his back. The stabbing eased, but not for long. "Introduce us."

With determined steps, he followed Antoine. Within a few feet, the plainly dressed woman Esteban assumed was the mentor turned and smiled. The woman named Phoenix kept her back to him as she spoke softly to the older man and woman.

"I'm tired. I want to go now." He heard the woman named Phoenix say to the older couple.

Then she turned and he saw her eyes through the scarlet shroud.

"I'll meet you outside at the limo, Abby."

A low growl bubbled up from Esteban's chest. *She can't leave.*

"Oh Merliah. Are you sure?" Abby asked as she placed a hand on Merliah's upper arm.

"Yes. Hi, Mister Rousseau. I enjoyed the show. Thank you."

"Oh, *ma chère*. I hope you did. Tomorrow we'll speak. I do believe I'll have good news for you." He winked and grinned, then stepped closer. He grabbed her shoulders, leaned forward and gave air kisses on both sides of her face.

Esteban grew sicker at watching the sight. Antoine was as phony as a three dollar bill in his opinion. *Merliah? I thought her name was Phoenix?*

"Aren't you going to introduce me to this mysterious beauty, Antoine?" Esteban asked, in order to keep the mystery woman from leaving.

"Oh, yes, yes, yes. Where are my manners? Esteban Freeman, Merliah…I mean Mademoiselle Phoenix. Mademoiselle, Esteban Freeman. He is a fellow artist here tonight."

Esteban extended his hand. She hesitated to accept.

"Pleasure to meet you…Merliah…Phoenix?"

His gaze drifted to the ruby red lips beneath the veil, tempting him in a way none other had before. They were perfect, the kind he'd desired to photograph for his canvases and never quite got right. He had to have her as his new muse, as well as discover the magic with her paintings.

"Merliah, be polite. You're not so tired you can't shake the man's hand," the older woman said.

"Mom, I was." Merliah glanced over her shoulder briefly, and then turned attention to Esteban. "Sorry. Pleased to meet you, Esteban. My name is Merliah, but I use Phoenix for my art." Her hand trembled as she reached to shake his.

He accepted her gesture and placed his other hand on top of hers, sandwiching her delicate one between his. "Unique name. Unique art. I'd like to speak to you more." His voice dropped to a husky tone.

She pulled her hand from his. "Perhaps another time. I'm tired and was about to leave."

"Yes, maybe I can set something up in a day or two," Abby interjected.

"And you are?"

"Abigail Mann, Merliah's friend and…mentor and teacher."

"Mr. Freeman, Abby takes care of my schedule. I really have to go now. Please let her make any arrangements." She turned her back to him, angering the beast within.

She snubs you and deserves punishment.

"Mom, Dad, help me outside."

"Um, I'm sorry. She's had a long day," Abby said.

"Too bad." The beast expressed his anger with a growl echoing in Esteban's ear. The bloodlust tugged at his core. He had to find satisfaction or he'd lose control. He couldn't do that, not here, not now. The plan didn't call for him going berserk in a public place. His chest rose and fell quickly as he began to struggle for air. The pain increased. "If you'll excuse me, I have to leave as well. Pleasure meeting you, Miss Mann. Antoine, I'll speak with you tomorrow."

Esteban left the gallery in search of a blood supply. Tonight, he'd forego any artistic pleasure and seek relief of the pain growing within. He continued to swear he had gone through another transition. The agony was unmistakably familiar. When he stepped outside the gallery, the humid night air enveloped his aching body. He couldn't breathe with the air so thick. Closing his eyes to gain control and calm his racing heart, he took a few deep breaths and then opened his eyes. A petite redhead caught his eye. *Human. She'll do nicely. Follow her, Esteban. I want to play with her. We can start with her and maybe have fun at the club later. We'll find the other one with Antoine's help. Now move!*

Chapter Seventeen

A Backroom Healing

Stefan led Sorin to the SUV waiting in the valet area outside the Rousseau Gallery. With the backup of vehicles, Sorin knew they weren't the only ones leaving the exhibition. Several vehicles were maneuvering to squeeze into the small space near the entrance of the building. Young men dressed in red shirts and khaki shorts ran back and forth, tagged keys in hand, retrieving vehicles while impatient humans waited. The large Escalade bullied its way into the fray and stopped curbside within a few feet of the two vampires towering over most of the guests.

Within seconds, the driver exited and opened the rear access. The two men climbed into the rear passenger seat.

"Gerrick, take us to Euphoria," Stefan instructed the driver.

"Yes, sir."

"I can't wait much longer, brother." Sorin barely got the words out. His breathing became labored and he clutched his stomach with both arms crossed over his abdomen.

"Hang in there, Sorin." Stefan rolled up the sleeve of his shirt, and then offered his wrist. "Here. Take some from me until we get there."

Sorin eyed the proffered arm with the pulsing vein calling to him. His vision blurred red. The pain became almost unbearable at that point. He didn't know if he could last another five minutes let alone the time to travel to the club. Neither did he care if the blood belonged to his friend and fellow MC. The hunger was so intense, he felt like his insides were turning inside out. He grabbed Stefan's arm and pulled the bared wrist to his mouth and sank fully extended fangs into the flesh, drawing with strong suction the remedy to his anguish.

After a few minutes, Stefan pushed Sorin off. "Enough or you'll make me weak. We'll reach the club shortly." Stefan then licked the wound, sealing it. "Gerrick, are we almost there?"

"Yes, sir. A few more blocks. I'd say another five or ten, depending upon catching any traffic lights. I'll pull to the front when we arrive, sir."

"Very good." Stefan turned his attention to Sorin. "Are you feeling a little better?"

Sorin leaned his head back on the seat headrest with his eyes closed. The pain had subsided from the worse he'd felt in a long time, but twinges persisted. He needed more than vampire blood, he had to have human.

"A little, but you know what I need."

"We'll be at the club soon. I'll set you up and then we'll figure out what brought this on."

Sorin opened his eyes and glanced over at his friend. He knew what caused this episode—Merliah and her painted world. There was no other explanation. He felt human, felt alive in there, with her, in the make-believe creation. The beast was silent, the fangs and desire for blood didn't exist. The warmth and brightness of the sun kissed his skin. The fresh air filled his lungs. The landscape reminded him of his home in the spring. The other painting depicted his manor home in the mountains. How did she know? Did she tap into his mind during the dreams they shared? Was she in fact an angel or a clever demon bent on eventually destroying him or sending him over the edge into the pit of insanity? *No, not my angel. I can't believe she meant to destroy me this way.*

"The woman." The words were almost inaudible. The pain began to slowly creep back. Holding the beast back from full-out release grew more difficult.

The Escalade came to a slow stop. Sorin bobbed his head toward the black tinted window and glanced out. They had arrived.

The driver came to a stop directly in front and exited the vehicle to open the back passenger doors. First for Stefan on the far side, and then he opened the other for Sorin. The two vamps were greeted at the door by a male vamp towering at least a couple inches taller than Sorin. At six-five and by most standards taller than average in height, he was surprised how the employee easily inched him out. Stefan nodded to him as the burly vamp opened one of the wooden double doors.

Despite the pain growing stronger, he had an image to project, and showing weakness made him vulnerable walking into the exclusive vamp sex club. As an MC, he had to show his power, so he mustered every ounce of strength to put on display for the benefit of any vamps who may have questioned his abilities. The sooner he satiated his hunger, the better off he'd be.

The lobby area had been crowded the first night in town and he hadn't noticed the remodeling job. Sorin suspected Stefan conducted extensive makeovers to all of Dragos' holdings since taking over the family. He'd have done the same.

"Master Stefan! I didn't expect you'd be here tonight." The female hostess behind the front desk popped up from her upholstered chair.

"You never do," he mumbled under his breath, but not so low Sorin didn't hear him as they both strode through the area and through the passageway into the main play area of the club.

"Master, can I get you anything?" Sorin heard the young woman ask as Stefan ignored her.

"Remind me later to fire her. She says the same thing every time I come here. The whiney, little girl voice drives me freakin' crazy. Plus, she just sits at the front desk and does nothing useful."

Sorin snickered. "Then fire her unless you can put her to work somewhere else."

"It's not worth it." Stefan gestured with his head grabbing the attention of a vamp seated at the bar in the center of the room. The man was dressed in black jeans and T-shirt. A red band on his right arm signified him as an employee. He walked at a brisk pace, stopping a few feet in front of them.

"Good evening, Master Stefan," the clean-shaven and short cropped haired vamp said. He nodded his head to Sorin. "Sir."

"Miguel, I need a room and three," Stefan paused and glanced at Sorin. "No, select four discrete female patrons. Preferably I want women who haven't donated tonight."

"I believe room eleven is available. I'll have the donors sent in immediately, master. Is there anything else you'll need, sir?"

"No, we'll be good. Thanks, Miguel." Stefan grabbed Sorin's upper arm and moved them across the room to the far side and down a dimly lit corridor.

"Patrons?"

"Yeah, the damned laws in this city have us working within the ridiculous rules for *volunteering* human blood. I thought the human law for blood consumption was bad in Virginia, but here is just as ludicrous. Blood in exchange for sex has been frowned upon since the skirmish leaked to the public about Dragos. Pretty sure someone from the local Vamp Hunters Coalition let the word out. Alex swears no one at the Bureau did. But, I don't know if that's true, or she's not privy to certain information."

Stefan stopped in front of a door marked "11" etched on a brass plate, then turned the knob and entered the room. Sorin followed and within a few seconds they were joined by the vamp Stefan called Miguel and four scantily clad women. Human females of varying attractiveness to Sorin's eye. He didn't give a rat's ass about their make-up adorned faces, length of hair or the curves on their body. He wanted, no hungered for, their blood. The only requisite was they were alive. The warm elixir of life would soon be his to satisfy the beast scratching for satisfaction within his gut.

"Thank you, Miguel. That'll be all," Stefan said. He turned his attention to the women seductively moving toward both of them. "Good evening, ladies. My friend needs your assistance. You freely give of your blood?"

The petite woman with brunette hair flowing over her shoulders to half-way down the curve of her back answered first. "I do and any other pleasures of the night you wish, Master." Her voice had the soft tone of a seductress, begging for more. Sorin had no intentions of giving, only taking what she willingly offered.

His body trembled in delight as another joined the small one, and together the two women fondled his body running their hands along the hard planes of his abdomen. "Are you joining in, Stefan?"

"No, you need this."

"Take her," he motioned with a nod of his head. "Three will do me. You need to refresh after helping me."

Stefan grinned. "You're right." He grabbed the taller brunette closest to him and snaked his arm around her waist, pulling her tighter into his embrace.

"No sex, baby? I thought that's why you brought us back here," the brunette cooed.

"Not tonight," Stefan said, then brushed the long tresses away from the column of her neck. His fangs dropped and in one swift motion he sank them deep into the pulsing vein below her ear. She moaned and fell against his body.

Without a moment of hesitation, Sorin wasted no time either. He leaned forward and possessed two of the three remaining women, curling a hand tightly into the long dark brown silken hair of the petite one and the other hand around the waist of the buxom blonde. He smelled their arousal, but more important, their blood titillated his nostrils and could wait no longer to taste the sweetness of young life-giving fluids burn in his veins. To his surprise through the blur of hunger, he was turned on. His primal urges reared as well. Out of habit, he pushed a mental mind command to each woman, demanding acquiescence and not to struggle against his hold. They were to identify the pain as pleasure when his embrace tightened, lowering his mouth to the exposed neck of the petite brunette. The beast could be cruel, and in his state of mind, he had no idea if he could control the monster once set free.

Sorin pressed forward, his fangs elongated and he bit hard into the warm flesh, sucking voraciously. After a minute, he pulled out from the abused neck, easing her onto the mattress of the small bed. Turning his attention to the other one, he licked the residual blood from his bottom lip and tightened his grip around her waist. She'd continued to fondle his body when he'd been otherwise preoccupied, and he enjoyed her attention. His mind began to race with the thrill of fresh blood coursing through his body. He felt like the first night he'd transitioned more than the night he'd been saved by Stefan and the other warriors. The euphoria made him dizzy for more blood and sex.

The second woman smiled then swooshed her hair over her shoulder with a flick of her head. His cock grew hard, but he resisted the urge to act on it. He loved blondes, and this one resembled his angel. *Fuck! Merliah?* His cool lips pressed a kiss on the plump lips of the mesmerized look-alike blonde, sampling, parting them. With a quick thrust of his tongue, he plunged inside her mouth with the force of a predatory animal, not gentle lover.

Bloodlust consumed him, wrong as it may be, he couldn't resist the tug, and the hunger still persisted. He jerked free from the blonde's lips and she stumbled back. He caught her in a tight embrace and scraped fangs along the length of her neck, the scent of her pulsing red elixir consumed him down to the bone. Drinking deeply, Sorin forced himself to stop as the woman's blood flow slowed. Withdrawing his sharp fangs and a sound like a groan escaped him as he lowered the blonde to lean against the other woman on the bed.

Standing back from the scene, he slid his tongue over his lower, engorged lip and felt a trickle of blood then wiped it away with the back of his hand. Turning for the third woman, he viewed through red-glazed eyes her position next to Stefan. The two remaining women were rubbing their hands along his friend's body and he'd already taken blood from one, her neck wounds raised and darkened blood covered the two marks.

Sorin moved closer to the group, coming up behind the unmarked woman. He pulled her back against his chest and brushed her hair to the side. Within seconds, he pressed sharp fangs to the creamy skin, piercing the pulsing vein. The blood flowed over his tongue, down his throat. By the third woman, gorging on the intoxicating liquid, he felt like himself again. After a few more minutes, he released his embrace and she swooned into his embrace. He lifted her in his arms and carried her to the bed. Stefan had already taken the woman he drank from and set her in the overstuffed chair across the room.

Slowly, Sorin turned and faced his friend, his mind clear and body refreshed. He wiped the dripping blood from his mouth with the back of his hand and sucked in a deep breath. His head fell back and he let out a low growl, then he dropped to his knees.

"Are you all right, man?" Stefan asked.

"What the hell happened to me tonight?" The storm raging inside him minutes before had subsided, and a soft breeze of content replaced the torrent of pain and raging hunger.

"I'm not sure, but your reaction took me aback. I see this type of behavior when someone goes through transition. Did something happen to you at the gallery? You mentioned the woman."

Sorin drew in a sharp breath, and then let it out slowly. "Merliah. I met her tonight. At the gallery. There's something...something very different about her."

"So, she's definitely real and not part of a dream?"

"Yeah. Let's get out of here. I need a drink, stronger than blood wine."

Stefan laughed. "Yes, and you'll have to tell me more about this Merliah. Maybe she had something to do with your bloodlust going on a rampage tonight."

"What about them?" Sorin gestured with his head to the women.

"Miguel will take care of them. He loves the clean-up, if you know what I mean." Stefan opened the door. "Miguel, take care of the ladies, please."

"My pleasure, Master Stefan."

The two vampires left the room and returned to the main area of the club, taking a seat at a booth near the back of the room.

"So, are you going to tell me what happened?"

Sorin leaned against the upholstered back. How could he tell his friend where and what he did with Merliah? Hell, he couldn't believe he ended up in a painting, making love to the woman he'd dreamt of over the past six months. Nor believe he felt the warmth of the sun on his flesh and the beast within didn't seem to exist. How could he explain this to Stefan and have him believe the story? Merliah was real, even though he hadn't seen her except in his dreams and the fantasy landscape. "I need a stiff drink. Any suggestions?"

"My favorite. I'll have a glass sent over." Stefan motioned to the waitress who stood poised at the bar several feet away.

"Good evening, Master Stefan, your usual?"

"Yes, and one for Master Sorin as well."

The server nodded and left the table.

"I was in a painting." Sorin blurted out the explanation.

"What?"

"I was sucked into her painting. That's where I was right before you walked into the room."

"Okay. Then where is she? Still in the picture?"

"I don't know. We left, remember. Something about pain and hunger."

Stefan gave him a sly smile. "Interesting. You realize what you're telling me sounds crazy."

"You think?"

The drinks arrived, and Sorin recognized the vampire cocktail. "Aw, I should have known, your special cognac." He hadn't had the drink in years. Blood wine had been his blood drink of choice. Relishing the intense bouquet when he lifted the snifter to his nose, he sipped the drink, letting the reddish amber liquid burn down his throat. It didn't erase the memory of what just transpired in the back room, but it didn't hurt either.

"She lives in the painting at the gallery?"

"No, she's the artist."

"The woman in the veil?"

"What veil? She didn't have one when I saw her."

"I've caught a glimpse of her a couple times at the gallery when I went to meet with Rousseau. Her name is Phoenix, I thought."

"That's the name she uses for her art. Her real name is Merliah. She has some kind of powers or magic for creating the world inside the painting. I felt the sun on my face, Stefan. My fangs didn't drop. Neither did the hunger for blood tug at my gut. I felt human again. Then, when I left, my existence as a vampire rushed back immediately, like I was born vampire again."

With the glass held to his lips, he paused as he watched the expression on his friend's face. *Fuck! He thinks I'm certifiable.* Then, he gulped the remainder of his drink, slammed the glass on the table and rose to leave.

"Sorin? Where are you going?"

"To the gallery to find her."

"Wait, no one is there, I'm sure. You could set off alarms and who knows what other trouble you could get in. This is my territory, Sorin. I have to ask you, as a friend, do not act rashly." Stefan's eyes narrowed.

The silence between them grew tense. "Isn't Rousseau delivering your purchase tomorrow? I'll make sure Alex is at the penthouse when it arrives and your package will be there when we awaken tomorrow night."

"And if she's not there, where do I search for her? I went to the facility Alex suggested from the database and I didn't find her." Sorin crossed his arms over his chest. "I need to get out of here. I'm in no mood to be around others."

Sorin really didn't need to socialize with other vamps he'd never see again, at least in this century. Once he found and solved the mystery of Merliah, he'd return to his home in the mountains. Hopefully, she'd be with him.

Chapter Eighteen

A Step Closer to a Reveal

Alex slid into the sedan, which pulled up in front of the Rousseau Gallery. *Dang! I hate leaving Stefan.* "So talk to me Johnson. What's up with the late night meeting with the locals?"

"No hello Johnson, how are you, before you jump into all business? Geez, Alex. I love you too."

"Oh can it, Scott. I thought we were past formalities. So, are you going to tell me?"

Johnson shook his head. "Nice dress, by the way. Sexy."

She tugged at the hem of the black sheath dress. The strappy red heel stilettos were killing her feet, but she didn't have another pair to slip into. She hated wearing such fancy clothes, but this had been Stefan's night and he wanted her dressed to the nines for his debut show. She'd been happy wearing dress slacks and flats, but he complained about not seeing her legs. Now, Johnson was ogling her. *Men! They fall over their dicks when they see a woman in a pair of fuck me shoes and a short dress. They're so damn predictable.*

"Don't go there. I had to dress nice for Stefan's show. He likes me dressing up."

"Well, that's one thing we have in common."

"Keep to business, Johnson. What's up with the late night meeting?"

"The lead detective on the case called the Chief with new info. Something about a blood DNA result and other interesting evidence came back from one of the killings. Vampire."

"Ha! Told you. I could smell it. We should have been called in sooner. A couple of those women wouldn't be dead if they had. There's a rogue on the loose and I'm surprised my buddy hunters didn't fill me in."

"You're not one of them anymore, sweetheart. You're part of the establishment and have to work within the confines of the law. If they told you anything, you'd tell."

"Hey, not necessarily."

"Please, I can't hear that. You're a hardcore agent now. I've watched you grow in this position. You may have been originally trained as a vamp hunter, but you're an FBI agent with the Vamp Squad."

"Yeah, yeah."

"What are you doing?"

"What do you think?" She turned her attention to him, noticing him eyeing her thighs. "Hey eyes on the road buddy. I don't feel like going to the hospital tonight."

"Sorry, I'm not used to you showing so much leg."

His gaze held hers for seconds longer than she felt comfortable. She slid out of the seatbelt and turned to look in the backseat. "Shoot, nothing! Did you bring my stash of Cheese Doodles and Cherry Coke, or not?" Alex continued to rummage along the backseat floor board looking for her favorite snack foods. The late night snacking was a bad habit she should give up. Especially since Stefan had been on her lately about the orange crumbs and fingerprints being everywhere in the penthouse. On New Years' Day, she made a resolution to give up the high caloric junk food, even drinking diet soda instead of regular. She lasted about a month.

"I thought you told me to stop enabling you. You said Stefan got tired of crumbs in the bed."

She snapped her head around to catch his profile and the smirk on his face. "I told you that? No, I didn't, did I?"

"Yeah, you did. Palmer's going away party, remember? You had a few too many and cried on my shoulder about your vamp."

"Well, I didn't mean it. That was an alcohol induced confession. You swear to me you'll never repeat what I said."

The quirky laugh he used when he teased, infuriated her. She knuckle-punched his upper arm.

"Hey! What's that for? I should report you for assaulting your supervisor."

"Oh, *please*. Tell me you promise never to repeat what I said, or I'll punch you again."

"Maybe you ought to take those anger management classes you mentioned to Stefan." He snickered.

"That's not funny."

"He's a vampire, Alex. They are all angry creatures. Granted, some of them are nice when they want to be, but ultimately they can turn and be nasty sonsofbitches when they have to be. Frankly, I don't know what you see in him. You could have had me, you know."

"Don't start again, Johnson. You know we're just friends. I like you and I'd even go so far as to say I love ya, a tiny bit." She lightly placed a hand on his arm and glanced at him. "But I don't *love you* in that way."

"So, speaking of Palmer. Have you heard from him? Does he like Headquarters?"

"He's enjoying his stay. Ass-kissing all the big wigs from what I've heard. He's definitely in his element in Washington."

"Hmm, I hope he doesn't kiss the wrong ass, or he'll wind up in Anchorage, Alaska next time."

He laughed. "Yeah, that'll really piss him off. Maybe he'd end up back here."

"I doubt it." She paused for a moment. "Hey, looks like a party's going on here too. Try not to park too far away from the entrance. I don't want to walk a long distance in these stilettos."

"I'll drop you off and meet up with you. How 'bout that?"

"Thank you. Special Agent Johnson, you're such a loving, caring partner. I'm not up to nursing blisters on my feet."

Johnson let out a huff.

While waiting at the entrance for Johnson, Alex ran scenarios through her head. So far, her instincts told her the Tiara Princess Killer was a vampire. DNA recovered proved her right. What other evidence could have been found to call her and Johnson in this late? Why didn't Stefan know about this vampire running rampant in his territory? Even if a rogue, he'd have heard or sensed something. Anything. If he did know, why didn't he tell her when she asked for his help?

"Okay, let's go," Johnson said.

The two special agents flashed their badges at the desk sergeant. A few minutes later, another officer escorted them to a conference room behind the secure door.

"Ah, good you're both finally here," Chief Rodriguez said, glancing up from the papers he was reading when they walked in.

"Chief Rodriguez. Nice to see you again," Johnson said.

Chief Manny Rodriguez stood about six foot, had a ruddy complexion, and appeared to be in his early forties. Alex found his appearance distinguished but hard around the edges. He seemed a bit more haggard than the last time she saw him during the holidays. Stefan had been invited to a political fundraiser and the Chief had attended.

Alex nodded.

"Ah, my favorite Vamp Squad special agents. Have a seat."

"This better be good, Chief Rodriguez. You pulled me from an evening with my...my boyfriend." Alex wasn't sure how to describe Stefan. The need to describe him to anyone outside her immediate sphere of co-workers and family never came up. "I was at his debut art exhibit."

"Oh, how nice for you, but I'm under pressure by the Mayor's Office to settle this case. I thought this vampire shit was a joke when you two were called in, but I guess not." He tossed a manila folder in front of them. "These are the results of blood we found in one of the first murders. Seems the perp got a little mad and punched a hole in the wall. The place had been systematically cleaned. He probably didn't think about the hole in the wall when he left the scene."

"Okay, we were called in before this obviously because you suspected a vampire was involved, now this confirms it. Doesn't give us any more than before. Why call us in at this hour? This could have waited until tomorrow." Alex became increasingly annoyed at having to leave Stefan to come and hear nothing new on the case.

"We discovered something else."

The door to the conference room opened. A familiar face appeared. "Sorry, I'm late. Oh hey guys." The man dressed in a white lab coat came in and sat down next to Alex.

"Matsui? What are you doing here? The chief called you too?" Alex asked.

"Yeah, didn't you hear?"

"Hear what?" Johnson asked.

"Blue. The toxicology report showed an unusual substance and I was called in to analyze and confirm it," Matsui said.

Alex glanced over at Johnson, and then returned her attention to the excited lab tech. "You're sure? I thought the entire drug supply had been confiscated and destroyed."

"Apparently not, Agent Carlton. From what I understand this is a nasty drug I don't want to see loose on my streets. I also understand you keep house with the head vamp in this city and he owns the company which manufactures this shit. Want to explain?" Chief Rodriguez asked, snarling as he spoke.

Both of Alex's eyebrows crinkled. "My personal relationship with Stefan Marin has nothing to do with how I conduct my business with the Bureau. He fought against the previous Master of this city who unleashed a deadly virus and the very drug you speak of. SGM doesn't manufacture Blue anymore because of Stefan."

"I personally know Mister Marin and he would condemn this rogue vamp. They take care of their own and this one would have been dispatched if those in their Blood Family were aware of his existence." Johnson spoke with conviction.

"Do you have proof? Who's to say Marin only tells you what you want to hear. Someone is using this Blue to drug the women before killing them. If the perp didn't get it from SGM, where is he getting it from?"

"Maybe someone who had access before the production was shut down. I'll follow that possible lead," Alex said. Then she turned attention to Matsui. "Is it possible this is a knock-off drug, maybe changed and not as strong?"

"I reviewed the toxicology report and compared it to the original sample you brought me. It appears the same, Alex. Whoever is doing this got ahold of some and is using it to incapacitate his victims. Then, he does the rest."

"If this dude is a vamp, why is he drugging the women? He could easily charm them into doing what he wants. After mesmerizing them, he could take their blood and disappear. Why is he going through the staging of their bodies, calling emergency services and tipping his hand? None of this makes sense," Alex said.

"Because he's a psychotic sonofabitch wacko! And I have the Mayor's Office breathing down my neck to get this solved. Election years, I hate them," the chief said.

"Where's the file? And I mean the complete file. What you gave us in the preliminary report doesn't have anything other than the first reports by the CSI and Coroner's office," Johnson said.

"Here are your copies of everything." The chief tossed a thicker file folder across the conference table.

Johnson opened the file and placed it on top of the table between him and Alex.

"Ohmigod! Stop. Go back to the previous photograph," Alex said.

A knock came at the door then a uniformed officer came in and whispered something in the chief's ear. Alex glanced up momentarily. She quickly pulled the picture from the file and held it, staring intently and shaking her head slightly. The woman in the scene was dressed in white lingerie and her face heavily made up with the focus on the lips with a vibrant red. She barely made out the fang marks on the neck. She flipped the photo over and made out the photographer's annotations. *Too bizarre and too coincidental.*

"Goddammit!" The chief said in a raised voice, startling Alex out of her thoughts.

"What?" she asked.

"Another body was found only this time on the streets and not dressed up like the others. We could possibly have a copy-cat killer or the perp is getting bolder." The chief pushed away from the table and stood. "You want to join me? I'm going to the scene."

"We'll follow you. Where are we going?" Johnson asked.

"In an alley between 25th and 24th Street. The area has been cordoned off. If we get separated, I'm sure you'll find it."

"That's down in the Wynwood Arts District. I was just there."

"Really? With your vampire boyfriend?" The Chief's tone of voice didn't set right with Alex.

"Yes, we were there for an art show. Stefan's debut as a matter of fact. That's why I'm dressed like this."

The chief harrumphed. "Interesting this happened in the same area. Did he leave with you?"

"What are you implying, Chief Rodriguez?"

The fortyish man stopped at the exit door and turned to face her. "Nothing, I'm just saying I find the situation interesting. Are you coming?"

"Hey, can I go? I don't get out in the field much and this might be a great time for me to help with the evidence." Matsui's expression was one of a little kid anticipating going to the candy store. Alex thought he looked like he'd jump up and down any second.

"Sure, you'll probably help out...for us."

Twenty minutes later, Alex walked with Johnson and Matsui along the yellow crime scene tape that cordoned off the alleyway between an office building on one street, the backside of another connecting to the street to the north. The area used to be all warehouses. Years ago a city project refurbished the worst of the abandoned buildings and repurposed them into art studios and galleries. Her gaze wandered over the brightly painted exterior walls, not remembering seeing them earlier when at the show opening for Stefan. This area was several blocks from Rousseau's Gallery. They parked a street over in a parking garage, coming up the other side of the street. She began to speculate if the victim was a guest at the show.

A uniformed policeman guarded the entrance to the alleyway off the main street. He stood in a business-like stance with legs braced and thumbs hooked under his gun belt. No one would pass without his approval by the expression and body language he presented. As they approached the taped off crime scene, he straightened his stance. The scattering of plain clothed detectives in the area outside the tape taking statements paid no mind.

"This is a restricted area folks," he said in an officious tone as he appraised the group. Alex reached into her clutch and pulled out her identification. The other two men did the same. The officer glanced at of the badges and then handed them back. "Okay, go ahead. Chief Rodriguez said you were authorized to enter when you arrived." He turned his head slightly and spoke into the radio at his shoulder. "Sanchez, tell the chief the Feds are here." Alex caught him looking at her with a wandering eye. The form-fitting dress she wore didn't help her position. She could only imagine what he thought about her, except she didn't care.

As they walked through the alleyway, Johnson spoke first in response to the security barrier. "What was that all about? Authorized us? I thought he was the one who asked us here. Asshole."

"Politics. He doesn't really want us here. The mayor does. Let's do our job and find this rogue," Alex said.

"I guess I'm not cut out to make it at Headquarters. Too much ass-kissing for my taste. Palmer is probably grooving on it."

"Probably, until he kisses the wrong woman…or ass."

The three laughed until they came within a few feet of the crowd gathered around the discovered body. A number of criminal scene investigators performed their various tasks gathering evidence samples, and taking photographs. A faint hum of voices whispered into crime techs' recording devices combined into an undifferentiated buzz both creepy and uncomfortably loud. Chief Rodriguez peered up and saw them and made a beckoning gesture with his hand, and moved to the side to reveal the covered body. A flashback came to Alex of the scene which revealed the young woman from the Euphoria many months ago. She'd grown accustomed to vanquishing vampires, but seeing humans ripped at her insides.

"This the victim?"

Alex had to smirk inwardly because Johnson wasn't a man of many words. He tended to cut right through the bullshit. Unfortunately, she'd never learned the fine art of embellishment as yet. *Must be a guy thing.*

Rodriguez bent over and flipped the cover from the body beneath. "Same as the others. Only difference is she isn't made-up or dressed up. Not the usual accompanying nine-one-one call either."

"Who found her back here then?" Alex asked.

"One of the employees in this building." Rodriguez cocked his head to the side, indicating the building facing the other street they entered. "He came out for a smoke and saw the victim."

"May I?" Matsui asked.

"Yeah, sure. Just speak with the ME before you touch or take anything. This is still an on-going crime scene."

"I know the drill, sir."

Alex hated the smell of death. She'd seen a few human bodies fresh after the happening, but the unpleasant and distinctive odor continued to roil her stomach. The indelible image and scent imprinted onto her memory. The moment Alex stepped into the alley the sickly-sweet odor filled her nostrils. Fortunately, the cooler early spring air slowed the decomposition to a minimum, but she still threw her hand up over her mouth and nose. Her guess was the poor girl died several hours or less ago. Alex inched closer to take a look at the face. The long auburn hair covered most of the side view of her face. Flesh showed through a section of the parted tresses. There was a wound—a two-hole prick mark on her neck. Blood made a trail from the puncture points, dropping slowly onto the concrete surface. The infliction was all too familiar. *Vampire.* She gasped when Matsui turned the victim's head slightly.

Bruises and cuts covered the woman's swollen face. Alex's throat tightened. This victim didn't look like the ones in the official police photographs. The young woman had been viciously attacked and left to die in the open. *Maybe this is a copy-cat killer like Rodriguez suggested.* She closed her eyes briefly to calm the queasiness.

Stomach acid surged into Alex's throat and threatened to boil over like the day she saw Haley spread-eagled on the floor of Euphoria. The same expression of pain and pleasure frozen on the woman's face with the blood trickling down the neck had all those emotions flooding back. Wrenching her gaze from the ghastly scene, she turned and smacked into the chest of Johnson. Grabbing her shoulders he asked, "What is it, Alex?"

"I recognize her. She was at the art gallery tonight. I don't know her name, but remember seeing her. Stefan even commented on how her hair was similar to mine."

"Interesting. Your Mister Marin again," Rodriguez said.

Fighting back her flaring temper, she responded coolly. "Yes, it is but he didn't do this as you're implying."

"I didn't say he did. I'm sure he has an iron-clad alibi." Rodriguez scowled.

Breathe, Alex. Stay focused. I know Stefan didn't do this.

Alex took in a deep breath. "I'm fine. Can I see the case file?" She extended her hand toward Johnson.

"Here. What is it? You've got a clue, don't you?"

"Yeah. Before the call came in, I recognized something." She opened and glanced through the photographs. "This one. I've seen this woman before too." Alex handed the shot to Johnson.

Rodriguez yanked the picture from Johnson's hand. "Let me see that. Hmm, and just where do you know her agent?"

"I'm not sure, but she is very familiar. Let me think on it and I'm sure I'll remember."

"We don't have time. This murderer has ramped up his killing. This is my case and like before, I'm not releasing jurisdiction no matter what the mayor says. I'm running out of patience with this bastard. Either help me nab him or stay out of my way." Rodriguez handed the photograph back.

As usual, Johnson maintained flawless tact and diplomacy when it came to handling sensitive situations between law enforcement agencies. "With all due respect Chief, we're more equipped to handle this situation now that a vampire has been determined as the killer. We'll keep you informed of our progress, as a courtesy. But, you need to let us do our jobs with your full cooperation of staff and evidence. If you need further clarification on this matter, I'll have my people call your people." Johnson pulled out a notebook and checked the time on his wristwatch. "We'll stick around and take our investigation evidence around your CSI team. If there's nothing else Chief…" He scribbled a few things on the paper, and then glanced up. "Alex?" He turned his back.

Alex followed suit. "That was ballsy. What's next?" she whispered.

"We need to follow-up on who you think the other woman is." He leaned in closer to her ear and murmured. "Tell me Stefan isn't involved."

Alex jerked back quickly and stared at Johnson, her partner and friend. Disgust snaked up her back, raising the hairs on her arms. *What the hell?* "Where'd that come from?" she asked curtly. "You know that's not possible." She glanced over her shoulder and met Rodriguez's cool stare. "He didn't do this and I'll prove it. I'll be in the car."

While walking back to the company vehicle, Alex mulled over what to do next. All of her hunter instincts kicked in. Something was odd about all these killings. She'd seen the women before, both here and in the photos. If she left the investigation up to the police, they'd find some convoluted way to blame Stefan. They may have been ill-equipped to deal with a vampire, but they were excellent at finding ways to make the evidence show what they wanted. The responsibility fell to her to find the real culprit. *What do they have in common? Think Alex, think.*

Her paced picked up and as she reached the sedan, she halted abruptly. Her breath hitched.

She remembered.

Chapter Nineteen

It's a New Day

After returning to the Institute close to midnight, Merliah decided to forego a shower and crawled straight into bed. Exhausted, mentally and physically, she was surprised she fell asleep so quickly compared to the past week. With the stress of the art exhibition behind her, plus the encounter with her dream man, the comfort of her bed lulled her into a blissful slumber.

The following day, she awakened late morning, refreshed and exhilarated.

Merliah pushed the bed coverings off her body and rolled to her side, tucking the pillow beneath her head. She fluttered her eyes shut and took a few moments to fantasize about Sorin, since she had no memory of any dream last night. Her heart beat fast thinking of the way he touched her, running his fingers over her aroused flesh, the soft whispers in her ear, and the musky manly scent made her dizzy. The time spent in his arms within the painting was her best experience since recovering from the accident and coma.

A tap on the door scattered the sensual thoughts like a flock of startled doves.

"Hello?"

The door creaked open. "Liah? Are you decent?" the familiar voice of her friend Abby sounded.

Merliah bolted upright, sitting on the edge of the mattress. "I'm good, Abby. You can come in."

"Oh, you're not up yet. I'm sorry, sweetie. Do you want me to come back?"

"No, I was up. Just laying here thinking."

"Well, I received a phone call from Antoine and he has very good news. The collector who purchased your landscape decided to buy the remainder of your collection. Isn't that wonderful?"

"All of them? Even the new one?"

"He said everything, so I assume even the new one."

"Who is this collector?"

"A European, Antoine said. He didn't give me a name, but he's waiting for the final payment to clear the bank before he releases them." Abby paused and had a concerned expression. "What's the matter, Liah? You don't look happy."

Merliah had slipped out of bed and limped across the room toward the window. She opened the blinds, and squinted as the sunlight charged into the room. "The wildflowers landscape and castle I want to keep. Mister Rousseau can sell the others. If the buyer wants the other two, tell him I'll create two identical ones instead." Merliah shuttered at the thought of an innocent person setting their hands on the paintings and being sucked into the surreal world she had created. *They'll freak out. I can't have that happen.*

"What do you mean? You can't do that, Liah. This doesn't make any sense. I can maybe understand the last one with the castle, but the other one? Why do you want to keep them and offer to make duplicates?" Abby walked toward Merliah. "What's going on? You didn't seem right last night and definitely are acting strange now. Did something happen you're not telling me?"

"Nothing happened. I just don't want them sold. They're...they're special and I can't let them go." She moved past her friend, the limping less noticeable. The need for stretching when first rising became less than the day before. The change she found amazing and remarkable. "Abby, I can explain to Mister Rousseau. I'm sure he'll understand. The buyer will have to as well. Now, I have to take a shower and eat. I'm starving. I'll meet you later in the dining hall and maybe you can take me to the gallery."

"This discussion isn't over. You're not telling me everything and I'll get to the bottom of this." Abby turned and reached the door. "I'll be in the dining hall, waiting." Then she left.

The behavior and way she spoke to Abby was uncharacteristic. In fact, downright rude and mean, but she had to. There was no way she'd allow the paintings to fall into unsuspecting hands. Smoothing things over with Abby wouldn't be difficult. Now, she had to convince her to go to gallery, retrieve the two pieces while she started work on new ones without the special touch.

Merliah still had no idea how she was able to create the internal space, the make-believe world came out of nowhere. Ever since coming out of the coma, she sensed something different inside, in her head and body. When she began to paint, she felt the energy radiate through her hands. Then the screeching sound began. The strangest thing that happened when she thought about expending the force into the painting occurred one late afternoon when she touched a finished canvas. When she expended the energy the first time, she thought she imagined the experience because the loud and painful noise in her brain forced her. With Sorin joining her last night, she realized escaping into the landscape wasn't only in her head. Others could find their way into her created alternative world and that could prove dangerous. The patients at the institute weren't a problem. They'd never tell her secret, but those on the outside would.

After stepping from the shower, she quickly wrapped her body in a bath towel. The stir of a slight breeze from the overhead exhaust fan caused goose bumps to blossom along her damp skin. With another towel she dried off and then tossed the towel to the floor. She stood before the full-length mirror attached to the back of the door. Fogged over from the steam, she wiped it down. Her image slowly appeared. Totally naked, she studied the reflection of her battered body. The ends of her lips curled down into a frown. Scars from the surgeries to repair injuries from the accident were now vaguely identifiable white lines crisscrossing her flesh. She ran her hands over her breasts and down her abdomen. Raising her eyes, she met the soulful gaze in the mirror. A tear formed. The face staring back was not the one she remembered as the young woman before the accident. Now, a battered visage peered back, several fine lines of raised flesh ran down the left side. They were the remains of the many procedures attempting, with mixed success, to repair the damage. A disheveled patch of hair, like an old threadbare mop, covered her misshapen head. "How can a man as handsome as Sorin, love someone as grotesque as me?" Shaking her head, she turned away from her reflection.

As difficult as the choice would be, she decided not to see Sorin again. Eventually, she'd have to tell the truth about her special ability and show him her real identity. The tears began to flow and she sniffled. "I can't let him see me like this. He'll be disgusted and I can't bear to take that heartache. Yes, this is best. I can't call to him again."

Dejected by her appearance, she scurried off to the bedroom and dressed then made her way to the art studio. Before leaving her room, she called Mr. Rousseau and explained her reasons for withdrawing the two paintings. She'd create pieces to exchange with the others today and have Abby bring her to the studio. He didn't seem pleased, and he'd have to contact the buyer, but he told her he'd do what he could. As far as Abby was concerned, well she'd have to wait, creating substitutes was more important and time was short.

Within an hour, she had completed half of the new landscape. If she had to spend the rest of the afternoon composing the two canvases, she would. The expression on Mr. Rousseau's face would be one of surprise, she was certain. Immersed in finishing the piece, she didn't hear the door to the studio open, until the footsteps tapped across the wooden floor. Startled, Merliah turned and inadvertently dragged the sable brush over the trees instead of the field of wildflowers.

"Abby, you scared me."

"I'm sorry. I thought you heard me come in. I got a call from Antoine. He said you called him and told him you weren't selling two of your pieces. Then, you didn't show up for lunch. I figured you were here painting."

"Did he sound upset with me?"

"Confused is more like it. So am I for that matter. Do you want to tell me what's going on?"

Merliah sighed and turned back to her painting. "I can't."

"What do you mean you can't? Liah, I'm your friend, not just your art teacher. I care about you and what happens. You've made such progress and then you do this. Something happened when you disappeared for several hours, didn't it?"

"No."

"I don't believe you. The tone of your voice says otherwise." Abby came closer and placed a hand on Merliah's shoulder. "You seemed really strange after you met Mister Freeman. Did he do something?"

Mister Freeman? Why would she say him? Merliah's anxiety grew. Abby wouldn't let go of why she decided not to sell the paintings. How could she explain to her friend about them? Could she trust her to tell the truth? She'd have to take the leap and tell someone eventually. *Better to tell Abby than a doctor or my parents, who'd probably put me away for another five years, if not more. No, I have to trust Abby will keep my confidence.*

"Abby." The hesitation in her voice combined with biting her lip for a second, had the expression on Abby's face show concern, worrying Merliah. "Abby, I've done something. I don't know if you'll believe me, but I have to tell someone."

The women had become more of a sister and friend than any Merliah could remember having before the accident. Abby grabbed both of her hands. "Sweetie, did he touch you inappropriately?"

"Huh? Who?" By the time Merliah figured out who Abby referred, her friend answered.

"That Esteban guy."

"Oh, no, he…he did frighten me. My pulse kicked up a notch and goose bumps skittered up my arm when he touched my hand, but other than that he didn't do anything other than give me the creeps. I definitely knew I had to leave the party." She paused and watched Abby's face before continuing. "Not him. There's another man. He kind of saved me. But, I thought I made him up, in my head."

Abby's brow furrowed. "You're not making any sense. Who did you make up?"

"Sorin. The man of my dreams. He rescued me from my coma and he came to the gallery last night."

"What are you talking about? A man you dreamt about saved you. From the coma? How? What do you mean he was at the gallery? Who is this man?"

"I told you. Sorin. I can't describe it any better. I have created a world within my paintings and he joined me there. At the gallery last night. I thought he was imaginary like I made him up or something so I could cope with my condition. He's real, Abby. A living, breathing, and incredibly handsome man made love to me in my dreams and followed me into the landscape. When he left, I don't know where he disappeared to because someone came in and I couldn't get out until after they left the area. I can't sell the paintings because someone else could innocently get transported into the landscape. You have to help me get them back and I'll give them the new ones."

"Liah, you're still not making any sense."

"Then take me to the gallery and I'll show you."

"I don't think going there is a good idea. Why don't I get Doctor Wright? Maybe he can give you something to calm you down."

No amount of convincing appeared to work with Abby. Persuasion wasn't her best suit, but Merliah took a deep breath to calm her agitation and tried again. "Abby, please. Take me to Rousseau's. I don't need to see Doctor Wright. I need to retrieve my paintings."

Abby didn't speak for a few moments. "All right. Let me make the arrangements for you to leave. Stay here and finish the new canvases. I'll be back in a little while."

"Thank you, Abby. Thank you."

Merliah watched her friend depart the studio and then turned her attention back to the duplicate landscape. She furiously worked to finish at least one of the paintings. The one with the castle would probably have to be completed later, after she had the originals in her hands.

Time seemed to pass slowly as she diligently brushed on the vibrant colors of paint, bringing the new painting to life. The only difference would be the lack of the energy she imprinted when she finished.

Thoughts drifted to Sorin as the final touches were placed on the stretched canvas. Last night had been glorious. The intimate times she spent in her dreams with him were exciting, but to be with him in the flesh was beyond magnificent. The mere thought of how his skin against hers brought tingles to her core.

Squirming in the seat, she mentally chastised herself for thinking about him again. Any opportunity she had with him would be short-lived once he found out how she truly looked. As much as the thought of never seeing him again hurt, she had to forget contacting him again. Her life was doomed to an existence of being alone, veiled to strangers and loved by no man. Only family, a few close friends, and her doctors would know the real her.

The door to the studio creaked open.

"Abby?" Merliah asked as she swiveled on the chair. "Doctor Wright?" She glanced at Abby, and from the expression on her friend's face the trip to the gallery wouldn't happen.

"Merliah, I understand you're having some anxiety. Why don't we go back to your room and I'll give you something to calm you," Dr. Wright said.

"How could you, Abby? I told you there's nothing wrong with me that I needed to see him." Merliah's heart raced when two nurse's assistants appeared around the corner. *This isn't good.*

"I'm sorry, sweetie. But, you were talking about strange things. I had to tell Doctor Wright."

When Dr. Wright pulled out a syringe from his pocket, Merliah panicked. "No, no. Don't do this. There's nothing wrong with me. Please, doctor, I'm fine. Really I am. I have to go to the gallery. I have to get my paintings. Please, please don't do this. I'm an adult and I can leave here anytime I want."

"Unfortunately, Merliah, that's not true. Your parents are your legal guardians. I contacted them after Abby discussed your story. They've authorized this until they can arrive and we reevaluate you. This will help calm you and won't hurt a bit."

"No, no. This isn't happening. You can't do this."

There was no use struggling at this point. The two men had moved to either side of her and restrained her with their arms around her waist and each holding one of her arms. The doctor drew closer and rolled up the sleeve on her shirt, swabbed the outer bicep of her left arm and then inserted the needle into the muscle. Within moments, Merliah's vision began to blur and her body relaxed. She tried to speak, but the words to her own ears didn't register as decipherable.

No! Please, someone help me. Sorin, if you really can hear me, make them stop. You aren't a dream. Come and tell them, you're not made up.

Then blackness overtook her consciousness.

Chapter Twenty

It's a New Night

After rising from his day of restless sleep, Sorin walked into the kitchen of the penthouse and found Stefan there. "Did my delivery arrive?" In the back of his mind, he'd hoped the voice of Merliah ringing in his head the middle of the day had been her trapped in the landscape, calling for him to help her out. Maybe what I heard were her calls from there after the delivery to the apartment. *I can only dream.* He chuckled to himself.

"Good evening to you too, brother."

"Good evening. Well?"

"I haven't checked yet. Your deliveries aren't a priority when I awaken. Check with Alex when she gets up."

"Fine. What nourishment do you have available tonight? Or do I need to go out?"

"Actually, I have a couple donors that should be here any moment. No need to go out." Stefan moved from around the center island and sat on the stool positioned behind the raised granite bar. "Did you rest or have another dream with your imaginary woman?"

"She's not imaginary. I told you last night. She's real and I'll prove it to you. Tonight. If I have to return to the Berger Institute, I will."

"Okay, okay. I believe you. But, I need to check with Alex before I take off with you."

The plod of bare feet striding across the wooden floor drew Sorin's attention. He snapped his head around over his shoulder and saw Alex sauntering into the kitchen. "Check with me for what, Stefan?"

"Ah, *prinţesa mea.* Did you sleep well?"

The red-haired woman looked from his friend then to him and back. Alex may have been irritating, but Sorin had to admit, nothing got past her.

"I did, but that's not why I feel this great. I need you to come with me to the gallery."

"Why? I have business to take care of and no time to schmooze with pretentious humans who think they know art."

"I got a lead on the serial killer last night. There was another murder and I have an idea. I need to go back to the gallery and check it out."

"Why didn't you go today?"

"I would have, but I fell asleep and when I woke up a few hours ago, I figured I'd wait until you rose because this killer is a vampire. He's in your territory so I'm giving you the opportunity to bring the rogue to justice."

"Who?"

"I need to confirm my suspicions, but I think I saw one of the victims in a painting at the gallery. Now, how do you think that's possible unless the artist was there at the scene of the crime?"

"*Prinţesa.* If another artist at the gallery were a vamp, I'd have known it. Which one are you accusing?"

"Wait, bro. Last night there was a moment I sensed another. Remember?"

"You two noticed something? When? Before or after I left?"

"Shortly after, but I didn't get a good look at him. He disappeared around the corner to another room. Sorin wasn't feeling great and I was more interested in getting him out of the gallery."

"Since when do vamps get sick?" Alex stared at Stefan then to Sorin.

"I wasn't sick, just in need of a quick blood fix."

The stern expression on her face took Sorin aback. "Tell me you didn't hit the streets, say close to the gallery and went a little too far."

"Alex! What are you implying? I took him to the club and took care of everything there."

"Sorry, it's just there was another murder last night. A woman was murdered not far from the gallery. Her blood was drained. I recognized her from the show." She turned to Stefan. "You'd have recognized her too since you made the comment about her having hair like mine. Remember?"

"The redhead in the emerald dress. She's dead?"

"As a door nail. Found in an alley behind a building several doors down from Rousseau's. Bite marks, blood, the whole vamp MO. Just to give you a heads up, Chief Rodriguez thinks you have something to do with it." Alex walked to the refrigerator, opened the door and pulled out a can of Cherry Coke. "Of course, I told him that's nonsense. And, if you found out there was a vamp in your family violating the law, you'd take care of him." She turned and stared at Stefan. "Right?"

"*Prinţesa*, where is this going? You don't trust me?"

"Oh, I trust you. But, I have to wonder if there isn't someone trying to set you up." She turned and walked to the pantry. "You know, trying to take over the family. Maybe one of Dragos' former members is behind it. Have you thought about that? Manny Rodriguez seemed pretty convinced you had something to do with the murders. He keeps saying the mayor's office is pushing for resolution. I think that's where we should look. Maybe the politics of vampires and humans is raising its ugly head again. Dad always told me to either follow the money trail or know there's sex and politics involved." She returned to the breakfast bar with a bag of Cheese Doodles and sat down on a stool next to Sorin.

Every cell in his body craved the warmth of a woman. Not any woman, his angel. "She's right, Stefan. Did you vet the remaining vamps after the take-over? Personally, I would have ended their existence immediately. If this is political, the tentacles could run all the way to Washington. Or even the High Tribunal. Dragos humiliated and made a mockery of the elders. This could be their way of getting rid of you as a roundabout way of seeking revenge. You are his heir, after all."

"Technically, you are too, my brother."

"Yes, but I live in Europe, far away from their governing powers. I answer to the European council, not the North American. The idea has merit, but I can't imagine they would do this to you."

Stefan rubbed his chin. "No. I don't believe any of this is possible. I know I would have heard some chatter through my network if the council voiced displeasure with my governing. No, this is the work of a rogue and I'll get to the bottom of it. Sooner than later and more like tonight. I will not have humans dictating how I run my family." Stefan stood and pushed the barstool forcefully, nearly knocking it over. Sorin caught the edge and broke the momentum.

Alex jerked in her seat.

"Stefan. Chill. I'm not accusing you. I have a gut feel as to who is responsible, but I need your help. Come with me to Rousseau's and I'll show you."

"What's at the gallery?" Sorin asked raising a brow.

"I have to check out a painting I saw."

Sorin squirmed, his heart dropped to his stomach. He swirled his barstool around to face the woman. "What painting?"

"I don't want to say yet. You can come along if you want, Sorin."

Sorin and Stefan exchanged apprehensive glances. Sorin didn't have a good feeling about this situation. Was Alex referring to the painting by Merliah? *She doesn't look like she could harm an insect let alone another human being.*

"Of course, I'll go. Speaking of the gallery. Did Rousseau deliver my paintings today?"

"I don't know. I went to bed late and slept all day. Security would know though. Have you checked with them?"

"Not yet."

"I'll check, Sorin. Alex, get dressed and we'll go. I have to get to the bottom of these murders. This rogue is toast."

An hour later, the driver pulled up in front of the Rousseau Gallery with the three. Sorin had an uncomfortable and uneasy gut feeling about Merliah since awakening. The bizarre reaction to entering the landscape canvas the night before, craving blood to the point he nearly lost control unnerved him. Couple that with not hearing her call for him during his rest had him on edge. Now, this rogue vamp brought havoc to Stefan's territory. The trip away from his homeland hadn't turned out the way he'd hoped.

"Oh, my. Did we have an appointment tonight?" Antoine Rousseau walked toward the group. "Mister Bochinsky, was there a problem with your delivery?"

"Actually, yes. I'm missing two of my purchases. Would you like to explain?"

Practically falling all over himself to make clear, Rousseau appeared confused to Sorin. "I left you a message. Did you not receive it? There's...there's been a miscommunication with the artist deciding not to sell the other two pieces. She was supposed to be here this afternoon to replace the paintings with others, but she never showed up. I'm assuming she hasn't finished the substitutions."

"When did she contact you?"

"Around noon. She said Abby would bring her later in the day, but like I said, she never showed up."

"Abby? Who's she?"

"Oh, sorry. Abby, Abigail Mann is Miss Phoenix's teacher and I guess you could say her manager."

Sorin realized he stood alone with the gallery owner. At the far side of the room he caught sight of Stefan and Alex. He sensed unrest with Alex. "Excuse me. Let me finish with my friends and then I'd like to continue this conversation."

With quick strides across the marble floor, he came up behind the other two just as they stopped in front of a large mix media portrait hanging on the wall.

"Oh...my...god," Alex said. She pulled a photograph from a folder. "Look, forget all the accessories. It's the same person. I knew this looked familiar."

"Let me see," Stefan said.

Sorin peered between the two. He glanced at the art on the wall, then to the photograph Stefan held. There was a strong resemblance, he had to admit.

Alex turned on her heels. "Antoine, who's this artist? Or better yet, I need to know everything about him. An address, phone number, and his entire file if you have one would be a great start."

"But...but, I can't give out private information about my clients." Rousseau stumbled over his words as he approached.

"You can and will. This is part of an FBI investigation." She reached into her trouser pocket and retrieved her identification.

"Okay. Follow me, but I really don't know what you're looking for. Mister Freeman is a very nice man. Strange, but nice."

"Well, we'll see about that," Alex said, crossing her arms across her chest.

Sorin followed behind until the group past the area where Merliah's paintings, now his, were. Without any indication to his friend, he slipped away and headed to the smaller gallery.

* * * *

Sneaking out wasn't difficult. *Hell, how many times have I done it the past several months to paint?* Merliah stared out the cab window into the night landscape whirring by and watching blindly as the city lights slowly came into view. The institute slowly fell behind. The nurses were used to seeing her come and go at all times of the day and night. She waited until the shift change when there was always less attention paid to her. Being a model patient/resident of the institute didn't hurt either, but she took no chances. The fact she'd been drugged may have changed protocol in her case.

As the driver maneuvered the cab through the traffic, Merliah strained her memory to determine if the driver really was headed in the right direction. Not that time was of the essence, but the sooner she returned to the gallery and remove the two paintings, the better she'd feel. She hoped and prayed no one had touched them since last night.

The evening before with Sorin had been a mistake, in every way. He never should have found her in the painting. She created the scene as a special place for her alone. Never in her wildest dreams had she expected anyone to find her and now someone had purchased the landscape and could find out the secret. In her limited experience, she honestly couldn't imagine anyone would buy her work. She'd only been painting for a few months. Who mastered painting enough to have a show and sell their art in such a short period of time? *No, none of this should have happened. My paintings aren't good enough to sell. I can't believe Abby talked me into doing this.*

The driver brought the cab to a rolling stop in front of the Rousseau Gallery. "Would you mind waiting? I shouldn't be but a few minutes."

"Sure, but you know the meter continues running," the gruff voice came from the front seat.

"Yes, that's okay." Merliah climbed out of the back seat with ease and proceeded to the entrance. After adjusting the veil covering her entire head, she wished she'd taken the time to put on a wig to cover her head and only wear the smaller mask. The full veil drew more attention to her than she liked, especially wearing only jeans and a T-shirt with a black shroud. She knew the outfit stuck out like a sore thumb in this neighborhood of upscale shops and art galleries, but her true appearance would have drawn far worse than curious looks.

Over the past several days, her need for a cane to support her gait improved to the point tonight she didn't even notice at first the walking stick wasn't needed. Therapy had been going well, but considering she'd been drugged and slept most of the day, her muscles should have been tighter. Except, they weren't. *Hmm.*

The nagging in the back of her mind about how she acquired the mysterious abilities and her miraculous recovery from the injuries resurfaced. How could she go from a coma six to seven months ago and accomplish the physical dexterity now? The therapists were always remarking how they were amazed with her recovery. And then her painting was an entirely different subject. The only thing that came to mind was what Dr. Wright had said about her brain activity. *There have been some changes, but nothing significant.* Could the vampire blood have changed her? The little amount she remembered Robbie saying he gave her after one of her surgeries couldn't have done this to her. If so, why weren't more humans like her?

The gallery had an eerie lack of sound as she entered. Surprised no alarm went off and no employee had been near the entrance. She glanced around and since no one was there to stop her from proceeding further, she walked toward the area where her paintings were on display.

Entering the unlit room, her eyes slowly adjusted to the darkness. Feeling along a wall she found a light switch. The drop lights came on, shining spots on the white walls where her artwork once hung. Her jaw dropped. All the paintings were gone, except the two she came for. The remaining two paintings were propped onto easels. She crept closer and lifted the landscape from the stand. "Oh thank goodness. They're still here." Getting them back safe with her had been her main priority. Standing here looking at the landscape brought back fond memories of the night before. With Sorin.

"I'm glad they are too." The familiar deep voice out of the blackness from behind startled her.

Merliah squeezed her eyes, hoping she heard wrong. Setting the framed piece aside, leaning against the wall, she pondered what to do next now Sorin stood so close. Why did he have to be here now? After taking a shaky breath, she turned around, her hands trembling and faced her worst scenario of seeing Sorin again. She adjusted the veil. The day was bad enough, now the night promised to be no better. "I'm not stealing my own paintings if that's what you're thinking."

Sorin cursed under his breath. "I didn't say you were, angel. But, the problem is, I've purchased them and they should have been delivered today. You wouldn't have anything to do with that, or is that why you're here?" There was a hint of humor in his tone. "Merliah? Why are you wearing a veil?"

Her heart beat hard as she watched her dream man move closer. If only she could escape before he touched her or tried to remove the veil, because she knew he would try. The situation was deteriorating at supersonic speed. She had to come up with something to get out of there. Quick. Her mind went blank. What could she say that wouldn't seem strange? *Yes, I wear a veil because I'm a hideous monster to look at and don't want to scare the shit out of you. No, that's not good.* She brought her hand to the veil. "I…uh…had a facial peel today and my face blistered. I wouldn't want to scare anyone if they saw the way I look right now." *Yeah, that was good and I hope he bought it.*

Even with the dim light, she could make out his splendid features. He looked the same as he did last night, maybe better, even with the scar on his cheek. Lord, she wanted to reach up and pull him to her, but that would be a mistake. A really big mistake. She had to get out of there, with her paintings, and return to the Institute. Severing all contact with Sorin would be her only salvation. He could never know her true self or her special abilities. Another, more beautiful, needed to be standing by his side, not her.

"A what? I'm not sure what a *peel* of your face is, but your skin is flawless. Why in the world did you do something that would blister your beautiful skin?" He took another step forward and she backed up. His eyes narrowed. He had to be confused by the explanation, she decided. *I have to get out of here quick before he finds out.*

"I had...some...discolorations. You couldn't tell because of all the make-up I used to cover the flaws." She turned to the remaining painting on the easel.

"You have no flaws to me, Merliah. You're an angel."

Instant dizziness shook her to the core with fear and excitement from being alone with Sorin. She would have to do whatever it took to get out of the gallery before falling prey to his attentions. Then, she felt him step up behind her, his powerful torso just inches from her back. He gently ran his hands up and down her arms, then over her shoulders, brushing the veil. She hitched a breath.

"Dammit, angel," he growled low under his breath and the vibration of his deep tone rumbled through her entire body. "What are you doing to me? Playing the mysterious woman who haunts my dreams and waking hours, to tease and taunt me?" His hands came down and patted across her hips and down her buttocks, then glided along her thighs. Merliah moaned involuntarily at the sudden need she felt in her core. She struggled to keep her hands from wandering to touch his body, to keep from turning around and lacing her arms around him.

When he pressed his body against hers, holding her back to his chest, her breath caught in her throat. She felt his massive erection pressing against her lower back and her knees almost gave out under her. "I...I'm not doing anything to you."

"Then why aren't you selling the paintings to me? They are special and I consider them my personal favorites, especially the wildflowers."

She turned in time to catch him winking. Certainly didn't help that he followed up with a wicked grin, making her insides flutter and knees almost give out from under her. "You're right they are special, but last night shouldn't have happened. No one can know what happens if they touch the surface. It...it could be very dangerous. We were almost caught." *You're very dangerous, but I don't know why.*

"I didn't feel threatened with you there with me. I've never felt so at peace than when we're together in the woods behind the field of wildflowers in the make-believe world you created. When I came out was the real bitch. That's why I wanted to take them. For safekeeping, of course. They will be our special place."

Closing the distance between them again, he stepped forward and encircled her in a loose embrace.

Merliah shook her head, pulled from his grip and stepped back, slightly bumping the easel. "No, you stay away. We can't be together again, Sorin. You can't have my paintings either. They're not for sale. I told Mr. Rousseau I'll replace them, but you can't have these." She paused at the realization that he was the collector who purchased all of her paintings. "You? It was you who bought all my art pieces?"

"I am. Now tell me what is wrong, angel. Why can't we be together? I came all this distance to find you and I did. This can't end. We just found one another after all these months."

"No, I mean I'm sorry. Abby said I sold them, but you didn't know I was the one who painted them?"

He shook his head. "Not exactly. All I knew was your name. Phoenix. I knew there was something special about your work before I followed you last night. Merliah, why can't we be together? What aren't you telling me?" He took another step closer.

"Stay back. Please don't do this, Sorin. I'm grateful for you saving me and now I know you're real and not my imagination or that I'm going crazy, but we can't be together. Please, let me be and let this end here. You...you just don't understand I can't do this. I'm not good enough for you." Tears began to form, but she fought from having them spill over and show weakness more than she already was.

"Where is this coming from, angel?" He reached his arms out to her and she jerked away. "Tell me. Why are you afraid of me? Do you know who and what I am? Is that what's causing you to pull away?"

Merliah looked at him quizzically. *What is he talking about?* She didn't know how to answer. Did his questions center around the scar on his face, which as she remembered, didn't exist within the painting? His blemishes disappearing were no different than what happens to hers when she entered the other world. "I don't fear you. I did at first, but not anymore. Who are you?"

"I could ask you the same thing. You have magical powers I can't even begin to understand. I've been around a long time and have never seen the abilities you possess."

"The make-believe place, you mean?"

"That and how you were able to get into my mind, my dreams I shouldn't be having."

"You got into mine. I was in a coma. How...how did you do that? I don't understand how you brought me out of the pits of hell, the darkness, and touched my unconsciousness. I thought you had the powers."

"I saved you only because you called to me, angel." The volume of his voice trailed off. He paused and stared at her. She didn't like the way he leered at her. More like shock and curiosity. "Merliah, what has happened to your hair?" He touched her shoulder, brushing the veil aside.

"Please don't." She placed her hand over his. Electricity sparked between them. Merliah couldn't let him touch her or she'd fall under his spell. All logic flew out of her head when his mesmerizing and erotic gaze captured hers. "What are we doing? I don't even know you. What we had last night was great, but it's over. That's that, and nothing more."

"You don't believe in us? What has happened to us has touched me in ways I never thought existed anymore. I know you feel the same, angel. Trust in us."

Get the paintings and leave before you give in Liah.

As she reached for the paintings, he snagged the sheer fabric and pulled it away from her head. In shock, she snapped around and for the longest moment, they stared at one another. With heart beating hard, she panicked. All she could think about entailed getting away as quickly as possible before he could ask any questions. Embarrassment. Fear. Anger. Every emotion raced through her body and mind. She ran as fast as her disabled legs could take her. Considering their condition, she moved fast. As she ran from the gallery, she clutched the edges of the painting so not to touch the surface. She made it to the front entrance and pushed the door open. Fortunately, she spied the taxi still parked only a few feet from the door.

"Merliah!"

She glanced over her shoulder and saw Sorin closing the distance between them. With one last push forward, she made her way to the vehicle and safety.

"Let me get that for you." Came a man's voice from behind, out of the dark, and startled Merliah. Not Sorin's for sure, and she remembered the cab driver's voice having a Hispanic accent.

She peered up and saw the face matching the voice. *The scary, strange man from the night before.* The one who made her skin crawl. "Uh, thank you," she murmured, too stunned to say more.

"Merliah!" Sorin called out, standing at the door to the gallery.

She slid into the backseat of the vehicle, followed by the man. "What are you doing?" Her voice cracked. She held the painting close, but not enough to touch the surface. Then she realized she only picked up one, the castle and mountain scene. *Oh, no. I hope no one gets to the other one.*

A tap on the window drew both their attention. "Take me back to the institute, sir," she said as she viewed Sorin's visage pressing against the glass pane. "Quickly, please."

Shivers skittered up and down her spine as she caught the wicked grin on the creepy man's face. His thigh grazed hers. The slight touch sent goose bumps to the surface. The sensation didn't cause arousal, but it certainly did something to her, something she didn't quite feel comfortable with.

"So, Phoenix, or should I call you Merliah? Tell me, who are you exactly?"

"Merliah is fine. Who are you?"

The corners of his mouth turned up in a wicked grin. She shuddered.

"Tell me, how did you create your *special* paintings, princess?"

Chapter Twenty-One

A Princess in Danger

"Merliah!" Sorin cried out as he slammed his fist on the back of the cab pulling away from the curb.

"Sorin? What's going on?" Stefan asked, patting Sorin on the shoulder. "Who was the woman?"

"Hey, what's all the yelling about?" Alex asked.

Sorin flicked attention to his friend's woman, then back to Sorin. "You saw her?"

"Not really. I only caught a glimpse of the backside of a woman running out the door with a painting. Was she stealing your landscape?"

"No, not really. She's the artist."

"Who was the man? He looked familiar."

"His name is Esteban. The artist you were inquiring about, Miss Alexandra," Antoine added as he sashayed beside her.

"Are you sure?" she asked.

"That man is your suspect, Alex? This isn't good. He's a vamp," Stefan said.

"He must be the one we sensed last night. How can we find out where that cab is going? Merliah is in danger." Sorin answered even though Stefan directed his inquiry to Alex.

"I want him as bad as you do, brother. He's a rogue, in my territory, killing innocents. He's soon to be a non-existent vamp if I have my way. I'll do what is necessary to find him, and the woman." Stefan walked toward the entrance. "*Prinţesa*, can you work with me on this? We have an address and we know he's a vamp which means we can track him."

"Oh, *mon Dieu*. Are you serious about Esteban? He's a vampire? That's why you asked all those questions, isn't it?" He flailed his arms and the look of terror crossed his face. "He...he could have bit me at any time. Oh, *mon Dieu*! I think I'm going to be sick." Antoine rushed into the gallery covering his mouth with one hand and the other his stomach.

"What's with him?" Sorin asked of Stefan.

"Hell if I know. I thought he knew who and what we are. Evidently not."

"Okay. I've got Johnson on his way here and we've got the cavalry following. Do you boys want to go ahead and I'll meet up with you at this suspect's apartment. Here's the address." Alex pressed the small, wrinkled paper into Stefan's hand.

"Will you be safe until your partner arrives, *prinţesa?*" Stefan grasped Alex's hands, and then bent to kiss her.

As much as Sorin liked to see his friend happy with his woman, he saw the exchange of affection between the two a waste of precious time while Merliah was in danger. He pushed away his growing anxiety and tried several times to make a mind touch with Merliah, but nothing happened. Probably, he thought, because he couldn't concentrate with all the outside noise and distractions. The high humidity of South Florida felt like a sauna against his cool flesh and didn't help his agitated state. "Stefan, we have to go. I sense Merliah is in danger."

Stefan turned and gave him a steely glint. "Fine, let's go. I want this rogue tonight." His friend reached into his jeans pocket and pulled out a cell phone. A few minutes later, the driver pulled to the curb.

As the SUV sped down the side streets, weaving toward the main street, Sorin settled into the backseat. *Why didn't I take her in my arms when I removed the veil? Shock, that's what I expressed instead of love. Now I understand what she meant by scars. Fuck! What have I done?*

Lying down, he closed his eyes and began to tune out the white noise of the engine and concentrated on touching Merliah's mind. He had to get through to her and say how sorry he was. Everything began to make sense with their encounters. The paintings were her escape and she reached out to him in a way no one ever had. Then, when faced with the reality, he froze. He failed her and their love. *Fuck!*

With a calming breath, he cleared his thoughts and called for her. *Merliah. Let me in, angel.* He paused. *Merliah, please let me in. I'm sorry I reacted the way I did. Forget that for now. Merliah, let me come to you. You are in danger.* He ceased his calling to listen. To sense her, something, anything so he'd be able to get through to her. *Merliah, the man I saw get into the cab with you is a...he's dangerous, angel. You have to get away from him.*

"Anything yet, brother?"

Sorin's eyes snapped open, and turned his head, meeting his friend's concerned expression. "No."

"Keep trying. If there's any way to see her surroundings to help us scope out an advantage, I'll take it."

"Let me be so I can concentrate, Stefan. I know what I have to do. Let me know when we arrive." And with a gruff command, Sorin resumed the psychic appeals to his angel. Somehow he had to convince her to listen. Her life depended on his getting through. He chastised himself for reacting the way he did at the gallery. His lack of saying anything in response to the unveiling and no doubt the expression on his face had to have said more than any words could have. For a few blurry moments he couldn't think straight enough to make sense of what he'd seen. A scarred and battered woman stood before him who sounded and acted like Merliah, but her appearance wasn't the same as the night before. His mind raced trying to put all the pieces together. A rehabilitation facility. A make-believe world. Dreams. Reality. Darkness. Scars. They shared dreams, scars, and a make-believe world where they could escape and be what they used to be away from the reality of their horrendous existences.

Merliah. Please, forgive me and let me touch you. Let me come to you, angel. Merliah? You have to hear me. You are in danger from Esteban. Still no answer came and he had to take another tactic. Soft pleading words weren't working.

Merliah? Answer me. I command you to let me inside your mind. Now, Merliah! You are to do as I say. Answer me. I have to see where you are. Open your mind and eyes so I can save you.

The silence began to unnerve him. Crossing his arms over his wide chest, the breaths he took caused a rise and fall in quick succession as he attempted one more plea for her to answer. Focusing on her image, he launched all his imprinted senses of her to concentrate his mind touch. *Merliah. Hear me. I demand you allow me into your mind. I'm on my way to rescue you. Stay strong. Merliah, answer me. Now!* The demand was clear and forceful in his voice.

Sorin?

The sound of her awaited response was barely audible in the deep recesses of his mind. But he answered. His eyes popped open. "I have her!"

* * * *

Merliah's head ached, her skin tingled, and the man who insinuated his way into the cab at the gallery was the same one she met the night before at the exhibition. The one who gave her the creepy-crawlies sat within inches of her in the backseat. At first he was a welcome reprieve to forget what happened in the gallery. The astonishment on Sorin's face spoke volumes as to his reaction seeing her true appearance. He was shocked by the widening of his eyes and the tensing of his mouth. She panicked and bolted out of the gallery. She retrieved one of the paintings, but the other remained, still a problem if anyone touched it.

Fighting back the tears, she tuned out the man named Esteban. The throbbing in her head didn't subside. As she rubbed her temples, she watched his mouth move as he spoke, but couldn't hear a word he said. Something about him frightened her beyond reason, and she struggled to calm her racing heart. Then, the sound of an annoying gnat tickled her ears and she swore a voice called to her. A man's voice? *Sorin?*

How was he contacting her? Normally, she was asleep and initiated the dreams where they met. Up until last night, she thought they were only dreams, never reality. Now, she heard him calling her. Closing her eyes, she focused on the buzzing in her head. In the other ear rang the natter of Esteban. His tone ratcheted up to annoying making it difficult to hone in on Sorin's voice.

"Why are we stopping here?" Merliah leaned forward, resting her elbow on the back of the front seat. "Sir, this isn't the Berger Institute."

"I'm sorry lady. Your guy gave this address after you got in. I thought he was with you. If you wanta go back to the institute I can take you, but will cost since I have to backtrack." The gruff driver turned his head, glancing over his shoulder.

"I don't care. I have to get back."

Merliah felt the creepy touch of a cold hand resting on her forearm. She snapped her head around.

"You're coming with me, Merliah." He flipped a couple large bills at the driver, locked onto her wrist and tugged her close.

Shivers ran up and down her spine. *Ohmigod! Sorin help me.* The grip on her wrist tightened. "Let me go. I'm not going with you."

"My little princess, you will." His voice lowered, and then he bared his fangs. "Take this," he said as he extended a finger, with the tip covered in a small amount of blue liquid.

Merliah gasped. "No."

"Take it!" He smeared the fluid over her lips. "Lick it, now!"

"Jesus, Mary and Joseph. You're a...a vampire." The driver stuttered and fumbled with the door latch.

"Please, don't hurt me. I'll do what you want." At this point, Merliah shook like a leaf on a blustery day. She licked the bitter solution, anything to try and stay alive by doing as the maniac demanded.

"Bring the painting," Esteban said and exited the cab. "Wait over by the door while I take care of the driver."

After taking a hard swallow, she took a deep breath, grabbed the painting and exited on the street side of the vehicle. For a second, she contemplated running as far and fast as her legs could carry her down the street screaming for help. The thought vanished quickly as she realized he'd catch her before she traveled ten feet. He was a vampire. From what little she knew about them, they were lightning fast while she only recently learned to walk without a cane. She'd existed in darkness over four years and didn't want a repeat engagement. By the time she reached the entry door to the building, she felt a cool rush of air graze the back of her neck. She closed her eyes and called to Sorin in her mind. He had to hear and find her before this man, this vampire, did something she couldn't bear to think about.

"You listen well, princess. Now, you're going to tell me everything about you. Let's go." Esteban wrapped his arm around her free arm. The other held the painting.

The adrenaline, laced with fear and terror, surged through her veins. She made several more internal pleas for Sorin to find and help her, but she began to feel strange, like her body floated. Then, as Esteban guided her through the lobby to the elevator, she had an awful and disconcerting thought—the question of how she could communicate with Sorin mentally and while awake. In the recesses of her memory, she remembered Robbie telling her about his experiences with his friends and the vampire club they frequented. Vampires had powers, supernatural type abilities which surpassed any she'd ever heard of in humans. Could one of those skills be telepathy? Is that how she'd contacted him the first time to save her from the pitch black existence of her coma?

"You're contacting him, aren't you?"

"I–I'm not saying anything."

"You are. I can see it in your eyes." He stepped closer and stared into her eyes.

She felt a sharp pain shoot through her head and closed her eyes.

His hands cupped her face and held tightly. "How are you doing this? You're not letting me in. Hmm, another interesting ability."

The elevator dinged.

As if in a trance, she entered the lift with the stranger's grip wrapped around her arm again. She glanced down at the castle painting in her hand. *Could I hide in there when he's not looking? If I disappear into the picture, can Sorin hear me? What if he is a vampire, surely he will have the abilities to save me from this lunatic sure to do me harm.*

The ding of the digital bell when they reached the designated floor and followed by the doors sliding open drew her out of the escape thought possibility. With a tug on her arm, she followed her captor. She had to hold on in hopes Sorin would find her in time. There was no indication what this Esteban man wanted other than the secret of her art, and she'd be damned if she told him, but her will to not say anything grew weak. *What's wrong with me? I feel so strange.*

With an expression cold and fierce, he leaned into her. "We're here. Do not try and run away. I'd catch you before you got ten feet." He released her arm and dug into his pants pocket and pulled out a set of keys. He inserted one and turned the latch to the door with twenty-three in three-inch brass numbers attached to the red painted entry. Grabbing her wrist, he yanked her over the threshold and the two stepped into the dark apartment. With one quick flick of the switch, recessed lights illuminated the room.

"Is this your place?"

"I'm not here with you to socialize. I'm in no mood for such frivolities. Now, get over there and sit. I have to prepare."

Merliah swallowed hard. *Prepare?* "For what? Why are you doing this? I don't know anything." Her words came out slurred, her head hurt and she felt like she was floating.

"Oh, I'm sure you know quite a lot. You're going to tell me how you disappear into the painting. I was inside, in the field. I saw the sun and didn't die. I want to know everything." He grabbed her arm and pushed her to the couch.

She stumbled and dropped the painting. "I'm not helping you."

"You will or I'll take care of you like the others."

"The others?" she asked in a low voice. *Oh, Sorin hurry. I'm scared now.*

He laughed. "Yes, they thought they were getting sex and blood from a vamp, but I showed them. They got exactly what they wanted and more. They are immortalized in my work."

"Ohmigod! The women in your paintings are...are really dead? You...you killed...them." She pulled her legs close to her chest, wrapping her arms around them. "What are you going to do with me?"

"For you, princess, I'll do something special, but only if you give me what I want. I didn't plan to do this, but when I first saw you come out of that landscape painting at the gallery and then you cavorting with the hideous vampire creature, I knew you had something powerful and special. I want it *and* I'll get it." He turned and left the room, walking down a hallway to where she assumed had to be a bedroom.

The throbbing pain burst into her head again. She rubbed her temples. *Ohmigod, what's going on?* She attempted to glance around the room to see if she could find something, anything to protect herself with. A heavy book, a sharp instrument, or maybe just pull herself together and leave. She pushed up from the sofa, felt a bit wobbly, but managed to stand and began to walk. Halfway to the door, she felt his hand on her shoulder.

"Princess, where do you think you're going? Do not make this more difficult."

"Pl–lease, let m–me go." Nerves and fear ramped up and her voice cracked.

Forcefully, he turned her around. "You're not such a tough woman, are you?" He stepped behind her and massaged her shoulders, edging up to her neck. "You are one ugly human, princess. No self-respecting vamp would want to be caught dead with you. Unless you can offer him something. Like me."

Tears tumbled over the edge and down her cheeks.

"If you think that filthy creature at the gallery loves you or will find you, you're sorely mistaken. We'll give you what you deserve."

"I'm not ugly and he...he loves me." She shrugged off his hands and turned. "You don't know me, or him. He's on his way here to save me. You'll see."

"I know who and what he is and I'm not stupid, princess. You're bullshitting me. He doesn't know where to find us. I'm not one of his little puppets in his ridiculous blood family." His voice elevated to shrill as he pushed her forward. "Move."

She stumbled and fell to her knees. As she looked up she saw the painting. *I can get there and hide. Sorin, if you can hear me, please hurry.* She crawled a few feet before a large hand fisted her top and yanked her to her feet.

"You blood whore, you think this fucking vampire is your long-lost savior, your knight in shining armor? He can't save you because I'm smarter than he is. All of them. They created me and I'll make sure they pay, just like the stupid humans who made fun of me." His words squealed in her ears as a feeling of euphoria swept through her body. "You're going to tell me who you really are and what kind of powers you possess. What's with the disappearing into that painting?" He squinted with an evil glare at her, and a vein pulsing in his neck.

With what doggedness she had left, she yelled at him, but even to her ears sounded weak, not strong. "You're crazy! I'm not telling you anything." She may have been frightened, but she would fight for as long as she could. With every part of her being and last ounce of strength, she pulled against him to break free of his embrace.

"You will." A low growl came from deep in his chest. He grabbed her wrist and spun her around, and she flopped onto her back.

Rip. Her cotton T-shirt shredded like tissue as he yanked it up over her head, exposing her bra. She struggled to get free, flailing her legs and arms, but his free hand pressed across her stomach, holding her in place. "You will pay for this, you freaky-looking bitch."

With one more surge of energy from deep in her muscles, she broke from his grip, turned and took a couple steps toward the painting, diving forward with her arms outstretched in front. With the tips of her fingers, she managed to reach the edge of the canvas as she fell flat to the floor. Within seconds she was sucked into the vortex and the dizziness, whirling and blackness overtook all her senses.

The ground became solid beneath her body, and she opened her eyes. Now inside the landscape of the painting, she scrambled to her feet and ran toward the distant stone manor house. She'd never been in this painting and wasn't sure what she'd find, but she had to hide there until Sorin found her. When she painted the building, she imagined being there. Within the walls she could find shelter and safety from the madman chasing her. With a quick glance over her shoulder, she spied the confused look on Esteban's face, still outside in the apartment. From his position she knew he stood peering down at her. As soon as he touched the painting he'd be inside and after her. Resolutely, she made a push to the small castle.

As she reached the entrance, she heard other voices. "Sorin, what the fuck was that?" *Sorin?* Someone else who sounded familiar was with him. Her heart raced from more than the run across the field of wildflowers leading to the far away castle. All she had to do was stay hidden long enough until Sorin could reach her. Surely, he'd follow into the painting. Before entering through the large double wood and metal door she peered in the direction of the voices, back to the portal between the two worlds. The small figure ran in her direction. *Esteban?* Pushing the door shut behind her, she didn't see a lock or latch to prevent her pursuer from gaining access. Abandoning the idea, she quickly looked around and saw a large, curving staircase.

With her new found strength, she charged up the stone risers two at a time. At the top of the landing, a vague sense that she'd been in the dwelling before overwhelmed her. She hesitated, and then chose to follow the hallway to the left, to the end. Just as she reached for the lever to open the door, she heard the latch at the front entry. *He's here!*

Slowly, she pushed the handle down trying not to make a sound and give her location away. Pressing against the door, she opened it enough to slide between the doorframe and the edge of the door. Once inside the dark room, she felt along the wall for a light switch, but found none. She eased into the room taking small steps, shuffling along the floor and extending her hands chest-high in front of her. Almost instinctively, she moved straight without moving right or left until she reached a fabric-covered wall which when she moved the material revealed a window. Light filtered into the room, enough to help her see the layout of the room. A bedroom or more like a sleeping chamber from a time past. One that appeared even more familiar than she could believe, even though she couldn't remember why.

She heard the voice of Esteban and panicked. Finding a place to hide until Sorin arrived was paramount. As her eyes adjusted, she scanned the room. Her attention held onto the canopy bed a few feet from where she stood. Closing her eyes, she felt paralyzed by the sight. Spinning around the entire room was familiar. She'd been there before, not here in the painting, but in her dreams. With Sorin. *Is this his house, his bedroom, where we met and...*

"Ohmigod," she murmured. "I created this from my dreams of him."

Merliah's heart pounded hard in her chest. She took a deep breath and turned away from the bed continuing to scan the room for a place to conceal her presence. Then, there in the far corner a large wardrobe. Hopefully, the cabinet would be large enough to hide from Esteban. Just as she closed the door, she heard a tap on the bedroom entrance. She couldn't breathe, her heart beating so fast she thought she'd have an attack.

The turn of the lever made a slight sound and the hinges squeaked. Obviously, whoever entered didn't care about stepping into the room quietly. She closed her eyes and said a silent prayer in hopes Sorin would find her before Esteban did.

Footsteps crossing the wooden floor could be heard, even from the makeshift closet and Merliah couldn't tell where in the room the owner of the noise traveled. A sudden streak of light slipped through the sliver of space of the armoire door and frame. She took another deep breath to calm her runaway heart and breathing. *What was that?*

"Come out, come out wherever you are." The childish, sing-song voice of Esteban's echoed in the otherwise silent room. The steps grew louder and then they ceased. Her breathing hitched as the door slowly creaked open. Blinking, her eyes couldn't adjust to the brightness outside the confines of her temporary sanctuary fast enough to make out the dark figure standing in front of her. The gleam of white teeth and reddened devilish eyes glowed were the only features she could identify.

"There you are, princess. Didn't you know you couldn't hide from me?" With a rapid thrust of his hand forward, he seized her arm and snatched her from the wardrobe. Tripping over her own two feet, she stumbled back from the force pulling her out of the cabinet. Her heart hammered against her chest. She pressed a hand on her chest as she took a deep breath to calm her nerves. After taking another step back, she gathered her wits and turned to run, praying the nightmare would end with Sorin coming to her rescue.

But, that didn't happen the way she hoped. Esteban's hand on her arm stopped her movement.

"You're becoming more trouble than it's worth." He growled softly. With a quick jerk, he dragged her several feet to the bed and then flung her onto the mattress without regard to the strength at which he did so. He moved over her and his hands tightened painfully on her arms, and she winced from his grip.

"Please don't hurt me," she cried out, then tried to scream but he covered her mouth then pinned her body with his.

Whack.

The slap across her face stung her skin and was hard enough to make her eyes water instantly.

"You're going to tell me how you created this place or I'll beat it out of you. Better yet, maybe I'll fuck it out of you. Would you like that, little blood whore?"

Remain calm, don't panic. Be brave. Sorin will come for me. She tried in vain to struggle against his grip, flailing her legs and twisting her body, but he was too strong. With whatever that blue stuff was he made her take in the cab still had a slight grip on her. Dizziness and a sense of ecstasy came on fast. *This isn't right.* When she couldn't fight the assailant off anymore and felt her mind drifting to a black abyss, she thought she heard another man's voice calling her name.

    Sorin?

Chapter Twenty-Two

A Knight in Shining Armor to the Rescue

"Merliah!"

Sorin and Stefan burst through the front door of Esteban's apartment just as Sorin witnessed Merliah falling into the picture. The suspected killer hovered over the art about to follow her.

"Who the fuck are you?" The angered perpetrator spit the venomous words out, almost hissing as he did.

"I'm Stefan Marin, the Master and Commander of this region's blood family. You are in violation of my rules. Stand down."

The rogue vampire laughed. "You're not my master. You're a disgusting creature who walks lock-step with the tyrannical leaders of our kind. I answer to no one." Then, he turned and leapt into the painting.

"Shit! Where did he go?"

"Stefan, I don't have time to explain. I have to save Merliah. She's in danger." Sorin stepped toward the landscape lying on the floor. He turned back to Stefan, examining his friend's confused expression. "They are in the painting. I'm going in. Stay here. Wait for Alex and the FBI. I'll need you to be here to grab that whack case when I bring him back."

He turned attention back to the painting and as he knelt down, he glanced over a shoulder. "Oh, and don't touch the front of the painting or you'll find yourself on the other side." He smiled then reached his hand and touched the center.

"What the..." were the last words Sorin heard before plummeting into the vortex. Upon landing, he took off in a full-out sprint toward the manor house. The small figure of the crazy rogue vamp was mere seconds ahead.

When he found his angel the first time among the trees of the other landscape he'd lost any advantage of being a vampire—the speed and strength, but not his ability to fight. And fight he would, to the death if need be. He didn't know why she appeared different when he'd removed the veil at the gallery earlier. All the other times he'd seen her, she was beautiful. A vision unlike any woman he'd been with. His angel. His salvation. His love. No longer feeling on the brink of insanity, unless he was crazy in love, he brushed aside the questions of who she really was in favor of saving her now and querying later.

As he approached the stone façade of the castle, he marveled at the precise details. Had Merliah created a duplicate model of his home from only their trysts in dreams? How accurate were the interior features? If they were true and correct, then there could be weaponry available to battle the other vamp. *If he's like me, he doesn't have his vampire abilities and can fall prey to human fallibility.*

Entering the reception hall transported Sorin back to his home in the mountains. The similarity was remarkable. Instinct had him going to the weaponry chamber hidden behind a tapestry of his family's coat of arms. The lapis, crimson, and gold colors were slightly faded. The replication remained impeccable. He pushed aside the edge and pushed on a carved stone which released a latch and an opening in the wall revealed another chamber. He squeezed through the slight space not wanting to alert the other vamp of his presence. After a few seconds, he retrieved the weapon he sought—his Templar knight sword.

The piece was magnificent and brought back many memories. Before unhooking the blade from the wall, he ran his fingers over the scarlet cross carved into the pommel. Weapon in hand, he left the room, not bothering with pushing the wall back into its closed position. No sound indicated where Merliah could be.

"Will my mind connection still work in here?" He closed his eyes and concentrated.

Merliah? Do you hear me? Where are you? Answer me, angel.

Faintly, he heard her voice. *Sorin? I'm upstairs, the bedroom at the end. Yours, I think.*

I'm coming, love.

Unsure if she heard, he took the stairs two at a time, then ran down the east wing hallway to the end. To his bed chamber.

The door gave way beneath a surge of strength engendered by love rather than from vampire ability. From the expression on the rogue's face, the surprise move worked. Sorin raised his sword. "Let her go!"

Esteban fisted a hand into Merliah's hair and yanked hard. Whipping her around, he wrapped his arm around her neck and braced his hand on the opposite shoulder. Continuing to grasp her hair, she fell back against his chest. "Come any closer and I'll break her pretty little neck."

The look of fear glared in Merliah's eyes. A low, guttural growl broached from deep in Sorin's throat. He made determined steps, cutting the blade through air, twisting and turning several times. His gaze focused on the rogue, trying to figure out an advantage without harming Merliah.

"Give it up, Esteban. Your vamp powers don't work in here. I have the weapon and you are no match for me."

A low chuckle came easily. "Ah, but I have her and the way I see it, she's more powerful than that antiquated piece of steel." He shuffled a few steps, dragging Merliah and maintaining a tight grip. "I swear I'll kill her right now if you come for me. Put your sword down. Now!"

Sorin's chest tightened. His free hand curled into a fist as the other gripped the pommel tighter. He couldn't let this bastard harm his angel. The situation was at a stand-off. Talking the rogue down would be his only choice. "Look, man, I'm putting my weapon down," he said as he dropped the sword. "You can let her go and walk out of here and I won't follow. You can slip out and vanish, just free the woman." If he convinced the maniac of this choice, the freak would run into Stefan and possibly the FBI on the other end. Sorin could remain with Merliah until he knew it was safe. He'd leave her in the safety of the castle until everyone departed. She then could exit and no one would see her true identity. *Yes, that is a good plan if the rogue accepts.*

"Do I look like I'm stupid? If the other grotesque creature and pathetic artist named Stefan isn't here with *you*, he's still in the apartment and waiting to attack me." He jerked Merliah and she whimpered. "She comes with me."

Tension coiled inside Sorin, threatening to spring forward in full out panic. He couldn't allow Merliah to follow the maniacal vamp back to the real world, not with so many possible witnesses to see her true identity. Once Esteban reached the other side he'd turn into a vicious and ravenous vampire again. He had to think fast. *What else might work?*

"We go together and I'll keep my friend from taking you, just let her go." Different scenarios ran through Sorin's mind as to how to get out of the dilemma. One idea could work. It sucked without having his preternatural powers. The one which seemed to function was his mental connection with Merliah. If he could cue her in on the plan, together they could make it out of the situation without a scratch. He studied Esteban's face for a reaction to the suggestion to leave the painting together.

"Fine. You lead the way and don't try anything funny. One wrong move and I'll snap her neck. Now, move."

Sorin met Merliah's tear-filled eyes, and then moved toward the door. As he left the room and began the trail down the hallway, he concentrated on tapping into her mind, to no avail. He continued to assail the barriers she put up most likely from fear. He'd called to her before and had to succeed again. Amazed at her strength, he couldn't understand how such a human anomaly had escaped the vampire world. How he was able to communicate with her without ever taking of her blood confounded every doctrine of his kind. Merliah was special and when everything settled out tonight he promised himself to find out more about her. But, first...

We have to get out of here and to the other side without incident. Stefan on the other side was an advantage. They'd work together to subdue this rogue.

At one point as they departed the castle and walked across the field, he glanced over his shoulder and caught her attention. She smiled and his heart sank, knowing she had heard him. The exit portal's undulating wall lay ahead and came into focus the closer they came. Sorin listened for any sign of distress from Merliah and heard none, but since he'd been unable to touch her mind completely, he doubted he'd hear anything at this point. His angel held up well under the duress. Looking forward, he saw nothing of Stefan, only the lights from the apartment. Hopefully, his friend along with Alex and other FBI agents would be lying in wait, out of view, to take control of Esteban the second he stepped out of the framed canvas.

Ten feet lay between the real world and the created one. He stopped and turned to face Merliah. "You okay, angel?" he asked in a soft voice.

She managed a confined nod. Esteban maintained the tight grip along her neck.

"She's fine as long as you do as I say. The first sign of anything underhanded and she's gone. We go together to get out of here and your friend better stay clear. You understand?"

If Sorin began to feel anything like he did the last time he'd returned from this world to the next, he knew Esteban had to go through the same reaction. He'd have a short window to act or the excruciating pain of hunger would overwhelm him as well. Keeping Merliah safe was his only priority and he'd suffer through the torment. "Understood. On the count of three?"

"I said move it, *now*."

Within seconds, the tumbling, blackness, and whirling came and went. Sorin landed on the floor of the apartment with a thud, followed by two more loud thumps. He glanced around and saw Merliah rolling on the floor, no longer in Esteban's stranglehold.

In a split second, Sorin leapt to his feet. Pain in his gut pulled him up short as he hobbled over to her side. As the agony faded into a dull ache, he grabbed her wrist and pulled her into his arms. Her body went limp and she dropped her head on Sorin's chest, burying her face from everyone's view.

"You're safe, angel. I have you and he won't hurt you again, I promise."

The killer writhed on the floor and then Sorin heard the shuffle of several feet clumping across the room.

Stefan rapidly pinned Esteban to the floor.

"You okay, bro?"

"Yeah."

"Silver him Johnson," Alex said. "And be careful not to *accidentally* touch Stefan with the cuffs."

Johnson squinted and shook his head as he knelt down and cuffed the suspect's wrists.

"Esteban Freeman, you're under arrest for the kidnapping and murders of Chandra Thomas, Claire Benson and five other women." Alex began to speak, reading from a card she pulled from her jacket. "Esteban, you have the right to remain silent. Anything

you say can be used against you in a court of law." Alex read off
the Miranda Rights and as she started reciting the next one, she
was interrupted.

"You blood whore, you'll never get away with this." Esteban
cried out and struggled against Stefan's hold.

"If she doesn't have the right, I do. This is my territory and
you've violated our edicts. Hold still or I'll end your existence
right now and we won't have to worry about going the route of the
human laws to convict." Stefan peered up at Alex and smiled. "Go
on, *prinţesa*."

She returned his smile and continued. "Esteban Freeman, you
have the right to have an attorney present now and during any
future questioning. If you cannot afford an attorney, one will be
appointed to you free of charge if you wish. Do you understand
these rights as I have recited to you?"

"Fuck you!"

Whack. "You don't talk to her that way, asshole." Stefan
raised his hand acting like he'd take another swing at Esteban.

Merliah pushed back from Sorin's embrace and peered up at
him through tear-filled eyes. He clasped her face in both hands. He
was shocked by the bruising on one side of her face and it was
serious enough that he wanted to screw the human and vampire
laws and stake the bastard who did this to her. He cursed under his
breath when he felt her shivering.

None of this would have happened if he hadn't reacted with
shock seeing her true appearance. She blindly ran from the gallery
and Esteban was there to take advantage. The bastard was
responsible for the abuse she'd suffered and he'd pay.

Taking off his jacket, Sorin placed it around her shoulders and
spoke softly. "Merliah, I'm sorry. I—"

"Get me out of here, please."

"Shh, angel. I will." The pain of her words pierced to the core
of his being. Two fingers slid under her chin, exerting enough firm
pressure to tilt her head up until she was looking into his eyes. He
sought her lips with his, brushing them softly at first. The passion
at having her safe in his arms in reality and not in a dream urged
him forward. Her arms reached up and encased his neck.

Breaking the kiss, he took a deep breath, and ignored the familiar hunger building in his core. He brought her body tighter against his and looked over at his friend.

"Stefan, that's enough. Leave him to us," Alex said.

"Fine, but if he says another word, I won't be held responsible for what I do next."

"Bro, let them handle him." Sorin turned slightly to conceal Merliah. "I need to get Merliah out of here. Can I take your vehicle and driver?"

"Stefan, go with him. Johnson and I can handle this one. He's in silver cuffs and shouldn't give us any trouble," Alex said.

"No. No way am I letting you escort this sick piece of shit rogue without me."

"Stefan, we'll be fine. I've called for back-up and they should be here shortly. This guy isn't going anywhere," Johnson said.

"I'm going," Stefan said, then turned to Sorin. "You need to take care of yourself because I can see you're not doing well."

"See, you need to take care of Sorin. Go with him," Alex insisted.

The pain flared again in Sorin's gut. He needed blood, the beast within clawed at his insides demanding satisfaction. Merliah's heartbeat thundered in his ears and his mouth ached to sink his fangs into her flesh. The faint sound of the other two humans in the room beckoned as well. He wanted to get out of the apartment as much as Merliah did, but for other reasons. The look on his face must have shown the distress welling up.

"What's wrong, Sorin?" Merliah asked as her eyes widened as he leaned over her.

"He needs to feed. I think that's what happened at the gallery," Stefan said.

"Feed?" Merliah pulled from Sorin's embrace. "Esteban said you were a vampire. All the strange things I saw in my dreams, is that how you spoke to me and brought me out of the coma? Robbie told me your kind had special powers, but I never believed him." Her breath hitched.

Through the red vision, he saw from her expression and knew she saw his eyes change too. "Yes, angel. We have an unusual bond." He ran his hand over her cheek, then down her throat. His fingertips pressed against the throbbing vein and his nostrils flared. "Hungry, I'm so hungry," he murmured.

Merliah stepped back, exposing her true identity for all in the room.

"Jesus, what happened to you?" Stefan asked with a shocked tone in his voice.

"Stefan, that isn't nice," Alex said as she took a step toward the frightened woman.

"You want to take my blood!" Merliah's face went pale with disgust, and she covered her head with the jacket, attempting to run.

Sorin took a few strides to stop her, but he doubled over from the gnawing pain. His breathing came in short gasps and he clutched his stomach. "Ack! Merliah!"

Merliah snapped around at the doorway.

"What's happening to him, Stefan?" Alex asked.

"I need to get him out of here. I hate to leave you, *prinţesa*."

"I'll make sure she's safe," Johnson said, joining into the conversation after confining Esteban.

"You better keep her that way or I'll personally make sure you never see the light of day again, Johnson," Stefan said.

Stefan put his arm around Sorin. "Hang in there, brother."

"Merliah? I won't hurt you. Please don't leave." Sorin barely got the words out. Escaping into the paintings had to stop if this was the aftermath. Either that or have a fresh supply of blood available to stave off the excruciating pain that flared up after returning.

"I'll take her to the penthouse until you're recovered." Alex put her hand on Merliah's arm.

Merliah jerked. "I–I have to go to the institute."

"Look, Miss Travers. I know you're scared and have been through a traumatic experience, but I'm human and a FBI agent, not a vampire. You'll be safe at our apartment."

"Let me get you to the SUV and then I'll give you my blood until we get to the club, Sorin." Stefan put his arm around his friend's shoulders.

"No, the penthouse." Sorin's vision turned to vivid red as he stared into his friend's normal eyes. At this point, the discomfort he experienced was secondary to what Merliah had been enduring. Blood could wait, his angel couldn't be exposed to further danger.

"Fuck man, no can do. Look, let me get you settled in at the club and we'll return to the apartment right after. You're in no state to be left alone or go out on your own. Remember, you're in my territory and need to abide by my rules. Alex will look after her."

"No, now." Sorin's tone elevated from the normally deeper tone.

"Hey, don't make me go ape shit on you. Shut up and let me handle this. After, you can tell me what's up with that freaking painting." His friend meant business, and frankly he didn't have the strength to fight. Alex was good people and would make sure his angel would be taken care of. His heart and mind was put at ease.

The door swung open drawing everyone's attention. Several men dressed in uniforms charged in nearly knocking Merliah off-balance. She nudged against Alex.

"Hey, what's wrong with you, Thompson?" Alex yelled.

"Sorry, ma'am. We heard the loud voices and thought—"

"That's your problem, you thought too much. Assist Johnson with the suspect. He's been silvered and read his rights, but be careful he doesn't try something unexpected," Alex instructed.

"C'mon, buddy. We have a nice shiny silver room for you downtown," Thompson said as he bent down to wrestle Esteban to his feet. "Aaron, cordon off the elevator and hallway. Radio downstairs to clear the area."

"Yes, sir."

"Time for you to leave before it gets crazier around here. I'll take care of Miss Travers," Alex said, then turned toward Merliah. "Let's go and get you cleaned up."

"My painting. Don't leave it here," Merliah softly said. "Hold it by the frame and don't touch the surface." She held her head and wobbled on her feet.

"Are you okay?" Alex asked.

"I feel a little dizzy. I think from that blue liquid he gave me."

"Blue liquid? Oh no, don't tell me?" Alex glanced at Stefan and Sorin.

"Get that shit out of her system, Alex and don't touch the surface of the picture, or you'll...," Sorin's voice trailed off to a curse. The pain became almost unbearable. He needed sustenance or the beast would explode and he wouldn't be able to control it. "Just don't..."

Before he could finish, Esteban jerked around and broke from the silver cuffs, the acrid odor of burning flesh filled the room. He growled loudly and screamed. "If I can't have her and the painting, no one will." He surprised the agents and pulled first one, then the other toward him and sank his fangs into their necks. Quickly the agents were incapacitated and Esteban turned his attention to Merliah, lunging for her in one swift movement.

With a flurry of bodies thrashing and screaming, the two male vampires moved with inhuman speed and wrestled the rogue vampire to the ground. "You sonofabitch! I'll take you out now and forget protocol," Stefan hissed, as he kicked the rogue in the ribs. "*Prinţesa*, are you all right?"

"Yeah. Johnson? You got him?"

"For once I agree with Stefan. I say we end this miserable bastard's existence now."

"No, he will get his just due. We have to follow procedure," Alex said.

"Merliah?" Sorin pulled Esteban from her body. The air in his lungs escaped with a whoosh. "Merliah!" With his heart racing, he gasped when he saw her throat ripped open and blood gushing from the wound inflicted by the rogue. She lay on the floor, lifeless and barely breathing.

"Ohmigod, Merliah," Alex glanced down. "Stefan, help her."

Sorin pulled Merliah into his arms, holding her tight against his chest. "Easy angel, I've got you. I'm here, Merliah. I'll always be with you." He pressed a hand over the wound, her blood oozing through his fingers. The scent pierced his nostrils, but the fear of losing her overrode the craving pain. He held her tight and leaned down and kissed her forehead. His personal agony clawed at his insides as well as the realization he was losing her. He was losing her. "No, this can't be happening. Merliah! Come back to me. Don't leave me."

Merliah's eyelids fluttered and for a second they opened and gazed into his eyes. At that moment Sorin had clarity. He rose with her embraced in his arms and ran toward the painting resting on the sofa. To save her, he had to escape into the landscape. Before falling forward, he glanced over his shoulder to his friend. "Take us back to your apartment. I'll meet you later, brother." He touched their bodies to the surface.

It was better this way, my angel. But soon, Merliah, I'll explain everything and we can be together again. Don't leave me.

Chapter Twenty-Three

Hard Decisions

The vampire's fangs had driven deeply into the fleshy column of Merliah's neck. The swiftness and shock of the act paralyzed her. She struggled to speak, to tell him to get off, but nothing escaped her throat. The earnest effort to wriggle her body out from under the decay-smelling man on top of her was to no avail.

Agony tore through her as the relentless assault went deeper. Glancing upward, she caught a glimpse of Sorin's face just as the vampire closed his teeth together on her neck. The jaws of the psychotic artist tugged hard, and she heard the sound of flesh ripping. She managed to eke out a scream. The weight lifted and she could breathe, slightly.

The pain overwhelmed Merliah's awareness. In the distance, someone called out. A woman, she thought.

Oh, God, I hurt!

With one last act of will, she pressed her hand against the torn flesh to ease the pain, but instead she felt hot, stickiness over her fingers. A sudden surge of cold shivers seeped into her body. Fear swamped her and she lost track of the world beyond the pain and cold enveloping her.

Why does this feel so familiar?

The world exploded into a cacophony of sights and sounds confusing her foggy mind. Shuffling feet, hisses, and screams filled the air, but she didn't have the energy to open her eyes to find the source of the noise. Merliah floated in a cool, dark place, growing more tired as the sounds retreated further into the distance. A bothersome voice warned her she might be dying, and this time Sorin wouldn't be there to protect her from the inevitable.

The beckoning darkness sucked her down into the familiar black abyss. The pain that arced through her body moments earlier began to wane. Not since the car accident had she known such agony. The circumstances were different, but the results the same.

Then, Merliah felt a strong wall of muscles wrap around her. *Sorin?*

Brought back from the cool surroundings, Merliah fluttered her eyes and inhaled his scent as she relaxed into his embrace. The agony seemed to fade. Was this a dream? Or was she imagining the warm contentment covering her? It felt real and smelled real, but she'd been like this before. The memories of those times frightened her.

His lips pressed against her forehead, and he squeezed her gently. "Easy, angel, I've got you. I'm here, Merliah. I'll always be with you."

Dizziness hit her hard, and she felt her body go limp against his chest. The same white noise she'd heard while in the coma rang in her ears. The pain of the attack resurfaced and she gritted her teeth against the urge to empty her stomach. Then she felt movement mixed with distant voices.

The awareness of Sorin's embrace put her at ease. The warning her body sounded that something else was wrong cut into her mind. The memory of the dark place before his rescue flooded her with a sense of foreboding. *Not again! Help me, Sorin.*

The murky memory of the coma came into focus. She concentrated on casting the thoughts from her mind, but the pull of the viscous dark power called to her like a siren's song. She couldn't resist. Sorin's distant voice seemed to struggle to keep her from leaving, the plea desperate.

She immediately wanted to soothe the fearful sound of his deep heartfelt voice and worked hard to pull herself closer. Sounds intensified, and light pierced the shadows in ragged tears, demanding her attention. Merliah struggled to reach for the light, but her body felt weighed down, and she began to sink away from it.

Help me, Sorin!

She didn't want to fall into the darkness again. She didn't want to be trapped there forever, lost in the black blankness of pain and sorrow. She wanted to live. With Sorin. She screamed her silent terror. A voice reached deep down into her darkness and yanked her toward the bright light surrounding her, dragging her back to consciousness.

"Merliah Travers, come back to me. Don't leave me. Reach for me, my angel!"

She groaned and slowly opened her eyes.

The bright light blinded her, and she squinted until the pain receded. Details of the room around her settled into focus. Her eyes took in an elegantly decorated room in deep reds and gold, a burgundy coverlet over crisp white sheets draped around her body. One stone wall appeared beyond the massive footboard and made a solid background to the man seated on the mattress beside her.

Merliah recognized the handsome man from her dreams. Her heart fluttered with excitement. *Am I dead or alive? Wait, where am I?* Her eyes snapped to the bedspread again and parts of the room. This wasn't her bedroom at the institute.

"Sorin? Where am I?" she asked as she struggled to sit up, but aborted the effort when pain shot through her neck.

"Just rest for now, angel. You're alive and healing." His familiar voice eased her uncertainty and fright.

"What happened? Why do I hurt and feel so weak?"

The pain felt like she'd been stabbed in the neck by a twelve-inch butcher knife. What was wrong with her? She hadn't felt this bad, even after the car accident. She pushed her hand up to check the injury, but she couldn't feel anything.

"Don't you remember, angel? We were at that creep Esteban's apartment and I found you and him in the painting."

All at once, the events came crashing into her brain. The content feeling he'd come and rescued her put her at ease when they exited the painting. He held her close and she savored the scent of his skin and the warmth of his body. Until...

She closed her eyes and shook her head to clear the cobwebs of the painful memory.

"I brought you here so you could heal. You were losing too much blood and short of turning you, I...I couldn't lose you, angel. Here, you could mend from the wound inflicted by Esteban. Do you remember that?"

No. Wait. Yes, she remembered the terrible burning and sharp bite to her neck and how she'd fallen to the floor with the scary man on top of her. Then the darkness and cold surrounded her. The memory played out in a reel until it ended with red eyes staring at her and the searing pain at her throat.

Merliah's eyes flew open, and she stared at Sorin with dawning unease. His expression filled with concern and compassion, his eyes a deep chocolate brown. No sign of red anywhere. The eyes of her nightmare weren't his, but Esteban's.

"You saved me again."

"Yes, my love." A smile flitted over his lips.

"And you brought me into the painting? I'm not dead or dreaming?"

His black eyebrows crinkled, one tendril of his dark hair fell across his face. It looked soft and smooth, and she wanted to push it behind his ear. His smug look banished any tender feelings his face expressed.

"You were bitten and your throat torn, I brought you to my manor home, the one you created so I could take care of you. There wasn't time to take you to the hospital. You're awake and doing fine."

Bitten? Esteban took her blood? Gasping, she thought she'd be sick at the thought. She reached for the inflicted area again and felt nothing. Then she ran her hand over her face and down her chest. Of course, she was perfect in this world. Sorin knew that would heal her. The vague pain had to be the after effects of the healing process.

"When can I leave? I need to get back."

"Soon. We'll stay here until I know it is safe for us to return. I've asked Stefan to transport the painting with us to his apartment. We'll return when you've healed properly."

"I have to go. Abby and my parents have to be worried sick about my disappearance. I snuck out of the facility and no one knows I went to the gallery." She tried to sit up again. She'd make it back to the only home she'd known in years. Come hell or high water. Goose bumps zinged along her leg when it appeared out of the covers.

"Hey! I'm naked!" She jerked her legs back under the sheets and stared incredulously at the man sitting next to her. "Where are my clothes? Did you try and take advantage of my situation, mister?"

He coughed and had the grace to look chagrined. "Forgive me, but I had lascivious thoughts as I sat close to your naked beauty and restrained myself from devouring you, because your recovery superseded those desires. All I've done is sit here and watched your breathing for the past several hours."

"Really?" She groaned, frowning. "You have to bear with me. I've just gone through one hellacious evening. I find out you're a...a vampire lover of my dreams and reality, kidnapped by a psycho artist, and bitten with my blood almost completely drained. And to top it off, I'm in a painting of my creation recovering, naked in bed with said lover who swears he didn't take advantage of my situation."

He laughed, the kind of laugh that comes from deep in the chest. "I see your humor has returned. That's a good sign, but you have to rest. Sleep and heal. We can talk again later."

He tucked the covers around her body, leaned over and placed a soft kiss on her forehead. Uneasiness crept through her as she stared hard at him, clutching the covers. Fear and yet comfort filled her. The loving gesture confused her. He'd saved her, but deep down she knew what he was capable of as a vampire and that fact alone scared her.

"Thank you." She managed to say as she cleared her throat. "Thank you for what you did, but when I'm better you promise to take me immediately to the Institute, right?"

He cocked his head to one side. His lips tightened and with a sigh before he rose from the mattress and strode across the room toward the door. "You have only been here a few hours and I promise I will return you when you heal, whether a day, a week, or a month." He opened the door and gazed back at her. "Good night, my angel. I'll be back. Now rest." Sorin smiled without showing his teeth. The corners of his mouth curled upwards, and his eyes crinkled at their edges, making her heart flutter. She didn't want him to go, everything was happening too fast and she needed him. But, he did depart, leaving her alone. *Damn, he's so sexy.*

Merliah settled in, rolling onto her back and gathering the covers around her chin. She was confused, fatigued and exhilarated all at once.

Sorin. He admitted being a vampire, although deep down she knew there had been something different about him since the first time they met. Now the difference was confirmed. He scared her, but he also made her heart and body sing.

Glancing around the impressive bed chamber, she had to admit it was a lot nicer than her tiny ten by ten room at the Berger Institute. If this was a true representation of his house, she was intrigued.

Sorin. Why couldn't she fall in love with a normal guy? Robbie had seemed normal, but look how he turned out. Turned tail and ran as soon as he saw who and what she really was after the accident. Sorin had been shocked, at first. But, he did rescue her and brought her here. Robbie wouldn't have been so caring. Sorin was a vampire. *Oh, God. I'm so confused.*

The woman at the apartment acted like she was with Stefan, the other artist from the exhibition and he was vampire. She was an FBI agent, an intelligent and strong woman. She didn't seem to have a problem with them and obviously loved the guy. But then there was the evil one, Esteban. She shook her head to get the image of the menacing creep out of her mind.

Killers. All of them. That was the scariest revelation. Alex kept saying "alleged killer" in regard to Esteban, because the vamp hadn't been tried and convicted yet, she supposed was the protocol in such matters. With her testimony though, the whack job would be put away for a long time if she had anything to do with it.

Merliah had her doubts. From what she knew about vamps she'd learned from Robbie. Other information came from the stories she read in magazines and the local newspaper, vampires weren't to be trusted. They used humans for their own perverted purposes. She didn't run in those particular circles, among humans who indulged in blood and sex. But, now she found herself smack in the middle of a murder or two and a kidnapping case.

Merliah came to the conclusion she didn't like vampires very much. She couldn't put her finger on the reason other than she had been abducted by one and the changes in her brain were caused by the vampire blood Robbie gave her after the accident. The dislike came at a different level with the fact they were parasites. The creatures lived beyond the lifespan of normal humans. They seduced, mauled and took what they wanted, namely blood, without regard to how their actions affected the real living beings. There was something unnatural about their existence. *Unfair? Jealous of their longevity and powers?* Maybe, but despite her growing feelings for Sorin, he was one of them.

Granted, he'd saved her from the Tiara Princess Killer, and maybe he brought her out of the coma, but did that trump the fact he seduced her in her dreams and in the fantasy realm of her paintings? Reconciling the facts with feelings wasn't going to be an easy task.

Sorin was handsome in a rough around the edges kind of way. He was mysterious and dark with scars and hurts she only began to see. *Not unlike my own, but he was powerful and charming when he wanted to be.* She suspected all the characteristics were his way of trapping prey. His allure and attractiveness seduced the unsuspecting victims. *Dammit! He's just too sexy for his fangs. That is so wrong.*

Her life was simple, up to the point Sorin materialized as a real person. Before him, she concentrated on becoming stronger, returning as close to her life before the car accident as she could. Then the special abilities that were graced upon her changed everything. In a matter of six odd months, her life had accelerated from blackness, trapped in the coma and solitude of her damaged brain, to vast panoramas of imaginary worlds she created through painting, to falling for the fantasy lover of her dreams who turns out to be a vampire.

I'm falling helplessly in love with a vampire. A sexy vampire who could have any woman and fall in love with all of them. Well, I'm not falling for his sexy allure. No, not me. When she had the opportunity to see him again, she swore she'd give him a piece of her mind, kick him in the shin and tell him she never wanted to see him again.

A knock came to the door, jerking her upright.

"Hello?"

The door creaked open. "Merliah? May I come in?" The familiar woman's voice piqued her interest. She wasn't aware anyone else was in the painting.

"Sure." Merliah pulled the comforter tight around her chest. "What are you doing here?"

"Hi, I'm Special Agent Alexandra Carlton. I'm investigating the vamp serial killer. We kind of met in his apartment. Do you remember?"

"Uh, yes, I remember you Miss Carlton. You didn't answer why you're here, in the painting. I can't believe Sorin would have permitted it."

"Well, I have influence and this is important to my investigation. I can wait and come back when you feel more up to it, but I really would like to wind this up as soon as possible."

Merliah hesitated, but something about the woman made her think she could be trusted, especially since it was obvious Sorin said it was okay for her to be there. "No, stay. I'll try and help as best as I can."

"Great." She moved to the side of the bed and pulled out a notepad and pen. "Let's first start with calling me Alex. Everyone does."

"Okay, Alex. I'll try and tell you what I can."

"How did you know this alleged murderer and kidnapper Esteban?"

"Well, I didn't really know him. I saw him at the gallery a few times while I prepared for the show. He seemed strange, but not a killer. Unless you call when he brought me to his apartment and dragged me in here. Then, I knew I was in trouble."

"Speaking of this place, I've spoken with Sorin, but he can't quite explain this. Can you?"

"My world? I don't know. One day at the Institute I went from sculpting in clay to picking up a paint brush and...and this." Merliah raised her arms and flared them in the air.

"Yes, this is quite a place. Nothing surprises me anymore with what I've seen when it comes to the paranormal world. Is there anything else you can tell me, anything you remember about Esteban? Did he tell you anything about other victims?"

"No, not that I remember. He was more interested in my painting. I got the impression he had been inside before. He may have at the gallery. Anything was possible with it on display without anyone guarding it. That's how Sorin found me there. He saw me and followed. Maybe Esteban did too."

"So no one else knows? Other than you, me, Sorin, Stefan and...Esteban."

"No, not even my friend Abby knows." Merliah paused. "No wait, there are a few patients at the Institute who might, but they wouldn't say anything if that's what you're hinting at."

"Merliah, this is an incredible discovery. If you can create a place like this, a place where vampires can become human, or at least not have their preternatural powers, and can heal a human body like what has happened with you, can you imagine the ramifications of this?"

"Alex, no one can find out. Ohmigod! I could become an experiment or something. Please, please, promise not to tell. Ah, my head hurts."

"I'm sorry, would you like some aspirin?"

"No, I'm fine. It's been a long night."

Alex shook her head. "No problem. I have many nights like this, well maybe not exactly like this, but I do have some interesting ones. Is it Sorin? I mean is he trying to contact you telepathically and that's why your head hurts? Stefan does that with me all the time. Gives me such a headache after a while."

"How do they, I mean no he's not now, but do they read our minds?"

"Oh, well I'm not sure of the mechanics but they can't always make a connection. Depends on how strong the bond is I guess. Stefan has been able to tap into my thoughts since the beginning of our relationship. I finally got him to teach me how to put up barriers so I can have a little privacy. You know a girl has to have some secrets from her guy." She grinned.

Merliah joined in the amusement. She began to really like Alex. Merliah found her smart, witty, and a caring person. They were close enough in age, perhaps they could become friends. The only other girl-type friend she had was Abby, but that was a little different.

"Look, don't worry about me saying anything about this *world* of yours. Stefan and Sorin have already sworn me to secrecy even though it makes doing my job difficult."

"By the way, what exactly does the FBI have to do with vampires?"

"I'm with the Special Vamp Unit here in Miami. The Vamp Squad some call us. I first worked as a vamp bounty hunter. Family business and all, then I met Stefan and one thing led to the other and now I'm here with the FBI."

"Really? You fight vampires? But, I don't understand you're with…"

"Yeah, crazy isn't it?"

"A little. By the way since I didn't get an answer from Sorin, do my parents or the Institute know I'm okay so no one calls the police again and we have an uproar again about my disappearance?"

"The police? I'm not sure. What happened before?"

"Oh, yeah. A couple nights ago, I left my room because I couldn't sleep. I went to the studio a couple buildings from the residence quarters to paint. Actually, we're in that particular one now. Evidently, some man broke into the facility, specifically my room, and the entire facility went on lockdown when they couldn't find me. Police were there, my doctor, the nurses and staff were running around, it was kind of funny when you think about it. If Abby had been there, she probably would have suggested looking for me in the studio." Merliah shook her head. "They never found the man who broke in. I heard the security cameras didn't even show anyone entering. Real strange."

"What night was this?"

"The night before the gallery show. Why?"

"Ha. The man was Sorin. He was there looking for you."

"Really?"

"Yeah. He was pretty disappointed when he didn't find you."

Merliah blushed. He did find her later that night, in her dreams.

"Hmm, he did eventually find you, didn't he?"

Merliah dropped her eyes. "Yes, he did," she murmured.

"Ha, I knew it. I had the same look on my face, at least that's what people tell me. When I first met Stefan I had to keep telling myself to look for scars and warts because I couldn't believe how instantly I was attracted to him. Like I said earlier, I'm a hunter by profession. My parents were vamp hunters and my brothers took over the business about six months ago. Believe me, falling for a vamp wasn't what I intended. I hunted them, mainly the rogue-types. Stefan became my exception. Listen to me, rattling on. So what's up with you and Sorin?"

Yes, I think I really like her, but I still don't know if I can trust her. "Um, I don't know. I think he likes me because of my special abilities and well this is one of my precious gifts. Creating a world where he is normal. Like human again."

Alex's eyebrows crinkled. "I think there's more than that going on with him. He likes you. I mean *really* likes you. This place is just a bonus."

Merliah hesitated, but the honest eyes of the new friend told her talking about her feelings about Sorin would be okay. "I like him too, but I'm afraid of him. How do you get over the fear?"

"I don't know, I just did. Love for the man hidden deep inside and not his outward persona makes the difference. I love him and that's all that matters."

Merliah nodded. After a long debriefing by Alex, Merliah was exhausted and tried to cover her yawns so not to be rude. After the formalities and the clever transition talking about personal information, Merliah wasn't so keen on discussing Sorin's and her relationship. Sorin. The name she'd told herself not to think about.

Sorin. Damn, I'm so confused.

Listening to Alex talk about her life with the Master and Commander of the Florida Blood Family like he was a god of unsurpassed sexual prowess reinforced Merliah's opinion of vampires. The woman sitting before her was captivated by vampires, especially Stefan. Although she appeared to Merliah as an intelligent woman, how could she fall prey to the creature? Even though the woman obviously was in love with the guy, Merliah didn't know him other than he was one of the other artists from the gallery and she shouldn't make such strong judgments without knowing all the facts. But there was the killer Esteban who also was an artist and he turned into a creepy, sick monster. Couldn't Stefan? Or Sorin?

"Hey, I can tell you're tired and need rest. We can talk later. I think I have enough information for my report." Alex turned to leave, and then stopped. "You know. Vamps, at least the good ones, aren't so bad once you get to know them. They have special powers that can make life with them special. Your abilities could certainly complement Sorin's. Don't throw a good thing away out of fear." She smiled, and then slipped out the door.

Left to the silence of the bedroom, Merliah seriously thought about what Alex said and decided tomorrow would bring answers. Her head hurt and she needed sleep, which eventually crept up on her before she realized it, the last thoughts before blackness entered were of Sorin making love to her. *So much for a kick in the shins.*

* * * *

"Merliah?" His voice filled the room. She'd awakened early and had made her way down the steps into the grand room on the first floor. With only a sheet wrapped around her body, she was surprised how warm the large stone manor was. But, then again, this was her creation, not reality.

Ohmigod! Just saying my name makes me melt like chocolate. Am I the only one he affects like this? She glanced over and watched him walking toward her. They were in their own world she created and never wished for it to end.

Her breath hitched as he drew closer. His eyes shimmered as he locked onto her gaze and didn't let go. After a moment of calm breathing to bring her thumping heart under control, she still felt paralyzed and swallowed hard when he stood within inches of her body.

All anger and fear flew out of her head as his hands slid down her sides, barely brushing the swell of her breasts, and ending at her lower back. He leaned in and lightly touched her lips. She craved his touch. The fire of arousal shot straight to her core and she recognized his as he pressed against her body. "Sorin? This isn't what I expected. Shouldn't we talk first?"

"We'll talk in detail later, right now all I need to know is that you're okay. With me, with us. I want to be with you. Make love to you, right here and now."

She sucked in a deep breath and let it out slowly. "I don't know. I'm scared and confused. I thought I'd never see you again when that crazy person took me. I ran because you looked at me with shock. I couldn't bear to have you see me like that. You knew me as the beautiful woman of our dreams and the fantasy world in the painting. In the real world, I'm a scarred and deformed girl. Frightened of my future dealing with the scars and pain, I'm not the perfect woman a man would want. Why would you be any different than Robbie and leave me when you saw how ugly I was?" Tears welled threatening to drop down her cheek. She closed her eyes to fend off the impending answer she knew he'd give to her question. *You're right, Merliah. I would only use you for blood and sex. I could never love you. Yes, that's what he's really thinking.*

Sorin kissed her brow. "You're not ugly, angel. You're beautiful to me. After the shock wore off, which was only seconds by the way, I realized none of that mattered. Look at me, angel. My scars run deep and beyond what you see. My existence has been fraught with pain and death as well." He drew her into his arms. "Angel, you are precious to me and beautiful inside and out. Your physical appearance has nothing to do with how or why I love you. You've shown me your world. Let me show you mine." He lowered his head and kissed her with a gentle brushing then raised his head and focused on her face waiting for an answer.

She didn't know if this was his seductive vampire demeanor talking or what a man says to a woman when he's in love. Merliah felt so out of practice. For the past five years, she'd been virtually non-existent when it came to love. She remembered her relationship with Robbie before the accident. When she realized he didn't love her, they settled into a friendship with perks. How bizarre all the ups and downs of her life turned out to be. *The first man I hook up with after coming out of the coma is a vampire? What the hell is that all about? I thought I was on the verge of insanity. Turns out the man I'm in love with is a card-carrying, certified member of the Undead Club. A head honcho vamp on top of everything else. What am I going to do?*

"Be my woman. Love me. That's what you're going to do?"

Her eyes widened. "You…you read my mind? You can't do that. It's not fair."

"Probably not." The ends of his mouth curled up. Wickedly. "Angel, as far as I'm concerned, nothing has changed between us. The only difference is we don't have to meet only in dreams. You know who and what I am, which is what I was before, except now you know it. I see who you really are, but that doesn't change the way I feel about you." He reached for her hand and threaded his fingers into hers. "Come. Let me show you how much I love you."

* * * *

Sorin led Merliah down the hallway off the second floor and back into the master bedroom, his room where he'd spent many a night alone, but never again as long as he had Merliah. The hour was late, after midnight, but he had many hours to deliver on the promise to show her how much he loved her. Tomorrow night he'd make arrangements to bring her back to his home, his sanctuary in the Carpathian Mountains. She'd become his woman and eventually a part of his blood family. Excitement filled every part of his being. *How long has it been since I've felt such life flowing through my veins?*

Then, the thought struck him. *What if she doesn't want me to change her? Fuck!*

As they stepped into the pitch dark room and he closed the door behind them, she shivered under his embrace. "What's wrong, angel?"

"I'm frightened. This…is…is like when I was…in the coma." She shuddered.

Sorin sensed the fear growing within her. He recalled the first time she called to him. The darkness surrounded her and instinctively he reached out and led her into the light. The light she had come to show him. "You're safe here with me, angel. Hold close and I'll take care of you." He kissed the top of her head as he wrapped his arms around her.

"I trust you, but I'm also afraid of you."

"Oh, my darling angel. I would never harm you. We've been together almost every night for months. Have I done anything to frighten you?"

"No, but isn't that what vampires do? They seduce their victims and take what they want?"

He let out a deep laugh. "Yes, we do, but you're different."

"Different? How? Because I'm ugly and you don't care."

"No! Angel, you're beautiful and I love you. That's the difference to me. We have a connection like none I've ever had with any woman. You called to me across an ocean to rescue you. I don't know how or why that was possible, but we belong together for however long you'll have me."

"I don't know how I did all this either. I think the vampire blood my ex-boyfriend gave me had something to do with it, but I'm not a hundred percent sure."

"When did he give it to you?"

"Evidently after one of my surgeries from the accident. I wasn't conscious, so I had no idea he did it until after I came out of the surgery. Do you think that's it?"

"Possibly. Our blood has curative powers and other elements we've heard about but really pay no attention to. Now, enough talk. I think I have a promise to fulfill."

Even in the dark, he could feel a smile form on her face as she rested against his chest.

"Can you turn a light on? I want to see you."

"Hmm, I think we can have more fun without. Masking one of our senses heightens the others."

She shivered again. "You don't want to see me, is that it?"

"Angel, you need to stop saying you're not worthy, not beautiful, not what I want. Can you look into my eyes?"

"Uh, it's dark in here."

"Yes, but I can assure you there's no pity, disgust, or indifference." He held her hand and slid it down to his growing arousal. "If we were outside this world, they'd be red. The lust in my eyes is for you not for blood. Does this feel like I don't want you?"

"No," she said softly as she ran her fingers over his growing erection.

"I want you. That's what my body is telling you, angel." He found her lips and pressed hard, passionately.

She moaned into his mouth.

Their tongues intertwined and danced, thrusting in and withdrawing for long moments before he broke off the kiss. His cock hardened more than he thought possible, his balls tightened, and everything in him begged to rush this encounter, to make her submit to him and become his woman for eternity.

Merliah was precious and pure as a lily. Fragile. Delicate. He had to take his time with her. He softened the kiss, until she sighed again. His tongue explored each crevice of her mouth, tangled with her tongue, sucking it into his mouth to invite her to taste him.

His hand traveled from her back to her firm, round buttocks. He pulled her closer and shared her startled inhale as his cock pressed hard into her pelvis. Unable to keep himself from testing her sexual limits beyond their other times together, he scooped her into his arms and carried her to the bed and gently laid her down. He ran his hands up her sides, along her arms, and pulled them over her head. Holding her wrists with one hand, he pinned them to the mattress.

Her eyelids fluttered then opened, piercing him with a seductive gaze. The crystal blue glittered even in the blackness of his room. They were beacons calling him to swim in their desire-filled coolness.

"Do you like the restraints, angel?" He leaned over her with the full weight of his body against hers. His cock throbbed, pressing painfully against the zipper of his trousers. The heat between them taunted his sensitive flesh.

"I like…like the way you command me," she whispered, her breath came in short pants.

Sorin tipped his head and murmured in her ear. "Do you really? You like to be…restrained?" He grinned with knowing pleasure. His guess in the painting of the woods about her submissive nature hadn't been wrong. "Then your wish is my command, beautiful lady."

Pushing back onto his elbows, he took in her full vision. A soft pink glow radiated from her face as she peered up at him with half-closed eyes. He suspected the rest of her body blushed as well. "Clothes. They have to go."

Moving from the bed, he stood, and with quickness managed to remove his shirt and trousers, kicking his shoes to the side first, followed by his boxers and socks. "I know you can't see me, but trust me, you'll feel me soon enough, angel."

He could see her though. This world didn't take all his abilities it seemed. As he removed his clothing one piece at a time, he watched her eyes widen and body flush with desire. He recognized from the intensity they shed, she was turned on and ready to submit to anything he asked. Merliah's temptress within waited to escape, just like all the nights she came to him in dreams. Teasing, exploring sexuality that filled her very essence and gave him the most exquisite pleasure as she waited for him to make the next move.

"What about you, Sorin? What do you like? Tell me."

Leaning in for another kiss, he said, "What I want is you in my bed every night." He kissed her again. "My dominance over you is the only pleasure I desire. To please you." He moved over her, resting his weight on his elbows and knees straddling her legs. "But, tonight I want to show you how special you are to me."

The soft cry she let out followed by her entire body shivering beneath him touched him deeply. Every cell in his flesh responded. The desire to take her right now burst through every barrier he had erected over several hundred years. This was the woman he'd been destined to love completely. He took her mouth, desperate to show her what she did to him. How she made him crazy with the need to bind her and please her with stinging spankings and tight restraints. The kiss turned potent, so intense he forgot where he was, and the beast that lay dormant inside. Fortunately, within the painting he didn't hunger so he could refrain from taking blood from her. All he wanted was her sex, her love. He determined tonight was to be all about her.

"Shh, it's all right, angel. I'm going to give you what you want and more. You don't have to fear me here. My vampire powers don't work in here. I'm almost human." He nuzzled her neck and then rolled to his side, pulling her into his arms.

Losing her would never be an option, not when she was his salvation. He'd fight to his death to protect and keep her at his side. He may have brought her out of the depths of her dark prison of the coma, but she saved him with her light of life, her strength. Her love. His miserable existence now had meaning, and it was all thanks to the woman he loved. For the first time, he allowed himself to think toward the future and what it might bring for him.

He licked his way down her throat, across her collarbone, trailing fiery kisses down her skin until he reached her breast. She rocked her hips hard against him as he flicked her nipple with his tongue and reached between her legs with his free hand.

He lifted his head. "Keep your hands above your head. Do not move them or I will punish you. Do you understand?"

"Huh?"

"I thought you liked this, angel?"

"Um, I do, I do. I will do as you say."

"Good girl." When his tongue swirled across her nipple, she groaned and arched her back. He understood she was new at the submissive play, but soon, she'd comply with ease. She pressed herself against his mouth, encouraging him, and then, when he continued to tease and taunt, demanded his attention be harder. He cupped her breast, kneading her flesh as he drew her nipple into his mouth and suckled. His other hand toyed with her hardening clit. He alternated between pinching the nipple, rolling it between his fingers and sucking.

Then, he bit her nipple. The small, unexpected pain elicited a squeal of surprise which pleased him. With one last lick, he soothed the throbbing hurt, and moved down her body, his hands caressing her sides, his loose hair tracing tantalizing trails across her flesh. His tongue laved wet circles around her navel.

And lower still.

He pushed her legs apart and bent his head to her mound. He licked her, swirling circles around her clit, then along her damp folds. His angel's moans sounded like heaven to him as he plunged his thick tongue into her hot pussy. He continued to lap at her slit with diligence, and then slipped two fingers inside, parting her flesh wider. Continuing to stroke and flick his tongue over her clitoris, he sensed the gentle pulses building deeper and longer within her. He increased the rhythm of sucking and laving, harder and faster. Within seconds he felt her inner muscles clamp down on his fingers and her body began to thrash under his.

"Oh, yes, Sorin. That's it...don't stop, please."

She moaned her release as he licked and swirled his tongue around and around the tight nub while continuing to thrust his fingers until he felt erotic spasms in her pussy. Her legs quivered as he felt another rush sweep through her core with the tightening of muscles. Before she came completely down, he settled between her legs and spread them wider with his knees. He positioned the head of his erection and slid his long, hard cock into her with ease. She was extremely wet, and tight. Sorin thought he saw stars when she squeezed around his shaft.

She made a faint whimpering groan and clutched at his back. "Oh, yes."

Pushing deeper until he was fully immersed in her, he paused while she adjusted to his size. He leaned closer and kissed her neck, then nuzzled behind her ear. "Angel," he murmured. He kissed her lips, capturing her mouth in a primal dance. "I want you to come again with me."

His hot, hard cock began to stroke inside her, first slow, grinding his pelvis against hers. Merliah lifted her hips to meet each of his thrusts. The intense sensations built within him. She wrapped her legs around his waist, driving him deeper inside her depths.

She arched her back off the mattress in a silent gasp as he focused on his task of bringing them to mutual release. Her continued moans of pleasure spurred him on. Sorin couldn't wait to feel her squeeze his cock as she reached her peak of pleasure.

She jerked against him, her wails of desire growing louder as she thrust her hips up to meet his. He rode her, plunging deeper until she took the whole of him with ease on each down stroke. "I'm close, Sorin. Oh…yes."

"Not yet, angel. Do not come until I say you can."

He groaned, and fucking her sweet and sopping pussy grew more urgent. With a few more strokes he knew he was close. "Come for me, angel. Show me you love what I'm doing to you."

"Sorin!" She screamed as she reached her climax, coming hard around him.

"Oh yes, that's it my love, give me everything of you. You're mine, angel, all mine and no other's." The contractions pulsed hard, milking him to ecstasy.

His cock was slick with her secretions and he growled as he held her hips and thrust harder and faster. Her hands grasped at his back, and her legs tightened around his waist, digging her heels into his ass. The sound and feelings sent him over the edge and he called out her name and followed her into his own orgasmic bliss, pumping into her with force, grunting and spurting his hot liquid into her convulsing fiery pussy.

He collapsed on her, taking his weight on his elbows so not to crush her. He kissed her sweat soaked body. An electric force charged the air. *Is that her or my imagination?*

"Are you doing that, angel?" He whispered in her ear.

"Mmm, I felt it too. My special powers maybe. I don't know."

He snickered. "Yeah, I'd say *real* special. That was incredible whatever it was." He kissed her shoulder and collarbone as her hands played along his spine.

He held her in the darkness, content in the knowledge that this was his woman. They kissed, feeling the electricity continuing to arc between their lips, their bodies, and the air in the room. Everything felt right to Sorin, their love making, their ability to mentally connect, the unspoken bond between them. "I love you, angel. You're my salvation, my light to my darkness."

"I love you too, with all my heart and soul." They kissed again, a soft brush of their lips.

His body felt so right against hers, as it always should be. They were complete. Two lost and scarred souls, united as one and no longer alone.

They had each other, forever.

Epilogue

Six months later…

"Good evening, angel. Did you sleep well?" Sorin stepped onto the balcony through the French doors from their bedchamber. Filling his lungs with the evening's air, and gazing at the stars and the beauty of his woman, he nuzzled her neck and placed a soft kiss there.

Merliah moaned. "Yes I did, and you?"

"Never better when I have you by my side."

She giggled.

"I've sent Maks to pick up your parents from the airport. They should be here in a couple of hours." He turned her in his arms and gazed into her crystal blue eyes. *God, I'll never grow tired of them.* "Does this please you, angel?"

She smiled. "Very much so. Thank you for bringing them here. I just hope they get used to the others in the castle."

"Hmm, me too. I don't want them to scare off my knights. We need them for protection." He bent his head and brushed his lips with hers.

"I love you, Sorin."

"And I you."

She returned her attention to glancing out over the moonlit field of wildflowers on the pristine grounds of the estate. The lights in the garden were beginning to flicker to illuminate and caused a sense of security to resonate throughout the property. "I love this time of night, just after the sun sets, when all of nature is in transition." She peered up. "Don't you?"

"Yes, love. I do." He wrapped his arms around her swollen belly and rested his chin on her shoulder.

Silence fell between them for a few seconds.

"Sorin, what is the High Tribunal going to do when they find out about me? I don't want the baby to become an experiment or exploited for their own agenda."

"I won't let any harm come to you or our child. I don't know what they will do, but I'm more concerned with the rest of the global community learning of your powers to create a world where we vampires are temporarily human. We can procreate and can be considered a threat to humanity."

"If they find out about the abilities of my paintings and how they can regress vamps to human, but only while on the inside of them, I'll be used and experimented on. I just know it. Please, Sorin? Don't let anyone take me away from here, from you. Protect us. Promise me."

Sorin held her tighter. "Always. I'll fight every last vampire or human on earth to defend you and our child. That's also why I want your parents here, safe within my compound just in case word leaks."

"I'm so sorry. If I had known this could happen, I wouldn't have created my art for the entire world to see and you wouldn't have—"

He placed a hand on her chin and lifted it toward him. "Enough of those what ifs. What is done is done and I wouldn't have it any other way. I've been blessed with not only finding the love of my life, but to have a son after hundreds of years of a lonely existence. I thought I'd never experience the joys and pleasures of a little one of my flesh and blood running around this vast estate. I'd relinquished the idea of ever having a legitimate heir. Now, my love, you've honored me with both."

"But, if I—"

Placing a couple fingers over her lips, he said, "Shh, no buts, no regrets. Besides, if our son is born healthy, then Stefan has told me he'd like Alex to become pregnant. I never thought I'd hear him ever say such a thing. Of course, I told him you have to approve. He doesn't wish to put Alex in danger any more than you are at this moment."

She smiled. "Are you kidding? Alex and Stefan deserve the same happiness we have. Alex and I've talked almost every day since we told them the news. I've already begun sketching ideas for their special place. Oh, and she's insisted on being here for the birth. Will that be okay? I didn't say yes or no yet because I wanted to ask your permission first."

"Anything you want, my angel. Anything that makes you happy, I'm happy."

Sorin flinched. A movement in the underbrush caught his eye, a slight shift in the shadows. The movement reminded him of the urgency to feed.

"You're hungry. I can tell. Go, I'll be here when you return. We can talk more then."

"I'm not really. You're so sensitive to my needs. Are you sure you're not reading my mind, angel?

She let out a deep breath. "No, at least I don't think so. I'm learning new things about my abilities every day." She turned and gazed into his eyes. "Go. I'll be fine."

"You sure? I can have one of my knights bring a blood donor and I can return quickly. I don't like leaving you alone."

"Sorin, I'm not alone. There are your servants and I have my painting and I like my solitude when I'm creating."

"I still don't like you unprotected. Besides, when I'm awake I don't wish to miss a single minute away from your touch."

She smiled at him as hot tears spilled over her cheeks. "We'll be together forever, my love. An hour or two of separation while you take care of family business and other duties is but a millisecond in our lives. Go."

Pangs of hunger surged throughout his gut and as much as he hated to admit she was right, she was. The transition each time had become more bearable, but what he regretted most was the separation. Squinting his eyes and with fists clenched, Sorin sucked in a tight breath, then leaned in and kissed his woman with such passion as if he'd never see her again. With a heavy exhale, he broke from the embrace, turned and leapt off the balcony. A sharp, crack of air rushed out from under Sorin's muscular body as he hit the soft ground below. He growled, scrambled back, and stood prone. He glanced up and saw his beautiful Merliah standing at the edge of the balcony. She blew him a kiss. He raised his hands, caught the imaginary gift and brought his palm to his chest.

He touched her mind and told her he loved her. Turning on his heels and with sure foot, he stole into the late summer darkness.

As he raced across the landscape, his heart filled with such love and joy he couldn't believe that in a year his entire existence had changed. The fateful night just over a year ago when his angel came to him asking for help transformed him. In a few months, he would become a father to a son he'd never dreamed possible.

The Tiara Princess Killer almost took all his dreams away, but the rogue vampire had been put away quite appropriately. After the FBI brought him into custody and determined his crimes were more vampire related, they turned him over to the vampire community. The High Tribunal granted Sorin the right to determine the appropriate punishment. Sorin executed the verdict in private and with great pleasure. The wacko killer rested within the confines of a special painting of Merliah's. He then painted the surface solid black and hung it on a wall where no one would ever find it. As far as Sorin was concerned, justice had been served for the artist who liked to kill innocents and portray them in his art. He didn't have a hard time convincing Merliah to create the dark prison. Sorin took precautions to make sure the High Tribunal would never find out about Merliah's special abilities, especially in light of her present condition.

Sorin was Master and Commander of the Eastern Europe Blood Family and he had it all. No more existing only to hunt, fornicate and command. No more pain. No more subsisting only for blood and sex. No more monotonous gray solitude. He had a true family and would defend his woman and child to the death if need be.

Before stepping through the portal on the edge of the open wildflower field, he glanced over his shoulder. Merliah still stood on the balcony, the light from the bedchamber backlit her figure. He smiled and touched her mind. Upon arriving on the other side, he leaned against the stone wall of the bedchamber, careful to keep his touch from the canvas. He closed his eyes and sighed, trying not to hear her sobs or think of the damage he caused. He'd never intended to hold her hostage in the fantasy world of the painting. Originally he brought her there to keep her from dying. After she seemed to heal, the first attempt to leave brought on excruciating pain with bleeding which turned out to be a blessing when they found out Merliah was pregnant, so they returned to save both her and the baby. Once she gave birth, they hoped the transition back to the real world wouldn't be a problem. Staying there became her way of life until they could figure out how to free her from the self-inflicted prison. Then, the news of the baby brought new hope, but concern for both their safety.

Dammit! He almost slammed his fist into the wall, but restrained himself. She'd have heard him even from the other side. He stood on the outside, listening to her cry and feeling guilty as shit. He hated it when she cried. He felt so damn helpless. With all his power, he could do nothing.

An unearthly snarl escaped from Sorin's throat, and he clamped his lips together. He was supposed to save, not hurt her and by the powers of the universe, he'd find a way out of this mess.

Sorin sighed again. His son would also be born in the make-believe world. He'd hurt not only the woman he loved but the unborn child. The mere thought traumatized him. He wanted them close to him, always. As she was special, his son would be too.

He should go back inside and soothe her sad cries and apologize for his actions for the thousandth time, but what words could he offer to console her? He turned and pulled away from the painting resting against the wall. Blood tears filled his vision.

Frustration and fear bordering on despair flashed through him. Sorin ran a hand over his forehead and eyes, inhaling her lingering scent. *Fuck!* He shoved himself off the wall, turning to leave, but her voice called to him.

"Sorin?"

Peering at the painting, her face filled the frame. "What are you doing, love?" he asked, blinking back the tears.

"I changed my mind about you leaving right now. I came for you. The only thing that separates us is a layer of paint. I'll be fine. We'll be fine. I love you, Sorin. Be with me before my parents arrive."

He smiled knowing she was right. Nothing could or should keep them apart. The most important thing was he had her and the baby. Everything else would work out in the end.

Sorin reached for the canvas, stopping inches from the surface. She raised her hand to his.

Together forever, my love.

THE END

About the Author

Cynthia resides in Orlando, Florida, the land of magic, surrounded by the treasured gems in her life, a caring, loving husband, dutiful and loyal daughter, and precious, delightful granddaughter. Oh and not to forget her mischievous Yorkshire terrier, Thumper.

Cynthia was a "Navy Brat" calling a different port home every couple of years—from Southern California, to Boston, to Virginia, to Florida. She developed wandering feet and diverse interests, and passionately incorporates those experiences into her stories, bringing characters to life, and eloquently sharing the vivid images of her mind with her audience.

Cynthia's debut release, *Born to Be Wild*, came available January 12, 2011 and can be purchased at www.store.secretcravingspublishing.com. The list of releases available by her has grown. *Born Again in Dreams* is her twelfth release with Secret Cravings Publishing and more are on the schedule for release in 2012 and 2013.

http://cynthiaarsuaga.weebly.com

Other Books by Cynthia
Born to Be Wild
Born to Play
Top Dog
Love and Death in the Big Easy
A Gift of Love
Texas Heat
The Cougar and Her Vampire
Vampire in Paris
Echoes in Eternity
Nightfall: Fantasies Fulfilled
Christmas with a Stranger (Free)
Five Hearts Anthology

Secret Cravings Publishing

www.secretcravingspublishing.com

Made in the USA
Charleston, SC
05 May 2013